Reclaim My Heart

Other Titles by Donna Fasano

The Merry-Go-Round
Her Fake Romance
Where's Stanley?
His Wife For A While
The Single Daddy Club: Derrick
The Single Daddy Club: Jason
The Single Daddy Club: Reece
Nanny and The Professor
Return of The Runaway Bride
Mountain Laurel
Take Me, I'm Yours
An Accidental Family
Taking Love In Stride

Reclaim My Heart

Donna Fasano

The characters and events portrayed in this book are fictitious. Any similarity to real persons, living or dead, is coincidental and not intended by the author.

Text copyright © 2013 Donna Fasano
All rights reserved.
Printed in the United States of America

No part of this book may be reproduced, or stored in a retrieval system, or transmitted in any form or by any means, electronic, mechanical, photocopying, recording, or otherwise, without express written permission of the publisher.

Published by Montlake Romance, Seattle
www.apub.com

ISBN-13: 9781477817988
ISBN-10: 1477817980
Library of Congress Control Number: 2013917232

For my aunt, Dorothy B. Montgomery,
one of the first
college graduates in our family.
You continue to be
an inspiration to me.
I wanted to follow in your footsteps,
but what can I say, Aunt Dot?
I fell in love.

CHAPTER ONE

Although it was after midnight when she pulled open the plate glass door, rows of fluorescent bulbs lit up the police station as if it were noonday. The officer sitting behind the gunmetal gray desk cradled a telephone receiver between his shoulder and ear while he two-finger tapped a computer keyboard that was so old the letters had worn off the most used keys, leaving them a shiny black.

"Hmm...no record of him being picked up in our precinct, ma'am," the officer informed the person on the other end of the line. "Not tonight, ma'am." Then he murmured, "You're welcome." He hung up the phone, slid several papers from the tray of a nearby printer, slapped them into a manila folder, and dropped the whole works into a white plastic bin, all in one fluid motion.

The officer's gaze met Tyne's, but before she could get out a single word, the phone rang, and he lifted his index finger. He chatted briefly, transferred the call, then glanced up at her again.

Her heart thudded. "My name is Tyne—"

The telephone jangled and the officer cut her off again, this time with an upraised palm as if he were directing traffic at a busy intersection. Tyne's mouth flattened as she watched him tap, talk, sort, drop, and she wrestled down the urge to snatch the papers from his hand to get his attention.

The caller's problem sounded complicated, and as the seconds ticked away, Tyne's fingers curled deeper into her palms. Her attention strayed from the officer behind the desk to the dingy station lobby. A woman entered from a side door, her expression weary, the skirt of her gray suit creased across the thighs. She offered a vague nod as she passed by, and Tyne turned to watch her disappear down the hallway. A man slouched on the bench at the far side of the room.

The unmistakable clunk of the phone receiver hitting its cradle had Tyne spinning to face the officer, but the damn ring sounded again. He shrugged as he snatched it up.

This time, she took a step closer to him. Her thighs an inch from the edge of the desk, her hands clenched into fists, her shoulders knotted as she waited, her eyes steadily fixed on him. When he hung up this time, she placed her fingertips on his desk in an attempt to pin down his attention.

"I'm Tyne Whitlock," she rushed, fearing another interruption. "I received a call about my son, Zach Whitlock. I'm here to pick him up."

He turned to the monitor and began pecking at the keys. "Whitlock, you said? With an H?"

"Yes. Zachary. Whitlock." She emphasized the H so strongly it came out as a whistle. "Can you tell me what happened?" She inched even closer, blood whooshing through her veins, making her feel lightheaded. Or maybe it was just stress. "Is my son okay? Is he hurt? The officer who called didn't say much. Just told me Zach had been picked up and that I should come."

"I can't tell you what I don't know, ma'am. Take a seat." He gestured to somewhere behind her, his eyes never wavering from the screen in front of him as he reached for the phone. "I'll call the arresting officer—"

"Zach's been *arrested*?"

"Picked up. Arrested. Those are interchangeable for us. I apologize if the situation wasn't made clear."

Heat flushed her body and sweat prickled the back of her neck. "There must be a mistake. My son wouldn't do anything—" The rest of the sentence died in her throat when she realized that Zach had been doing a lot of unexpected things lately.

Life was hard enough all on its own; it only took one stupid mistake to screw up everything. She knew that firsthand. "He's only fifteen. Is arresting minors even *legal*?" She couldn't fathom why such an asinine question had entered her head. She watched the evening news.

The officer nearly succeeded in answering her with a straight face. "Ma'am, we arrest anyone who breaks the law. We picked up a seven-year-old today who took a handgun to the playground. He says a friend—a *friend*—called him a toad face." He shook his head as he reached for more papers in the printer tray, muttering, "I wouldn't want to be that kid's enemy."

Tyne flinched when the phone rang.

"Just take a seat. Someone will come for you." His curt tone held a clear dismissal.

She turned, her knees weak. The space between her and the benches lining the back wall seemed an interminable void. She took a couple of shuffling steps across the black and white industrial tile, worn thin in places by high traffic, scuffed and nicked and stained in others. Strange, the things you notice when your mind is on overload. The hollowness yawning inside her made her feel cast aside and helpless, as if she—and Zach—weren't worth anyone's immediate attention. And she *still* didn't know what the hell had happened with her son.

The man she'd noticed just moments earlier studied her with bleary eyes. The alcohol fumes billowing from him were nearly visible. As was his acrid scent. He offered a slack grin and attempted to rise, but the handcuffs securing him to the arm of the bench prevented him from standing fully erect. Bent at the hips, he swayed dangerously on his feet.

"Charlie, sit!" the officer barked. "Don't make me come over there."

Dutifully, the drunk followed orders, his watery, defeated gaze sliding to the floor.

She eased herself down on the corner of the empty bench, as far from *Charlie* as she could get. Tyne couldn't believe this was happening. Couldn't believe she was actually in a Philadelphia police station. Couldn't believe that her son had been arrested.

Zach wasn't a bad kid. Sure, he'd been having some problems lately. Acting out a bit. He was a teenager. Rebellion was normal at this age, wasn't it?

But... *arrested?*

Two policemen barreled through the front door, the woman sandwiched between them kicking and shouting her innocence, then yelling threats, as they dragged her through the full length of the lobby. The three of them disappeared down the hall.

Tyne felt her heart pinch, thinking of her son somewhere down that same hallway. Zach had never experienced anything like this before. He must be terrified. But in the same instant, a flash of annoyance jolted through her, buoyed by a devastating fear for her son's safety. What was he thinking leaving the house after dark? He knew the rules, knew there were reasons for them and that he was expected to follow them.

Was this her fault for trusting him to stay home alone? But he hadn't been, damn it. Not tonight, anyway.

Catering required her to work a lot of nights, overseeing the serving of the food she prepared and supervising cleanup crews of the parties of the people who hired her. Things had started getting a little dicey a couple of years ago when Zach began to complain that he was too old to stay with Mrs. Armstrong next door. Then her elderly neighbor had fallen, broken her hip, and had ended up in an assisted living facility.

Desperate for a way to keep her son from spending his evenings alone, Tyne had turned sneaky, and she refused to feel guilty about the babysitting gigs she'd set up for him, or the times she'd asked him to tutor the children of her friends. Keeping tabs on a teen was hell, but she did what she had to do. When he'd turned fifteen, she set a nine o'clock curfew. If she had to work later than that, she usually finagled some reason for Rob to drop by the house until she arrived. Tonight had been no different. Rob and Zach were supposed to watch a game on ESPN.

Tyne had arrived home around eleven forty-five to find Rob asleep on the couch, a replay of some violent kickboxing nonsense droning on the TV. She'd touched the power button on the remote, awakened Rob with a gentle shake, and they'd chatted for a few minutes. Rob had told her Zach had stayed in his room most of the evening. He'd said he'd tried to coax him out when the baseball game started but that he'd had no luck and that he must have drifted off sometime before the ninth inning.

The hours she'd spent on her feet tonight had exhausted her, so when Rob reminded her that he was meeting his sister for breakfast, she'd actually been relieved that he wouldn't be staying over. She'd walked him to the door and kissed him goodnight. She had been just about to go slip into her pajamas when her cell phone vibrated—and this nightmare had begun.

She glanced down the hallway leading to the back of the building. Was anyone ever going to come? On the adjacent bench, Charlie's chin had slumped to his chest, his snoring soft and rhythmic.

Tyne had been surprised by the phone call from the policewoman, but not overly concerned. She assumed the woman had chosen the wrong Whitlock in the phone book. In fact, she'd been so certain that the officer had made some huge mistake that she'd asked her to hold on, so she could check Zach's room. The sight of her son's empty bed made lifting the cell phone back up to her ear sheer torture.

And now here she sat. In a police station. Waiting to see her son. Her son who was under arrest.

Should she have seen this coming?

Sure, Zach hadn't been easy to deal with lately, but she hadn't had any serious problems with him. Not anything that would allude to this scenario, anyway. His defiant behavior had begun some time ago. He'd started smarting off to Rob and back talking her. Not all the time—just every so often. Then she'd noticed that he'd forget to do his chores, leaving his bed unmade, his room a wreck, or the kitchen garbage mounting in the can.

Tyne had called him on it, if not in every instance, at least often enough so that he still knew who was in charge. But his behavior hadn't overly concerned her. Defiance and moodiness were just part of growing up, especially with kids Zach's age. Teens saw pushing the limits as their primary goal: to make their parents, and every other adult they came into contact with, utterly miserable. To stick their big, hairy-toed feet out of the box as far as they could until someone shouldered them back inside the boundary lines of acceptable behavior.

The shouldering part fell under her job description. It didn't matter that she was a single parent. Well, she did have Rob, but he was her boyfriend. Wait. Her *fiancé*, she mentally corrected, thumbing the diamond ring on her finger. But Rob knew squat about raising kids, or if he did, he didn't let on. It was Tyne's responsibility to see that her son followed the rules, even when he felt those rules were unfair or harsh, or just plain "whack," as he would say.

She'd excused it all away as puberty, raging hormones and all that. But then his grades started to slip last winter. A frown bit into her brow as she realized this had been going on much longer than she'd first thought.

His history teacher had complained that Zach was missing homework assignments, that his class participation had taken a nosedive, and there had been several instances of blatant disrespect. Tyne had cracked down on Zach. Hard. Although she hadn't heard from the teacher again, it seemed as if her son had limped through the remainder of the school year, finishing with mediocre grades in all his classes.

Tyne continued to preach at him at every opportunity about the importance of education, although her lectures seemed to bounce off him like a rubber ball against a brick barricade. Now, with summer vacation in full swing, she'd tried to find something to occupy his free time. He'd been appalled by the idea of working with her. Even a paycheck hadn't been enough to persuade him. Apparently, cooking offended his masculinity; it didn't matter how many famous male chefs Tyne had reeled off. Until Zach found a business owner willing to hire a fifteen-year-old, filling out working papers was useless. She hadn't had too much of a problem with him hanging out with his friends at the mall or playing basketball in the park, as long as she knew where he was and whom he was with.

Absently, she reached up and smoothed her fingertips back and forth across her chin. She'd been confident that she knew what Zach was doing with his time.

Until tonight.

And she never would have thought he'd leave the house after curfew. Without telling Rob. Without phoning her.

Zach hadn't just left the house, the cold voice of reality whispered from somewhere in the back of her brain. *He'd snuck out.*

She'd be a fool not to acknowledge the truth. Was tonight the first time he'd done such a thing? Or the second? Or the twenty-second?

Doubt twisted in her stomach. She should have left the party earlier tonight. She could have made that happen, but—

"Mrs. Whitlock?"

Tyne snapped to attention. The uniform the female officer wore looked starched enough to stand up straight even if she weren't in it. The bright overhead lights reflected off her thick hair, the bulk of which had been secured at the back of her head, up off her shoulders.

"I'm Tyne Whitlock." She stood and approached the woman.

"Officer Perez. Follow me, please."

"Is my son okay?"

"He's fine." The woman turned and made her way along the linoleum-tiled hall. "He's been at my desk while I filed the report. I decided not to lock him in a cell with the others."

Gratitude rolled through Tyne in a huge wave even as her mouth went dry. She knew she should thank Officer Perez for her kindness, but instead she asked, "Others?"

"The boys your son was with. Three of 'em. They're older than Zach. By a couple years, at least. And all of them have been picked up before. I'm hoping that spending a little time in confinement might instill a little fear, but who knows with these kids."

"What did they *do*?" A fresh rush of dread didn't allow her to wait for an answer. "Zach didn't hurt anyone, did he?"

Perez shook her head. "It was a minor offense."

Tyne exhaled with relief.

"But don't get the wrong idea," the officer cautioned, pulling open a door and holding it for her. "Your son is in serious trouble. The boys he was with—"

"Mom?"

Only a mother could understand the flood of emotion that coursed through Tyne's body when she saw Zach's face, heard the fear in his voice, witnessed that he was whole and unharmed.

"Take a seat, Mrs. Whitlock." Officer Perez rounded the desk as she spoke. "And, Zach, I want to thank you for staying put while I was gone."

When he'd first spied Tyne, Zach had scooted to the edge of the seat, but now he sank back against the black padded chair back. Tyne lowered herself onto the only other chair available in the cubicle. She set her purse on her lap.

"Your son was picked up at the local high school," Officer Perez began. "He and the others spray-painted graffiti and obscene words on the gymnasium walls."

"Oh, Zach." Disappointment snagged in her throat. Her son refused to look at her.

"Mrs. Whitlock, we picked Zach up after eleven."

Tyne's attention swung back to the officer.

"Were you aware that your son was out so late?"

The officer's coal-black eyes were probing and filled to the brim with accusation.

"I was working." Defensiveness tightened every word. "I had to go in around three this afternoon." She glanced down at her son, tossing him a quick, narrow-eyed glare. "I'd left dinner for him. And then Rob arrived before nine. They were going to watch the Phillies game." Tyne spoke swiftly. "When I arrived," she continued, "it was close to midnight. Rob was asleep on the sofa."

"So Zach's father—"

"That jerk *isn't* my father."

Tyne gasped. "Zach!" Her tone was sharp with reproof. "Don't talk about Rob like that."

His chin jutted, his mouth a thin slash. He looked so much like his dad in that instance that she had to force herself not to look away.

"Zach, go sit over by the door. I need to speak to your mother."

Officer Perez's request was stern enough to brook no argument, and Zach pushed himself from the chair, lumbered across the room.

Tyne glanced down at her lap and saw that her knuckles were white from the death-grip she had on her leather bag. Her insides quaked. "I—I just don't understand what's going on," she murmured, pressing her palm to her forehead and closing her eyes for a brief second. "I don't know what's happened to my son."

"Mrs. Whitlock—"

"It's 'Ms.,'" Tyne corrected. "Rob and I aren't married. Yet." She glanced down at the diamond ring on her left hand. The stone glittered in the harsh fluorescent light and she noticed that she was once again clutching her purse tight enough to make the tendons in her hands stand out rigidly.

"Maybe he should be here with you."

Officer Perez's voice was so unexpectedly soft that it drew Tyne's attention.

"What?"

"Your fiancé," the officer said. "Would you like for me to call him?"

"No." Tyne shook her head, looking away.

"I think you could use a little support. He might—"

"No." She straightened her spine. "I'm fine. Rob has to be up early. I don't want to bother him. I'm just fine, Officer Perez. I can handle this."

The woman sitting behind the desk didn't look convinced.

Like tiny sparks of light, memories flickered through Tyne's head. Difficult circumstances over the years that— as a single parent—she'd had to handle on her own. Front baby teeth loosened in a fall on the playground. The wrist fractured in a bicycle accident. Teasing that turned into nasty bullying because Zach looked different; he wasn't white; he wasn't black; he wasn't Latino.

Raising her son on her own hadn't been easy. The responsibility had forced her to develop a steely resolve, an unfaltering tenacity, if not on the inside, at least in the brave face she insisted on presenting to the world.

She could handle anything life threw her way when it came to Zach. She was devoted to his protection, and she meant to nurture him and defend him and love him. No matter what. She intended to be the very best mother she could be. One skeptical police officer couldn't instill doubt about that.

When she lifted her gaze to Officer Perez, she knew she expressed more confidence, even if she still felt quite shaken inside. She'd just take the problem one step at a time.

"I'm sorry he painted the school building," Tyne began. "He knows right from wrong. He knows better than to deface property. I can promise you he'll face the consequences. We'll clean the building or pay to have it cleaned. Zach's a good kid," she insisted. "Yes, he's been showing a bit of defiance lately. And, no, he should never have left the house tonight. He'll be on restriction for that. But I don't believe his behavior is so seriously depraved that he needs to have a criminal record." Reality sunk in and she repeated, "A *permanent* criminal record."

Officer Perez's face held no emotion. None, nada, zip.

A flutter of panic threatened Tyne, but she held it at bay. "You said yourself that no one was hurt. He's never been in any trouble before. Isn't there some other way we can handle this? Is there anything I can do to get the charges against my son dropped?"

Without taking her eyes off Tyne's face, Perez straightened the reports on her desktop, gathering them together and tapping them into a neat pile.

"I wish I could help you, Ms. Whitlock. But the damage is done. The report is already on file. There's no way for me to undo it. It'll be up to the judge to determine your son's punishment."

Refusing to feel defeated, Tyne asked, "Okay, so what happens now?"

"We're releasing him into your custody." She set the papers down and splayed her palm on top of them. "Listen, it's very clear to me that you're a...a concerned parent. A *truly* concerned parent. I wish I saw more of those around here." Perez's dark eyes softened. "It's usually my policy to give a kid a warning. I like to give them a chance if I can. If Zach had been merely loitering, then I'd have brought him home. I'd have given both him and you a stern lecture. However, he destroyed public property. He had a can of paint in his possession. Orange paint on his skin. And not only that, the boys Zach was with have already seen their share of trouble. They're way past the warning stage. One of the boys spent thirty days in juvie hall. These are not the kind of kids you want your son hanging with."

Closing her eyes, Tyne clenched her jaw so tightly the joints began to ache. Taking up with delinquents. Defacing public property. Running head-on into trouble with the law. Earning himself a criminal record.

She'd taught Zach better.

"This isn't normal behavior for my son. You have to believe me."

Perez rested her forearms on the corner of the desk. "I'll tell you what I believe. Zach is disturbed about something. Angry would be a better word. I tried to get him to talk to me. Tried to connect with him. He was rude and disrespectful. I hoped that would change once we were away from the others. But even then, he continued to be uncommunicative. That's not what I'm used to from first-time offenders. They usually break down and express remorse rather quickly. Not your son. Then fear got the better of him, and he just shut down. It's been my experience that kids like Zach—" She stopped, then started again. "There's not an easy way for me to say this. I think your son needs some help. Professional help."

Tyne fought the insult that reared in her chest, but she couldn't fault the woman for stating the truth. She nodded, fighting to breathe around the knot that swelled in her throat. "He does need help. And I promise you he'll get it."

"I'm glad to hear that, Ms. Whitlock." Leaning forward, the officer's tone lowered an octave as she suggested, "The first thing you should do is find a good lawyer. Zach has a mandatory court appearance in front of the juvie judge. And it's soon. Our policy is to take care of these things as quickly as possible, so he's scheduled on the court docket for Wednesday morning."

"But that only gives me four days—"

"Three, actually," Perez corrected. "We're into Sunday morning."

Tyne sighed sharply. "How am I supposed to find a lawyer by Wednesday?"

Unwittingly, items on her work schedule zipped through her brain; the meeting this afternoon with that couple to finalize their wedding menu, shopping and prep for the Women's Association Tea on Monday, the Idea Exchange for the Small Business Owners Guild set for Tuesday morning.

"I can't just go to court with Zach? Explain things to the judge myself? Surely—"

The officer cut her off with an emphatic shake of her head. "Not a good idea. Judge Taylor plays hardball. He's a firm believer that a person is known by the company he keeps. It's his motto. You'll probably hear him say those words while you're there. He'll come down on Zach hammer-hard simply because of the friends he's chosen to run around with." Perez leaned forward, sincerity tempering her intense gaze. "Find Zach a lawyer, Ms. Whitlock. He won't fare well without one."

There were forms to sign and another firm lecture for Zach before Perez let them go.

The drive home was made in stony silence. Tyne knew she and Zach would have to talk, but her son wasn't ready for any more scolding. She'd seen him switch off when the officer reprimanded him before they'd left.

The teetering emotional triangle she was attempting to balance had her feeling very much off kilter. Concern for Zach weighted one corner. Another sagged with motherly guilt. And the third? Well, that corner was heavy with anger. She wanted firm control over her emotions before she talked to him about his actions, what had precipitated this craziness, and the legal repercussions he was facing.

She braked the car to a halt at a stop sign, looked down the deserted street in both directions, and then crossed the intersection.

Legal repercussions. The phrase sounded ominous.

Damn, she was tired. She wished she had someone to lean on. Someone to talk to. Someone to reason this out with. She'd traveled a solitary road for years.

There was Rob, of course. But although she knew he cared for her deeply, she also knew how he felt about taking on the task of raising a teen. He hadn't come right out and expressed his anxiety about becoming an instant parent, but Tyne sensed his hesitation. Who knew how he'd react if she dumped this problem on his shoulders? She certainly couldn't keep it from him, but she could handle the bulk of it on her own.

How would she handle it, was the question.

Find Zach a lawyer. He won't fare well without one.

The officer's advice hit her like a kick to the gut. Then another thought breezed through her mind; Lucas Silver Hawk was a lawyer.

No way. No how.

"What?" Zach's short, sharp question broke the quiet.

Startled to realize that she'd actually voiced the thought, she attempted to downplay it by murmuring, "Just working out some things in my head."

Zach's father wasn't just *any* lawyer. He was a prominent, high-powered attorney who made the city news often. Judging from what she read about him in both the business and society sections, it seemed Lucas was Man of the Hour in Philadelphia's courtrooms *and* in the bedrooms of a multitude of women. She rarely saw a picture of him when he didn't have a beautiful female nearby.

Acid churned in her gut, and she leaned a little closer to the steering wheel.

Lucas was part of the past. A past she'd grappled with for a hell of a long time. A past that, for years, she wasn't sure she would ever overcome. But she was beyond all that. She'd left it behind.

She pulled into the empty parking space on the street in front of the brownstone she and Zach called home.

Your son needs a lawyer.

"No!"

Zach plucked the car keys from her fingers and shoved open the car door. "Talkin' to yourself now? Mom, you're freakin' me out."

The slam of the door reverberated in her head.

She wouldn't go to Lucas. She just couldn't. What would she say to him? How would she explain?

"Lucas," she whispered aloud in the darkness, "I have something I need to tell you."

Guilt eddied in her chest. The thought of facing his questions—not to mention his fury—made her entire body flush with heat. But all of that was preempted by a stiff resentment when she remembered all the years she and Zach struggled and went without.

The far-off bark of a dog broke the silence and she sat up straighter.

Zach had found himself a heap of trouble. Tears stung her eyes, and she did her best to blink them away.

He'll come down on Zach hammer-hard.

Tyne could think of a dozen reasons why she couldn't go to Lucas for help, but then she swung her weepy gaze toward the porch where the treasure of her world was letting himself into the house—and she realized in that instant that there was one crucial reason why she would.

CHAPTER TWO

Summer sunlight heated the crown of Lucas's head as he wove his way through the tourists and business people crowding the sidewalk. Cars, taxis, and buses rumbled along Market Street, sending dust swirling in the sultry air. One perk he loved about working in Philadelphia was that his office was within walking distance of the courthouse. He thrived in the outdoors, and the trek he made, sometimes several times each day, offered him the opportunity to be out in the open air rather than cooped up inside.

Rain, snow, sun—it didn't matter. His colleagues thought he was nuts. They simply didn't understand his affinity for nature.

Today his steps were lighter than usual. The petition he'd just filed would assure victory in the Jamison case. Winning the complicated litigation would be a feather in his cap. No one in the office had thought it could be done, and that's exactly why he'd accepted the challenge. Life was good. No, he decided as he entered the revolving door of his office building, life was *great*.

He whistled as he crossed the high-ceilinged atrium and stepped into a waiting elevator that shot him toward the top of the high rise. He shifted his briefcase to his left hand as the doors slid open and he entered the bright and ultra-modern vestibule of Young and Foster.

"Martha." He nodded at the firm's receptionist, pausing at her desk.

"So"—excitement dripped from her sneaky whisper—"did you do it?"

He offered up a mischievous grin.

Her brown eyes glittered. "You're *in*, Lucas. You're going to be the youngest partner this firm has ever seen."

More importantly, the first of Native American descent too. The idea gave him a great deal of satisfaction, but he said nothing.

Martha beamed, and Lucas gave her shoulder a warm pat.

"I hope you're right, Miss Martha." He picked up an envelope that had his name scrawled across the front of it. "Any calls?" he asked.

"Six. Two need immediate attention. Three can wait." Her tone lowered. "One can be tossed into the circular file."

Lucas accepted the slips of paper. "You know I appreciate your skillful memorandum triage."

Martha flushed to the roots of her bleach-blond hair. "Larry and Nate are waiting for you in Larry's office. You've got an appointment in twenty minutes with the parents of the Reeves girl. They wanted to personally thank you for helping Shannon. I'll call the minute they arrive." Without batting an eye, Martha continued her list. "You've got a court appearance at eleven thirty. Lunch with the Jamisons at twelve forty-five. And you're booked solid until seven, but we can go over your afternoon appointments later."

Not only was she an extraordinary office manager, Martha made a great mother hen. She juggled the schedules of the entire "minor league," as the two senior partners referred to the group of attorneys in their employ. Lucas didn't know how Martha accomplished the countless tasks that would have surely overwhelmed anyone else, but he was glad she did. He'd be lost without the woman.

"Thanks, Martha. I've got to stop by my office; then I'll go talk to—"

"Oh, wait. There's someone here to see you."

He frowned. "I don't have time today."

"I know, I *know*." Martha looked apologetic. "I tried to explain that your schedule is packed, but she insisted on waiting—"

"She?"

Martha glanced down at a pad on her desktop. "A Ms. Whitlock. Tyne Whitlock."

Lucas stared. Blinked. Then he reached up and tugged at his tie, wondering who the hell shut off the room's air supply.

"She's waiting in your office. I tried to tell her your schedule was full, but—" Concern sharpened Martha's tone. "Are you all right? She said she knew you. That you were old friends. That she'd only take a minute of your time. Should I not have let her in?"

Martha droned on, and he watched her lips move, but he didn't hear a word of what she said. A blind-side punch wouldn't have stunned him more than hearing that name. He lifted his hand and nodded at Martha to let her know everything was okay, even though he had no idea if it was or not; then he turned and headed down the corridor.

"Don't forget Larry and Nate. They're waiting!"

Martha's warning sounded like a distant echo.

Tyne. Here. In this building. In his office.

What had it been? Twelve, thirteen—no, *sixteen* years. He scrubbed his fingers across his jaw.

He turned the corner and came to an abrupt halt. At the end of the corridor, the door of his office stood ajar. He saw Tyne's perfect profile as she sat in a straight-backed chair staring at something out of his line of view.

In an instant, Lucas was catapulted into the past.

Darkness surrounded them like a cloak. Tyne's soft sobs tore at his heart. Of all the girls he'd dated—and there had been more than a few—only she brought out in him a fierce compulsion to protect.

He swiped away her tears, the dark color of his thumb a stark contrast against her creamy white skin.

"I don't understand them, Lucas. I never will."

"Don't worry," he crooned. "It's going to be all right. Trust me, babe. They can't keep us apart. You'll be eighteen soon too. We can do what we want then. Go wherever we want."

He cradled her, his back supported by the massive pin oak. And when she stopped crying, she pulled away from him and gazed into his eyes. Her sweet face wrenched his heart and caused heat to spark his desire. Never had he wanted a girl the way he wanted Tyne. Raw need coursed through him.

She cradled his face between her palms and drew him to her. Her lips were hot against his. The kiss grew hungry, their breathing labored.

"Our love will last forever," she whispered against his mouth.

He heard the question in her quavering tone and responded to her need for reassurance.

"Forever," he groaned, tugging her down onto the mossy ground.

Lucas tilted his head to stare at the carpet in front of his shoes and gulped in the artificially cooled air as he dragged his way out of the past. The grip he had on his attaché case made his hand throb almost as much as the memory had caused his groin to go all achy and needful.

Of course, their love hadn't lasted forever.

He was within steps of the door when Tyne glanced in his direction. Nuances of various emotions passed across her face. And it was a striking face, Lucas couldn't deny it. The years had refined her features—

She stood, smoothing her palms across the fabric of her skirt.

—and ripened her body. Her eyes were the same vivid blue he remembered, and her white-blond hair was still long and straight. He could easily recall the silky feel of it brushing against his bare chest. As teens, he'd thought of them as the perfect juxtaposition: she, all sunshine and light; he, dark like the night.

He forced his gaze back onto her face.

"Tyne." He entered his office, puzzled by the strain in his voice. What really confused him was the fact that he couldn't seem to get his tongue to form anything more.

"Hi, Lucas. It's been a long time." Her lush mouth pressed into a nervous smile, and his gut tensed.

He wanted to smile back. He truly did. With every fiber of his being. To let her know that he'd survived the sprawling interim since they'd parted just as well as she obviously had. But he couldn't smile. Couldn't speak. Couldn't think.

Time dragged.

Damn! Move, man! The harsh command was nothing more than pure, self-preserving instinct, and he thanked heaven for blessing him with a healthy dose of it, which never failed to kick in just when it was needed. This time was no exception.

Lucas took several steps and set his briefcase, mail, and messages on his desk. He said, "Yes, it has been a long... long time."

"I know you're very busy. The woman at the front desk told me so. But I was hoping you could give me some time. Just a moment or two."

Grateful for a reason to break contact with her mesmerizing cobalt eyes, he snatched the opportunity to study his wristwatch. "I'm due in a meeting right now. And I've got clients coming—"

"Five minutes."

"My day really is jammed, Tyne. But I'll have Martha check my schedule. I'm sure I could fit you in within the next couple of—"

"Please, Lucas."

He couldn't dismiss the tone of those two small words, nor could he ignore the magnitude of emotion clouding her expression. He had no choice but to relent.

"Sit down," he murmured. He closed the door of his office and then returned to perch himself on the corner of his desk. He steeled himself before asking, "What's on your mind?"

She seemed to shrink a little as a thousand thoughts ran though her head. Seconds passed, and still she didn't speak.

Lucas witnessed the phenomenon almost on a daily basis. The people who wound up in his office often felt as if they were carrying the world on their shoulders. He knew her anxiety would eventually discharge, and from the looks of it, he wouldn't have to wait long.

Finally, she pressed her hand to her chest. "I can't breathe."

"Relax. Do you want some water?"

She shook her head, a lock of her long, platinum hair falling over her forearm. "No. I need to get this out. I promised you I'd hurry."

He couldn't keep his brows from arching a fraction. She hadn't kept her promises in the past. Why would he expect her to now?

Tyne ran her tongue along her full bottom lip, hesitated another moment, then blurted, "I need a lawyer."

Lucas closed his eyes and stifled a sigh. He could have guessed as much, of course. He'd worked hard to get himself into the privileged position of being able to pick and choose his clients. The last person he wanted to represent was Tyne Whitlock.

"A *good* lawyer, Lucas."

Common sense told him Tyne wasn't attempting to flatter him. She was speaking purely out of desperation.

"Look, Tyne—" Something made him stop. He sighed, and then he stood, taking his time rounding his desk and sitting down. The leather-upholstered arms of the chair were cool and smooth under his fingertips.

"I know some of the best attorneys in the city." He plucked a pen from the cup on his desktop. "And many of them owe me a favor or two." He reached into his inside jacket pocket, pulled out one of the business cards he always kept handy, and turned it over, poised to write. "Let me give you some names and numbers—"

"I don't want just any attorney." Her chin lifted. "I want you. Why *else* would I have come here?"

His gaze lowered to the small white card in his hand. With much deliberation, he set down the pen and the card, and then he looked her directly in the eyes.

Every muscle in her body appeared board stiff.

"Listen to me," he said, keeping his tone calm. "When people find themselves in trouble with the law, or victimized, or wrongfully sued, or unjustly accused, they tend to get lost in a strange—I don't know—franticness. A recklessness that they almost always regret. Believe me when I tell you that no situation is hopeless, and circumstances are rarely as desperate as they might be perceived. Whatever trouble you're in, don't let panic and fear haze your thinking."

"You don't understand."

"I think I do," he rushed to assure her. "I see it every day. Honest, hardworking people finding themselves in dire straits. And this unfamiliar territory throws them. They grasp at help from the first source that comes to mind."

"But—"

"Just like that old adage warning that only a fool acts as his own lawyer, it's also foolish to choose an attorney in haste. You and I have a past, Tyne, and even though all of that took place years and years ago, the fact remains that we have a history. I don't believe I would be the best person to represent you in a court of law. You need someone who'll be totally unbiased. Let me give you some names. I'll make some calls for you myself—"

"Stop!" She lifted her hands and scooted to the edge of the seat. "You don't understand. And I can't make you understand if you won't *shut up* for a minute."

His eyebrows arched, and the frustration in her statement had him leaning back a bit.

She frowned. "I'm sorry. Really, I am. I had to stew all day yesterday." She fisted her hands in her lap. "I didn't expect to reach anyone on a Sunday, but do you know that your firm doesn't offer an emergency number on the answering machine?" She exhaled with force. "I'm a nervous wreck just *being* here. *Seeing* you. But all that aside, I shouldn't have snapped at you. Please accept my apology."

He didn't react, didn't move. He just waited for her to continue.

"The thing is...what you need to know..."

Once again, she grew terribly cautious, and Lucas found that extremely curious. What the hell was it she found so hard to tell him? What kind of trouble was she in?

She blanched, but then her spine straightened. "I'm not the one who needs a lawyer. I want to hire you, yes. But I'm not the one needing representation. It's my son who's in trouble." A nerve at the corner of her eye ticked, but her gaze never veered from his as she added, "*Our* son, Lucas."

CHAPTER THREE

It was rumored that Judge Marvin Taylor ate a pound of ten-penny nails for lunch every day—right after putting the hammer to at least a half-dozen delinquent teens every morning.

Because he specialized in corporate law, Lucas had minimal experience representing minors, and those cases had been forced on him when kids of clients had wound up in trouble. Shannon Reeves was a good case in point. In every instance, though, he'd been successful in having the charges reduced or dismissed simply by finding the right words to say to the right people in the DA's office and by talking to the judge. However, the judge presiding over Zach's case had refused his calls. The man wouldn't even talk with Lucas about the charges his son was facing.

His son. The phrase made Lucas's gut clench, and he turned his head to glance for what felt like the hundredth time at the grim teen seated next to him at the defense table. There was no denying the kid was his.

Lucas faced forward when the gavel struck wood.

"No, Mr. Hawk, I will *not* meet with you in chambers. I like to do business out in the open. Where everyone can hear and know what's going on." The Honorable Judge Taylor peered over his eyeglasses directly at Zach. "I do like for people to understand exactly what's happening and why." He pulled off his glasses, took a moment to buff them on his sleeve, and then perched them back on his nose as he returned his attention to Lucas. "There's nothing you could say to me in there, Counselor, that can't be said out here."

So the man wasn't only hard-hearted, he was also a jackass. Lucas stood. "May I at least approach the bench?"

It was a desk really. The juvenile courtrooms were small, almost intimate, as public audiences were barred from proceedings involving minors.

The judge sighed, loud and long, and waved both lawyers forward.

"Thank you, Your Honor," Lucas murmured. "If you'll hear me out, I think you'll agree that this case has some...special circumstances."

The prosecutor from the district attorney's office was a woman, just short of retirement, whom Lucas had met with only once in another case involving a minor. He remembered her as being firm but fair. Her smile bolstered Lucas, but the judge remained silent and stone faced.

"Your Honor, I'll get right to the point. Zachary Whitlock is my son." He paused. "I met him for the first time this morning."

The opposing attorney's gaze widened, but Judge Taylor's expression remained unmoved. Not much fazed Lucas, but he hadn't expected indifference.

"I understand you have a reputation of being tough. Even on first-time offenders. But I ask you to bear in mind that—"

"What *you* need to bear in mind," Taylor countered, leaning forward and speaking loudly enough for all to hear, "is that this young man is in my courtroom today because he broke the law. Special circumstances or not. Go back to your seats."

Lucas felt stung as he made the short trek back to the table. Tyne's troubled gaze locked onto him. He would have liked to offer her some encouragement: a smile, a nod—*something*. But he couldn't find a reason to.

"Don't get me wrong." The judge slid his gavel several inches to his right. "I'm pleased that you're enjoying a family reunion. I sincerely hope something good comes of it. But that doesn't change the fact that the fifteen-year-old sitting, well, slouching there—"

Zach shifted in his seat.

"—*chose* to associate with three known criminals. He *chose* to deface public property. He's costing the taxpayers money. I am sick to death of petty crime, and I firmly believe that every criminal act that goes unpunished only paves the way further into a life of unlawful conduct. If someone doesn't give me a solid reason not to, I plan to punish this young man to the fullest extent of the law. Zachary Whitlock has admitted to behaving in a criminal manner. *That* is what we're here to discuss. Isn't that correct, Counselors?"

The assistant state's attorney said, "Yes, Your Honor."

"Yes, sir," Lucas was forced to agree.

"Fifteen years old and hanging out with common criminals at midnight." Judge Taylor leaned back in his chair and crossed his arms. "Mr. Hawk, you say you just met your son for the first time this morning."

"Yes, sir." Lucas nodded. "We had breakfast at the coffee shop down the block." Attempting to garner some sympathy, he added, "Although we were too nervous to eat."

Everyone except Tyne's fiancé. The man had chowed down on a stack of pancakes as if he hadn't a care in the world. Lucas might have felt a bit envious at that, if he hadn't seemed so rock-stupid. But perhaps Lucas had been too quick to judge, and Rob had simply been too damned hungry to offer a single constructive idea regarding Zach's problem.

"Tell me. What was your impression? Of your son, I mean."

Lucas didn't answer right away. He remembered the teen's "I-don't-give-a-damn" posture, his brooding air. Zach had scarcely said two words to him. Had barely looked at him, in fact, as Lucas and Tyne had quietly discussed the proceedings.

But the kid was on emotional overload. Who wouldn't be? He'd met his father for the very first time this morning. He was also facing a courtroom and a judge and criminal charges. When a person was down in a valley as deep as Zach was, he had nowhere to climb but up.

"He has great potential."

Taylor only nodded. "I'd like for Zach to explain what happened. Why were you out so late at night, son?"

"Excuse me, sir, if you would." Lucas slid his fingers along the full length of his ink pen. "I instructed Zach earlier that, as his representative, I'd be doing most of the talking. He's never been in this kind of situation before, and he's feeling apprehensive."

"I sympathize, Mr. Hawk. I do. But not enough to let you run my courtroom. I'd like to hear what Zach has to say for himself. He obviously thought he was man enough to go out and break the law. He needs to be man enough to explain himself. I'd like for him to tell me, in his own words, what he was doing. What was he thinking? Why was he consorting with delinquents?"

Zach looked at the judge, then looked away. He fidgeted in his chair. "I didn' *know*."

"You didn't know what, son? That it was too late for you to be out? That spray painting graffiti on a building that doesn't belong to you is wrong? That breaking the law has consequences?"

Lucas ground his teeth, hoping Zach kept his cool in the face of the judge's taunts.

"I didn' even know those dudes."

The judge nodded. "I see."

"I just met 'em," Zach continued. "They asked me if I wanted to hang out. Have some fun."

"Do you have any idea how often I've heard the 'I-never-met-those-kids-before' story?" The man tilted his head. "Why were you out so late in the first place?"

"I had a bad day. Had a fight with my friend." The teen shrugged. "I felt like I was crawlin' outta my skin. I needed to get out the house."

"So you needed to get out *of* the house. And where was your mother?"

"Workin'." Zach's chin dipped and his tone lowered. "She's *always* workin'."

The judge zeroed in on Tyne. "Is this true, Ms. Whitlock?"

"I'm a single mother, Your Honor. I have bills to pay just like everyone else," she said, her voice tight. "I own a catering company. I fix food for parties. People have parties at night. If I want to pay the mortgage and utilities, buy food, clothes, I have to work at night."

"Even though it means forfeiting your son's safety and well-being?"

Tyne was clearly taken aback. "That's not fair."

"Oh, I disagree. It's perfectly fair. You're his parent. Zach should be your number-one priority."

"He *is* my number-one priority. Why else would I work so hard? Six days a week, sometimes sixty hours a week. There's no other reason except to provide a roof over his head and clothes on his back. Do you have any idea how difficult it is to provide for a child these days?" Tyne clamped both hands on the arms of her chair. "And I'd like it noted for the record that I usually only work two nights a week. Friday and Saturday. And my partners and I try to schedule things so that each of us has one weekend off a month." She fumed. "Yes, I work long hours. But I have to earn a living."

Lucas picked up the file in front of him and tapped it lightly on the table to get Tyne's attention. He looked at her. Hard.

She took a deep breath, but her shoulders remained rigid. Then she muttered, "Do you have any idea how much sneakers cost these days?"

Judge Taylor ignored the question. He looked at the man sitting at the far end of the table to Tyne's left. "And, if I might ask, who are you? And what's your role in all of this?"

"Rob Henderson, sir." He stood. "I'm Tyne's, er… Ms. Whitlock's fiancé. I was at her apartment the night all this went down. But I fell asleep, so I really can't tell you anything." He sat down, but then he bolted back to his feet to add, "Your Honor."

Taylor studied Henderson for a moment, giving him far more notice than Lucas felt the man deserved. The judge told Rob to take his seat, before swinging his attention back to Zach.

"So, son, let's get back to that night. You met these *dudes*, as you called them. They asked you if you wanted to have some fun."

"Yes."

Lucas slid his foot over an inch and gave Zach's shoe a light tap.

"Yes, *sir*," Zach said to the judge. "They asked me if I had money." The teen shrugged again. "I told 'em I did, and they said we should go tag some stuff."

"'Tag some stuff,'" the judge said, resting his elbows on his desk and his chin on his fisted hands. "Meaning to spray paint your name or your gang sign on dumpsters or fences or buildings or whatever, correct?"

"I'm not in a gang." Zach quickly added, "sir." He swallowed hard. "And the taggin' was *their* idea, not mine."

"But you admitted to buying the paint. The police report states the receipt was in your pocket."

The teen lifted one shoulder and his voice went meek. "I was the only one who had any money."

Lucas could feel Zach's shame, his defeat. "Your Honor, I've already explained that I just met Zach. That I don't really know him. But he's never been in any trouble before. I think it's quite clear that he just got in over his head here. Those boys were older than Zach. I'm sure he felt flattered that they'd even talked to him."

Taylor glanced at a document on his desk. "Officer Perez noted in her report that Zach mouthed off and that he acted rudely."

"That was posturing," Lucas countered. "I'm sure he was doing that for the benefit of the other boys. You were fifteen once. Don't you remember—"

"*I* never back talked a police officer, Counselor."

Lucas laced his fingers and rested his hands on the tabletop. "Sir, I have no idea what kind of parenting Zach has had up to this point. And I'll admit that three unsupervised weekends a month would leave any teenager with way too much time on his hands."

He remembered his own youth. Those long lists of never-ending chores his uncle always had at the ready. Like any adolescent, Lucas had felt he was being treated with unfair harshness. But now he realized there must have been good motives behind his uncle's behavior.

"Good!" the judge said. "I'm glad we agree that Zach needs supervision. What we need now is a plan. A plan that will ensure that Zach doesn't show up in front of me again."

Lucas placed his palms firmly on the table. "That's not going to happen, is it, Zach?"

The teen adamantly shook his head. "No, sir."

"Promises are all well and good." Taylor looked from Lucas to Zach. "But I can tell you, son, that eight out of every ten minors who sit where you're sitting come in here to pay me a second visit. And of those, an even higher percentage pay me a third visit." His stern stare remained steady. "And the punishment is stiffer for each offense." He picked up his gavel, slid his fingers down the length of it, his gaze raking over everyone sitting in front of him. "Like I said, we need a plan for this young man. Or I'm going to have to come up with one of my own."

No one said a word for several long seconds.

Tyne leaned forward, twisting to face Lucas. "I could try to get someone to cover my weekends for a while."

"Ms. Whitlock," the judge said, "I understand your dilemma. You're a single, working parent trying to raise a teenager on your own. I empathize. But I would be derelict in my duties if I didn't stress that there'll be no *trying* in whatever strategy we make here today. We will *do* something solid. Something concrete."

Lucas spent most of his weekends reading briefs. But he couldn't see why the kid couldn't hang out at his place while he read.

"I don't think I've made you understand the importance of what's happening here today," Judge Taylor told Tyne. "If your son shows up in my courtroom again, you won't be seeing him for a while. Unless, of course, you go to juvenile hall for a visit. Do I make myself clear?" He narrowed his gaze at Zach. "Don't let the name fool you, son. It's a prison. With bars on the windows and guards who carry weapons."

Eight out of every ten minors.

Bad odds. Very bad odds.

Lucas stole a glance at Zach. Fear hummed from the teen like low-voltage current, but he was doing his damnedest to hide it behind a tight, "you-can't-hurt-me" smirk that would only get him into deeper trouble. The kid's badass attitude churned up startling emotions in Lucas: dread, frustration, guilt.

He could be sitting here staring at himself at that age.

"Your Honor, what if I were to take him out of town for a time?" The question surprised Lucas just as much as it seemed to surprise everyone else in the courtroom. All eyes turned to him.

"Some litigation I've been working on was recently settled."

Judge Taylor nodded. "I read about that in this morning's paper. Congratulations, Counselor."

Lucas nodded his appreciation, but his mind fixed on the almost impossible logistics of making his suggestion happen. "I only have a couple other cases I'm working on at the moment. I could pass them on to colleagues. Clear my desk. Zach and I could go to Wikweko. The town where I grew up." He glanced down the table, noted Tyne's stunned expression, but didn't let it deter him from asking, "Zach is out of school for the summer, right?"

Tyne's fiancé casually examined his cuticles, and an odd irritation flared in Lucas.

When Tyne didn't answer, Lucas looked at Zach. "You must have several weeks of vacation left, right?" Suspicion clouded his son's dark gaze.

Lucas turned to the judge. "Wikweko is a Lenape community near Lancaster. A month or so there, and Zach's life would change forever. I'm sure of it, Judge. There's plenty of open space. Hiking. Fishing. And community events— tribal gatherings. Zach could learn about his heritage." His heart started to race. The more he thought about this idea, the more it excited him. "You know, Your Honor, I haven't taken a vacation in…" He trailed off, and his short bark of laughter held an odd note. *Vacation? What the hell was that?* "I'm sure I could get away from the office for a month. They owe me that. I'd only need a couple of days to sort things out. Then we could head off to—"

"You're not taking Zach anywhere." Tyne's shrill voice sliced through his enthusiasm.

"You have a problem with your son getting to know his father, Ms. Whitlock?" the judge asked.

"I haven't seen this man for…for…years. *Many* years. I don't know what kind of person he is." Panic edged her words. "I refuse to allow—"

"Mr. Hawk is a well-respected attorney," Taylor pointed out. "An attorney with a plan. A plan that's sounding really good to me, actually. Healthy, outdoor activity, and father-son bonding time. What more could we ask for?"

Lucas leaned forward and looked down the table. "Tyne, you're welcome to come along. I'm only thinking of Zach."

"I can't just drop everything and leave the city for a month, Lucas." Her blue eyes narrowed and her jaw tensed. "I have a business to run."

"What about what *I* want?" Zach blurted. "Does anyone care what I want?"

Judge Taylor peered over his eyeglasses once again. "Sorry, son. You lost your vote when you ran the train off the track." He pushed at his glasses with his index finger. "Ms. Whitlock, if you own this catering business—"

"Co-own," she corrected. "I am co-owner of—"

"Even better." Taylor nodded. "That means the business doesn't depend on you alone. I suggest you do a little delegating." He shrugged. "Or stay in town and work. The choice is yours. As for Zach, I think some time with his father is just the ticket."

"Lucas!" Tyne whispered furiously. "Don't do this. Don't you dare take Zach—"

"It's done," Taylor stated. He looked over at the court clerk. "I grant Lucas Hawk custody of Zach Whitlock for thirty days."

"You can't do that!"

"Oh, but I can, Ms. Whitlock," the judge said. "The good state of Pennsylvania has granted me that privilege. Mr. Hawk, please utilize the time to do what you can for your son."

"I will, Your Honor. Thank you."

"Ms. Whitlock, Mr. Hawk, as parents of a minor who has committed a crime, you're responsible for making full restitution to the city to have that wall painted. I strongly suggest you see to it that Zach pays off the debt himself. But that's entirely up to you." The judge glanced over at the clerk. "You getting all this? Good." He looked at Zach. "We'll reconvene in thirty days, at which time I'll make my final decision on this case." He looked at the assistant DA. "You have any disagreements you want to raise?"

"We're fine with this, Your Honor," the woman said.

Taylor narrowed his gaze at the teen. "Zachary, I strongly suggest that you use this time to do some hard thinking. What's important to you? What do you want to do with your life? Which direction do you want to go in? And most importantly, what kind of person do you want to be? You need to get yourself sorted out. I'll see you back here in one month's time." The judge paused a moment before asking, "Do you understand what's happening here, Zach? I'm giving you a chance to turn things around for yourself. This is a rare occurrence in this courtroom. I need to know that you understand that this is a pivotal moment in your life."

Zach's gaze lowered. "Yes, sir. I got it. I mean, I understand."

"Good. That's it, then." A sharp thud rang out as the judge slammed down the gavel.

CHAPTER FOUR

Lincoln Highway shot straight through southeast Pennsylvania's lush farmland. From the backseat of Lucas's BMW, Tyne gazed out at grassy wheat fields, tidy rows of neatly trimmed fruit trees, and squat, windowless, mushroom houses. The blasting air conditioner did little to cool her temper. Shaking Lucas until his teeth rattled loose might give her some satisfaction.

She hadn't spoken a single word since Lucas had picked her and Zach up a little over an hour ago. A fire continued to smolder inside her. It had been sparked in that courtroom when Lucas had succeeded in turning her life upside down.

Yes, he had made his suggestion for Zach's sake. Logic wouldn't allow her to think otherwise. And Sandy, Chip, and Gina, her friends and partners of Easy Feasts, couldn't have been more supportive or cooperative about her needing time off to sort out her son's problems. It would make for longer workdays for a few weeks, but they were good people who knew Tyne would, in an instant, do the same thing for them. Even Rob, who rarely voiced an opinion about her son, had admitted that Lucas's plan might be just what Zach needed. But that was classic Rob, always going with the flow, taking the path of least resistance.

So why was she feeling so betrayed? The reaction might not make much sense, but that's what she felt. Betrayed. By her friends. By her fiancé. She wanted all of them to be as annoyed with Lucas as she was for forcing her to leave her home and her business.

She even felt betrayed by Zach.

Her son had been an absolute bear since that ill-tempered judge had exiled them for thirty days. Zach had snapped at her at every opportunity. He'd moped around the house; he'd groused whenever she'd spoken to him. He didn't want to be on this trip any more than she did. But then this morning Lucas arrived in his sleek, silver sedan with its black leather interior and tinted windows. The car was probably worth more than what she earned in a year, maybe two. Zach had been awed, and he and Lucas had talked horsepower, torque, and acceleration speed as they stowed the suitcases in the trunk. Tyne had settled herself into the backseat, her arms folded tightly under her breasts, savoring just a smidgeon of satisfaction that her silent treatment would prove to Lucas just how she felt about his stupid plan.

But he hadn't seemed to notice.

The three of them hadn't even left the city limits before Lucas had plied Zach with sports talk. Lucas did most of the talking about the Eagles. But Zach was crazy for football. How many arguments had she had with him during his preteen years over staying up late to watch the game? The conversation became more two-sided when the subject switched to the Phillies. If only Zach could remember algebraic equations as easily as he spouted off batting stats. He became almost animated. Well, as animated as a sullen fifteen-year-old will allow himself to become, anyway, when the conversation turned to ice hockey. All that talk of power play percentages and shot on goals and shutouts became as mind numbing as a hefty shot of Novocain to Tyne.

The fact that father and son were talking was a good thing—she exhaled loudly, cheeks puffing, bangs blowing—*wasn't* it? Brooding like a four-year-old was stupider than Lucas's stupid plan. She realized that, but she couldn't do a damned thing about the irritation chewing her insides.

They'd passed Lancaster not long ago, so she knew they weren't far from their destination. Wikweko, a tiny hamlet located due west of Philadelphia, was nestled in a beautiful valley between the Susquehanna River and the City of Lancaster. The Native Americans who had come together to settle Wikweko shared the fertile basin with the people of nearby Oak Mills. Tyne's hometown.

The silence that had settled over Lucas and Zach tugged at Tyne's attention. She glanced toward them, then saw her son dart two quick looks at his father. An odd, kinetic tension simmered inside the car.

Finally, he said, "So, um, I'm, ah, Lenape, huh?"

Her gaze clashed with Lucas's in the rearview mirror.

"Honey," she said to her son, leaning forward and placing her hand on his shoulder. Shifting in the seat gave her a chance to support her son, but it had also allowed her to avoid Lucas's hard stare. "You knew your father was Native American. We talked about it."

Zach went still. He didn't turn around to look at her. "Yeah. We talked about it. Once. For that family genealogy project I did back in *fourth grade.*"

She slid back into the seat, mindful of Lucas's gaze boring into hers in that small mirror. Tyne glanced out the window and saw the Wikweko welcome sign.

"We're here." Tension and anger and sheer frustration strangled her pronouncement.

"What's it mean?" Zach asked. "Wikweko. Is this place named after someone?"

Lucas shook his head as he turned onto the community's main street. "No, it's from our people's native tongue. Algonquin. It means 'place where something ends.' My great-grandparents and a slew of other Lenape families pooled their money and bought this land." He made another turn. "They'd been tossed out of their homes, their land confiscated by the government, or they'd been swindled by fast-talking reps of big businesses. Things were harsh for our ancestors. I'm sure you've learned about that in your US history classes. A lot of people spent generations feeling lost, like drifters without a real home. They named the community Wikweko, thinking this would be the place where their wandering would end."

"Algonquin, huh? Saa-weet." Zach twisted in his seat to face Lucas. "You know any other words?"

Lucas lifted one shoulder. "I used to. When I was about your age, my uncle taught me some. Hello. Good-bye. Sky. Sun. Moon. The names of a few plants and animals. That kind of thing." He looked at Zach and grinned. "Just enough to impress the girls."

Zach snickered. Tyne forced her gaze away from Lucas's striking profile, focusing instead on the passing scenery. She'd certainly been impressed by him all those years ago. He'd been so different from the boys she'd grown up with in Oak Mills. His swarthy skin and sharp bone structure. Those dark, penetrating eyes. His bad-boy manner. His self-assurance. His quiet yet unmistakably proud demeanor. She'd been attracted to him immediately. Tyne let her eyelids slide shut, and the past became as clear as the present.

Amëwë is what he'd called her, the soft syllables tickling across her skin when he'd whispered them close to her ear. "Little bumblebee" fit, he'd told her, because she'd stung him in the heart. She'd razzed him mercilessly about the corniness of it, but she remembered how she'd melted in his hands that moonless night.

The car jolted slightly when Lucas steered onto a pea stone driveway.

The familiar red brick ranch house had Tyne smiling. "We're staying with Jasper?"

Lucas shook his head as he put the car in park and cut the engine. "Uncle Jasper doesn't live here any more. The house is mine now. I'm going to renovate the place and use it as a rental property. As soon as I can get around to it."

The three of them climbed out of the car, and Zach looked at his father over the car roof. "I have an uncle?"

"A great-uncle," Lucas corrected. They congregated near the trunk. "My father died when I was nine. Uncle Jasper moved in. Took over the mortgage, the utilities. Raised me like I was his own."

Tyne tugged at the hem of her blouse, then smoothed her hand over her hair. "How is Jasper?"

"He's doing okay." Lucas shrugged vaguely. "I guess."

Lucas opened the trunk, and Zach pulled out his suitcase and backpack. "When do I get to meet him? My uncle. I mean, your uncle. My great-uncle." Zach paused after slinging the backpack over his shoulder. "Do I get to call him Uncle Jasper too?"

Tyne went utterly still. She hadn't seen Zach smile in a long time.

"Let's slow down a little," Lucas said, his chin tucked tight as he unloaded the trunk. "Let's go inside and get settled. There's plenty of time to do everything we want to do."

Zach turned and made his way to the front door.

She reached for her case.

"I've got it," Lucas told her.

"No, thanks." Her fingers contacted his on the handle, and his skin felt fire-hot. "I can take care of myself." She gave a little tug and he let go.

"Suit yourself."

"I will, thanks." She flashed him a plastic "*screw-you*" smile before turning and following Zach.

She shouldn't continue this infantile behavior. Really. But she didn't want to be here in Wikweko. Didn't want to leave her business. Didn't want to be forced to live under the same roof with this man for the next thirty days. Lucas would just have to understand where she was coming from. If he couldn't... *tough.*

Lucas slid between Tyne and Zach to unlock the front door. As soon as he entered, he set down his own suitcase and tugged off the sheet that covered the couch. The curtains were drawn, and white sheets still hid the remainder of the furniture, but a deep sense of nostalgia rolled through Tyne when she stepped into the living room. How many Saturday afternoons had she sat here watching television with Lucas? It had been a different couch, of course, but they had spent so much time together—in this room, in this house—getting to know each other, talking about their hopes and dreams.

"It won't take me long to clean this place up," Lucas assured them.

"We'll help." Tyne moved further into the room, nudging her son ahead of her. "Won't we, Zach?"

"Sure. I guess."

The petulance in his tone had her cutting a sideways glance of warning at him. "Of course, we will. Lucas, tell us where to stow our bags, and we can get to work."

Lucas matched two corners of the sheet while folding it. "You take Uncle Jasper's old room. Off the kitchen." He motioned the way with a tip of his head.

"I remember. But that's the big bedroom." The suitcases were beginning to feel like lead weights in her hands.

"You take it. That way you'll have your own bathroom. Jasper added one on. The men can share. That okay with you, Zach?"

Her son shrugged. "Got no prob."

Lucas pointed down the hall. "You take the bedroom on the left. That was my old room. I don't think my uncle's changed much in there. I'll take the one straight back. The bathroom is to the right."

"Sweet," Zach said, hitching his backpack farther up on his shoulder and trekking down the hallway.

Tyne didn't get it. Zach was Mr. Sunshine with Lucas and grumpy as hell with her. She thought she and her son should be sharing some solidarity. What was going on?

A couple of hours later, all the beds had been made up with fresh sheets; the dust covers had been removed from the upholstered furniture; counters and tables had been dusted; the carpet, vacuumed; and a soft summer breeze fluttered the curtains of the open windows.

Tyne finished shining the stainless steel sink, rinsed and wrung the dishcloth, and hung it over the faucet. Then she dried her hands and, still clutching the dishtowel, she went into the living room. Seeing Lucas and Zach sitting on the couch, she frowned.

"What's going on?" Her son didn't take his eyes off the bow in his hands, so she asked, "What's that?"

Lucas chuckled. "It's a bow, Tyne."

Heat flushed her body. "I know what it is. What's he doing with it?"

"He gave it to me." Zach clutched the thick wood of the bow's handle as he lightly fingered the taut string as if it were some sort of exotic musical instrument. There was wonder in his tone, in his gaze, in his touch.

"My uncle made it for me," Lucas told Zach. "Along with a quiver of arrows. There are only a few arrows left, but we can buy some more." Then he looked at Tyne. "I found them stored in the closet. I'd like Zach to have them."

The strangest feeling welled up in Tyne. "Oh, no." She shook her head. "No, no, no. He's not accepting that. That's a *weapon*. That could be deadly. You don't give a fifteen-year-old a dangerous weapon."

Lucas looked momentarily confused, but then he smiled and shook his head. Tyne thought her brain would explode from the frustration caused by his nonchalant attitude. Zach's jaw set and his eyes grew hooded.

"Don't be silly, Tyne."

"It's a *gift*." Her son jutted his chin. "And I *am* accepting it."

"And I said you're not." Tyne planted a fist on her hip.

"He has custody this month. He gets to say what I can do and what I can't do." Zach stared at her in an evident stand-off. But it didn't take long before his gaze broke from hers, and he set the bow next to the leather quiver. "Why do you have to ruin everything? Everything!" He stood then and bolted for the front door.

The metal screen slammed shut, the bang sharply emphasizing the silence he left behind.

"What the hell do you think you're doing?" Tyne glared at Lucas.

The man sat on the sofa, cool and collected. "I'm trying to win his trust."

"Win it? Or *buy* it?"

A tiny fissure cracked through Lucas's calm. "Not only are you being unreasonable, you're also being unfair."

As teens, they had often debated the injustices of society, focusing mainly on close-mindedness and discrimination. Tyne was often upset by the bias Lucas suffered at the hands of teachers, coaches, and even peers, treatment that Lucas usually turned a blind eye to. Apparently, the years had helped him develop insight.

"It's a reasonable assessment from where I'm standing."

He cupped his knees with his palms. "Look, Tyne, the kid doesn't know me. I'm a complete stranger."

"The kid? That *kid* is my son." Everything he said seemed to grate on her.

"*Our* son," Lucas pointedly reminded her. "I have a stake in this too. I want to help him too. But you have to let me."

"That thing is a weapon."

He slid his hands over his thighs. "It can be. But it's only a weapon if a person has a mind to use it that way. And a person has to know how to use it; otherwise, it's a pretty frustrating contraption. Besides, it's safer than the knives and guns that some of the kids his age tote around these days."

"That's a ridiculous argument." Tyne rested her hand on the back of the chair, barely aware of the faint scent of pine spilling into the room on the heated breeze. "Zach has nothing to do with guns or knives."

"I was ten when Jasper made my first bow for me. A short, stubby little thing." He reached out and touched the wood of the bow he'd given Zach. "This one was a gift for my thirteenth birthday. It was too big for me, and my uncle knew it. He told me to pull it. That it would develop my muscles and callous my fingers. That when I could shoot it properly, I'd be a man."

Lucas looked up at Tyne. "I pulled on that string every day, Tyne. I was nearly Zach's age before I was strong enough to shoot with any accuracy. Uncle Jasper taught me to aim only at what I intended to shoot and to shoot where I aimed. I didn't realize it then, but he was teaching me responsibility, self-reliance, and self-confidence. Zach needs all of those things."

"How the hell do you know what Zach needs? You've spent a total of four hours of your life with him." Somewhere inside her there was a tiny seed of understanding that Lucas's argument was logical and warranted her attention, but a thick haze of emotion choked off the perception and kept it from sprouting into anything tangible.

He stood and stepped over to look out the front door. Tyne's shoulders squared.

"That boy is in deep trouble," she said. "He needs to be disciplined, not rewarded with a new toy."

"First it's a weapon. Now it's a toy." Lucas shook his head derisively. Without turning to face her, he slid his hands into his pockets. "He's not a boy, Tyne. He's almost a man. And it seems to me that the discipline should have been started long ago."

"Stop it. Just stop." She slung the dishtowel over the back of the upholstered chair. "I won't let you, or that judge, criticize my parenting. I'm a good mother, damn it! You have no idea what Zach and I have faced over the years. What *I*"—she poked herself in the chest—"have gotten us through. With very little help. From *anyone*. So I don't want to hear another word of disapproval from you. You don't know. You just don't know."

Lucas sighed as he turned to look at her. "Listen, Tyne, I don't mean to assign blame, and the last thing I want to do is argue with you at every turn. We need to focus on the problem. Zach is in trouble and he needs our help. And we won't be able to help him if we're constantly at each other's throats."

Tyne kept her mouth shut, shifted her weight to her right foot, and crossed her arms over her chest. The raw edges of her emotions refused to allow her to acknowledge that the man had made a valid point or two. Her silence would have to suffice.

"I get it, okay?" he continued. "I get that you're angry. You're angry that you're here. You're angry about the past. I get it." He lifted one hand and rubbed the back of his neck. "For what it's worth, I'm not so sure coming here was the best solution. But this is where we're at. This is what we've got. We have to make it work. We have to make it work together, you and I. For Zach.

"And about the past"—he lifted both hands, palms up, then let them fall to his sides—"I've got so many questions, I don't even know where to begin. But I know asking them will only lead to more arguments, more blame, more anger. I think the best thing for us to do is focus on the problem. For now, at least." He glanced out the door, then back at Tyne, murmuring, "Let's just focus on the problem."

He moved back to the couch and picked up the bow. "I want him to have this, Tyne. If you say not now, then that's how it'll have to be. But I want you to know, I'll just wait until he's eighteen and give it to him then." Lucas set the bow down again. "It's perfectly safe, you know. And I'd be with him. I'd teach him to use it. Properly. We need something, Tyne. He and I. Something to help us connect. Some reason to be together. So we can talk. So we can get to know one another." Again, he sighed. "I hope you'll change your mind."

For long seconds she remained silent, her jaw clenched until it ached. Finally, she murmured, "Okay."

He shook his head, confused. "Okay what? Okay, we shouldn't fight? Okay, we need to work together? Okay, Zach can have the bow? What?"

She swallowed hard. "Okay to everything." She snatched up the dishtowel. "But I don't like it, Lucas. Any of it. Not one bit. I want you to know that. I want you to know exactly how I feel." She looked down to see that she'd stretched the towel taut. "We do have to work with what we've got. But I damn well don't have to like it."

Tyne turned, stalked straight through the kitchen, down the short hall to the bedroom and shut the door.

After stripping down to her panties and bra, Tyne sprawled out on the bed. Maybe a nap would help cool her anger. Everything she'd said to Lucas had been the truth. She had struggled as a single parent, and no one could understand the pitfalls she'd experienced. The situation that forced all of them into this damned exile galled her to the core. Her heart ached for Zach, yet at the same time, she hated that she felt disappointed in him, hated that his mistake shined a bad light on her mothering skills. She wished she didn't have to be here, didn't have to deal with this mess. But she probably shouldn't have lashed out at Lucas about it. As angry as she was, logic and reason told her he was only trying to help Zach. Why couldn't she give him a little credit for that?

She rolled over onto her back, splayed her hands on her stomach, and stared at the ceiling. As her breathing became more measured, her shoulders relaxed, and her eyelids fluttered shut. Her thoughts drifted to the past, as if she were transported by some plush and magical carpet.

The first time she and Lucas had spent the night together, they'd packed sleeping blankets, sandwiches, fresh fruit, and water, and they'd slipped off into the woods together on a moonless summer night. She had lied to her parents—blatantly and boldly—and she hadn't been bothered by a single twinge of guilt for doing it. Even now, she grinned at the monumental audacity she'd exhibited back then, when it came to finding ways to be with Lucas.

His ability to build a fire, construct a lean-to for shelter, and, yes, speak the soft syllables that made up the words of his native tongue had impressed her. But she'd been so utterly *in lust* with him at the time, she'd have agreed to spend the night with him at the complete mercy of the elements during a monsoon.

"It's so dark," she complained, right after a screech owl had let out a heart-stopping shriek. She snuggled up against him, and he chuckled at her fear. Then he assured her there was nothing in the woods that would harm them.

"I chose the night of the new moon for a good reason," he told her. "Less chance of us being seen." Then he slid his arm around her shoulders. "And it's also a night when the stars really put on a show."

They were miles away from street lamps and house lights, far from town and neighborhoods. The sky was an inky dome, a perfect backdrop for the stars that glittered like gem chips, sapphires, rubies, emeralds, and of course a multitude of diamonds.

Their kisses and caresses had been innocent at first, but when their breathing became labored, they had peeled off their clothes, with no inhibitions. Lying naked in his arms, beneath the dazzling stars, had Tyne experiencing a freedom like she'd never felt in her life.

His golden-brown skin rippled with muscle; his hands and lips on her body ignited powerful urges in her. His breath was soft against her cheek as he hovered over her.

"I can see the stars shining in your eyes," he whispered. "And you're more beautiful than a whole universe of stars."

She marveled at how comfortable he seemed voicing those kinds of feelings, compliments that could almost be poetic. It was curl-your-toes romantic.

He stroked his fingertips down her neck and chest, over her breast, and then he lowered his head and took the dark peak into his mouth. She gasped at the deliciousness of it, and it seemed like the most natural thing in the world to lift her hips and press herself against him.

When he entered her that first time, the pain made her eyes go wide. He'd apologized, hugged her, kissed her, and soon she was panting and writhing beneath him.

Their first time had ended a bit awkwardly, with both of them feeling unsure where to focus their gazes or rest their hands, but they'd fixed that by practicing for two full days. And even though they'd been young and inexperienced when they'd walked into those woods, they'd been quick to learn at least some of the erotic secrets the other held. Over the course of that long, lazy weekend, they'd made slow, sensuous love, and swift, sweaty love, and every other type of love they could think of to make.

Screwing hadn't been their only pastime. They'd walked through the lush forest and fished in a nearby stream. Lucas had laughed when Tyne squealed over having caught a fish. He'd cleaned it, and she'd done her best to cook it, and he'd pronounced it the most delicious fillet on a stick he'd ever eaten; she'd agreed.

They'd celebrated by getting naked and playing in the knee-high creek. When she saw the leech that attached itself to her calf, she'd screamed and run. Lucas had to catch her, and then he told her to sit tight. He'd gone to the fire, deftly lit the end of a thin twig, and then blew out the flame. One careful touch of the glowing ember had the slimy creature releasing its hold and dropping to the ground. Lucas cleaned the blood from her leg and kissed away her tears, and then they made love right there on the mossy bank.

That's when he'd called her Amëwë for the very first time. That's the moment he'd told her he loved her; he'd spoken the words with such intensity, Tyne had difficulty holding his gaze. Her eyes had welled with tears, and she'd been sure the very fabric of her heart would rip apart from the immense emotion swelling there.

Tyne blinked several times and shoved herself up from the mattress, the ache in her heart keeping steady time with the heavy throb between her legs. Damn it. Looked like a nap wasn't on the agenda, after all. Maybe what she needed was a cool shower. No maybe about it.

She reached for her robe and headed for the door.

CHAPTER FIVE

Wikweko's Artists' Alley consisted of a winding, brick walkway that ran a full block between Main Street and Water Street. Signs clearly marked the Alley at both ends, Lucas told Zach and Tyne, for the growing tourist trade. The three of them entered town on Main Street and swung around the block to park in the lot located on Water Street, so they were able to view the quaint lane of galleries from one end then the other.

Zach sucked in his breath as he opened the car door. "Yowch," he grumbled, gently shaking his right hand.

"Those blisters will callous over in no time," Lucas assured him.

Tyne shut her door and lifted her face to the bright summer sunshine. For three afternoons she'd been left to her own devices while Zach and Lucas had disappeared with a packed lunch, a jug of water, and the bow. Tyne wasn't sure where they'd gone each day, but they returned home in time to eat the dinner she prepared. They must have done a lot of hiking, because Zach seemed too tired to talk much in the evenings. Which meant he was also too tired to argue with or snap at her.

She couldn't remember the last time she'd sat outside and read a book. Already, the sun had tinged her skin golden, and she felt well rested.

Several times since arriving in Wikweko, Tyne had overheard Zach ask Lucas when they could visit Jasper. Each time, Lucas had either put him off or diverted Zach's attention to another topic. This morning, both Lucas and Zach had complained of sore fingertips, so they'd decided to take a break from archery practice. Again, Zach had posed meeting his great-uncle, and this time he refused to be sidetracked from the issue.

Tyne looked around at the shops. "The last time I was here, there was no such thing as Artists' Alley. Or a tourist trade. Water Street hadn't even been paved."

Surprise momentarily slackened the tension on Zach's face. "You were here before? In Wikweko?" he asked her. Tyne only had time to nod before her son turned to Lucas. "I assumed you met my mom in the city."

"No," Lucas answered easily. "We met here. Or rather in Oak Mills. A town a few miles down the road. That's where your mom was born. Where we both attended high school. But we spent a lot of time here in Wikweko."

Avoiding his mother altogether, Zach stuffed his hands into the pockets of his baggie jeans and hunched his shoulders as he quickened his step to forge ahead of them.

Lucas sidled up beside her. "A lot's changed around here in sixteen years, don't you think? Wikweko High School was built about five years ago. We have our own post office now. We have a weekly newspaper. And a Starbucks, if you can believe it."

She sensed his edginess, heard the tension in his voice. He hadn't even noticed Zach's surly withdrawal.

"Why don't you want to see Jasper, Lucas?"

He stopped short. "What are you talking about?"

She paused, lifting her hand to shield her eyes from the sunlight. "Zach has asked every day to meet your uncle and you put him off every time. The only reason we're here is because neither of you can pull the string on that bow because of blisters. My guess is that you've been avoiding Jasper."

"That's ridiculous." Lucas's clipped gait forced Tyne to walk fast to keep up. "I don't have any blisters. And I'm not avoiding anyone."

He called out to Zach. "You've passed the gallery. Uncle Jasper's place is here." Lucas rushed forward to open the door for them.

The stylish sign hanging above the door didn't display a name; it only portrayed a fierce-looking hawk that had been crafted from some silver-toned metal. The detail work of the animal was exquisite. A bell attached to the door tinkled when they entered, and inside, the shop was cool and still.

"Wow." Zach breathed out the word rather than spoke it. "Look at that." He moved to the large eagle, its wings spread wide, perched on a glass shelf in a well-lit corner. A predatory fierceness had been meticulously etched into every aspect of the bird from its glaring eyes down to its salient talons. The sculpture's surface had been polished to a high sheen that accented the wood's grain.

The air suddenly filled with a haunting flute melody accompanied by a single drum piped into the room over the sound system.

"I'll be right there," a masculine voice called from a back room.

In his mid-sixties, Jasper Silver Hawk had classic Native American features: high cheekbones, deep-set eyes the color of glossy onyx, a ruddy complexion riddled with crevices etched by a lifetime spent in the sun and wind. A regal face you might see stamped onto an ancient coin.

"Lucas," the man exclaimed. "I heard you were back in town."

"Uncle Jasper," Lucas greeted.

The men shook hands, and although their words were warm, their brief embrace looked awkward to Tyne as they clapped each other on the back.

"I'm sure you remember Tyne," Lucas said to his uncle.

Jasper's gaze fell on her, genuine affection pervading his quick smile. "Of course. How could I forget? Tyne, you've become a beautiful woman."

"And you haven't changed a bit," she told him, stepping into his open arms.

He hugged her tightly and murmured, "The years refuse to pass without leaving their mark." He didn't let her go immediately, and Tyne rested her cheek on his shoulder.

Whether it was the truth in his profound remark, the tenderness in his greeting, or the moving memories of a more innocent time, Tyne couldn't say, but unexpected tears stung her eyes.

"It's good to see you, Jasper." When they parted, she swiped at the moisture clinging to her lashes with her fingertips. "I wasn't sure you'd even speak to me. The way I left all those years ago. You know," she murmured, "without saying goodbye."

Voicing her doubts wasn't something she was in the habit of doing. Experience had taught her that revealing her fears only left her vulnerable, but Jasper's warmth had melted those remarks right out of her.

Her face flushed and she forged ahead. "Jasper, I, um, I'd like you to meet my son."

Zach had been standing off to the side, waiting to be introduced, but now he moved forward. Tyne put a hand on her son's shoulder. Having been unaware of the teen's presence, Jasper's expression widened with joy.

"Your son, Tyne? How wonderful." He reached out his hand and Zach clasped it with his own.

"This is Zachary," Tyne said. "Zach, this is Jasper Silver Hawk. Uncle Jasper."

"I've been, like, wanting to meet you, like, *forever*." Zach continued to shake the older man's hand heartily. "Well, ever since I found out about you, anyway."

Only a teen could make seventy-two hours sound like a lifetime.

"Silver Hawk. I get it now," Zach told Jasper, nodding. "The sign outside above the door."

Tyne looked at Lucas, silently urging him to say something.

"He's a fine-looking young man, Tyne," Jasper said. "Tall and strong."

Lucas edged up beside Zach and clamped his hand on his son's shoulder. "He looks like his old man, don't you think?"

Jasper went still, and then he beamed. He hugged Zach to him and clapped Lucas on the back. He looked from Zach to Lucas to Tyne and finally pronounced, "This is good."

Everyone was smiling and jovial, enjoying the moment, until it turned fuzzy and warm and uncomfortable. Tyne and Lucas caught one another's eye, and their smiles slipped. In unison, they inched backward, stepping out of the cozy family circle.

"Did you carve the eagle?" Zach asked Jasper, seemingly oblivious to his parents' uneasiness.

"I did."

"It's, like, *amazing*."

Tyne followed her son and Jasper to the window to admire the sculpture and stood long enough to learn that the carving was made from the trunk of a black walnut tree that had been felled by a lightning strike, that a chisel and mallet had been the tools of choice, and that it had taken months for the figure to take form. Lucas kept himself separate, studying the paintings displayed on the far wall of the shop.

The bold colors used in the landscapes were at the same time jarring and intriguing, teasing the observer into a closer look. And Tyne fell victim.

One painting in particular, with its orange sunset and sienna trees, drew her. "It's beautiful," she murmured to Lucas. "They're all beautiful. Really unique, you know?" She didn't expect an answer. "I remember when we were teens that Jasper painted, but I never realized he had such talent."

"Neither did I," Lucas said quietly.

"Guess we didn't pay enough attention."

He lifted one shoulder. "Guess not."

They stood for several long moments looking at each other, and then they focused their attention on the art.

Every time she even considered talking to him, she hit this solid stone wall. She didn't know if she'd built it or if he had. Oh, hell. She ought to be mature enough to admit the truth.

For the past sixteen years she'd done all she could to foster her independence. Knowing that she'd pretty much made her own way over the years and had raised Zach by herself offered her a deep sense of satisfaction. She'd thought she'd risen above the past. Thought it could no longer affect her. But every time she looked at Lucas, every time she tried to communicate with him, she was reminded of the stark truth.

The unhappy adolescent she had once been continued to haunt her. The passionate teenager who had surrendered herself—mind and body, heart and soul—to Lucas still lived deep inside. The young woman who had been forced to leave town in disgrace was coming out of hiding. She thought she'd dealt with all the hurts, bandaged all the wounds that had been inflicted on her so many years ago. But merely being in Lucas's presence forced her to see that, beneath the makeshift dressings, she was still raw and aching. Bitter. And furious.

"Zach and I will be right back."

Tyne and Lucas turned at the sound of Jasper's voice.

Jasper stood with Zach at the threshold of the hallway that led to the back of the shop.

"We're going upstairs for some goldenseal salve," Jasper said. "For Zach's blisters."

Lucas straightened. "I found the bow you made for me at the house."

Jasper nodded.

"I heard that you used to win the archery competition at every powwow," Zach said to Jasper. "Will you shoot with us one day while we're here?"

"I am out of practice." The elderly man directed his keen black gaze at Lucas. "There haven't been archery competitions for years."

"What?" Lucas's head tilted the tiniest bit. "But why?"

Jasper lifted one hand, palm out, fingers splayed. "Lack of interest." He glanced at Zach. "Come with me. I want to put some salve on those fingers so they don't get infected."

The two of them disappeared down the hall.

"Hold on just one darn second here," Tyne said. "Just a few minutes ago you were bragging to me about how Wikweko has grown. 'We have our own post office,' you said. 'We have a newspaper.' *We.*" She emphasized the pronoun with a small, derisive wobble of her head. "You talked like you share some kind of kindred spirit with these people, this community. But it sounds like you haven't been back, Lucas. How long has it been? You haven't even come home for powwows? That's a big deal to the people here. I know it is."

She waited for him to answer, and when he didn't, she let loose a sharp sigh. "Admit it. You share about as much spirit with Wikweko as I do."

"I care enough to subscribe to the paper." He leaned his hip against a display case. "So I can read up on what's happening. I don't think you have any right to give me grief. Your son didn't even know you were born and raised here."

She chose to ignore that comment completely. "Why haven't you been back, Lucas? You and Jasper were as close as father and son. What happened?"

He studied her face for a moment. Finally, he said. "Nothing happened, Tyne."

Sunlight drilled through the window behind her, heating the spot directly between her shoulder blades. "I don't believe that. I saw the two of you together. Awkward doesn't begin to describe what I saw when the two of you greeted each other."

He shook his head. "Look, it's nothing, okay? My job comes with a great deal of responsibility. It's hard for me to leave Philadelphia. As soon as Uncle Jasper and I spend a little time together, our relationship will smooth out."

Tyne stood there, frowning at him. He'd missed holidays with his uncle. Lots of them. *Years'* worth of them from the sound of it. He hadn't been to powwow. Those gatherings were sacred to the Lenape of Wikweko.

As a teen, she'd been fascinated by the rituals, the legends passed on to the younger generations; the large, smoky bonfire; the delicious food; the games of skill; the camaraderie. Lucas had taken her to several of the celebrations while they were dating, and people had come from all over the country, some of them traveling thousands of miles, to attend. Tyne couldn't fathom Lucas missing even one of these very special events. Especially when he lived less than two hours away.

"Lucas—"

"Give it a rest, Tyne. Everything will be fine between my uncle and me. You'll see." He stalked away from her, crossed the small gallery, and with his back to her, stood gazing at the magnificent eagle.

∽

"Does Uncle Jasper know why we're here?" Zach looked over at Lucas from the front passenger seat of the car and then darted a quick glance at Tyne in the back seat.

"I haven't said anything to anyone," Lucas said. "So I don't know how he could. Why do you ask?"

Zach shrugged. "I dunno. He made me feel a little"—again he shrugged—"self-conscious, I guess. When he was showing me his studio—which is pretty amazing, by the way—he said he spends the whole winter carving and then spends the summer selling his stuff." Zach shoved his hair back off his forehead. "Anyway, he told me that my grandfather would have been proud of me. He mentioned that my grandfather was an honorable man. He used that word twice. Honorable." He glanced out the window and his voice went soft as he added, "Made me feel...I don't know, kinda weird. Like maybe he was pointing out that he thinks that I'm not...or something." He looked over at Lucas. "Without actually sayin' it, I mean."

Tyne curled her fingers around the strap of the seatbelt to keep from reaching out to her son.

"If there's one thing about my uncle I do know," Lucas told him, "it's that he says what he means and means what he says."

They had spent another forty minutes at the shop before customers came in and began wanting Jasper's attention, so they felt they should leave.

"I don't believe Jasper knows anything about the trouble you're in." Tyne leaned forward. "How could he? We're the only ones here who know about it, and we haven't said a word to anyone." When Zach didn't pay her any heed, she reclined against the seat again to watch the passing scenery.

"'Honorable' is a word Uncle Jasper always uses whenever he talks about my father." Lucas shifted his hands on the steering wheel. "I think he wants my dad to be remembered with respect and admiration." He glanced over at Zach and then back at the road. "I can remember many, *many*"—he repeated the word with a chuckle—"times when my uncle explained the importance of honor to me. He felt that a man could have many things—wealth, prominence in the community, intelligence—what have you—but if he had no integrity, he had nothing worth having."

"Is that a Lenape thing? A culture thing?" Zach asked. "To lecture on honor?"

"Well, I guess you could say that, but..." Lucas shook his head. "There's not a single race of people I know of that would want their sons and daughters to grow up to become liars and thieves."

The comment made Tyne smile. "That's true enough."

"Speaking of culture," Zach said to Lucas, "Uncle Jasper invited me to the Community Center tomorrow night. He said the kids go to meetings every week and learn about the past. Uncle Jasper goes. And other members of the Council of Elders. He said they tell stories, true stories from history, and some folklore too. They teach the kids about the old ways, he said. How to make a rabbit trap or how to churn butter or grind corn—that kind of thing. He said this week they'll have a bonfire. That they'll teach the kids a special tribal dance." He reached up and scratched the back of his neck. "I told him I don't have the moves and ended up having to explain what that meant: that I dance like I have two huge left feet. He said I could learn to drum some of the rhythms. You think I could go?"

Lucas looked at Tyne in the rearview mirror. She nodded.

"Of course," Lucas said. "I think that's a good idea. You'll have fun and meet some other kids from the community." He grinned. "And you might learn something too."

Zach dipped his chin and shook his head. "I'm not *dancing*, that's for sure."

When he looked at Lucas again, his expression was serious. "Could we not tell him?" he asked. "You know, about why we're here?"

Tyne didn't wait for Lucas to answer. "It wouldn't be right to tell any blatant lies, son."

"Yeah, I guess." Zach's tone sounded defeated. Then he swallowed and squared his shoulders. "But if nobody asks, we don't have to offer, right?"

For the beat of several seconds all that could be heard was the whirr of the air conditioner.

Softly, Lucas said, "We don't have to offer. But unfortunately they aren't called skeletons in a closet for nothing. Secrets have a way of showing their bones."

CHAPTER SIX

Lucas crossed the lawn with two chilled beers in hand, heading for the picnic table where Tyne sat with her back to him. The small sliver of crescent moon hung too high in the night sky to offer much light, forcing him to make his way slowly across the cool grass.

He missed the reserved, almost bashful girl he remembered Tyne to be back when they'd been a couple. He'd had to work hard—coaxing and encouraging her—to get her to voice an opinion about whatever subject came up between them. Her self-consciousness had attracted him, made him want to draw her out. The memory made him smile in the darkness and pine for the innocents they'd been back then.

However, the confident, outspoken woman she'd become thoroughly intrigued him. The interest she stirred in him is what had driven him to leave the documentary he'd been watching and seek her out, even though he knew full well that their encounter would probably end up in an argument. She'd developed self-assurance in the years since they had parted, but she'd also grown prickly as hell.

He gave a polite cough to let her know he was approaching, and when she turned, he offered a grin. "Hey, there. You up for a cold one?"

"Thanks." She took the bottle from him and turned back to face the table when he straddled the bench. "I thought it would cool off a little when the sun went down."

"Zach complained about the heat, so I closed the windows and turned on the air. I hope you don't mind."

She shook her head. "Not at all. We'll all sleep better if it's cooler inside." She lifted her gaze upward. "Would you get a load of that sky?"

Stars glittered and winked like gems against the inky backdrop. "As Zach would say... 'sah-weet.'"

Tyne laughed at his spot-on imitation.

"You okay?" he asked. "You've been out here a long time by yourself."

She lifted the bottle to her lips and then cradled it between laced fingers. "Believe it or not, I've been watching the fireflies. When I was a girl, I used to go outside on hot summer nights and catch as many as I could in a jar. I would sit on the grass and watch them for hours."

"I caught them too. In an old mason jar. I used to set them on my bedside table and they'd glow all night long." He grinned. "Uncle Jasper made me let them go in the morning."

Her mouth cocked to one side. "I wasn't allowed to bring them inside."

Remembering her parents, he chuckled. "No doubt." He took a couple swallows of the cold beer, then said, "So what has you reminiscing about bugs?" She continued to stare at the glowing insects hovering and darting in the yard, and he couldn't figure out whether she hadn't heard him or she simply intended to ignore the question. Feeling the need to say something, he murmured, "Every kid catches fireflies."

Tyne shook her head. "Nope," she said quietly. "Not every kid." She avoided his gaze. "Listen to those peepers out there. A couple of times tonight that sound became deafening. I've heard them every night since we arrived. I'd forgotten what it was like to fall asleep to the sound of tree frogs." Then she glanced at him. "Do you know there are no tree frogs in the city? Oh, maybe along Kelly Drive out near the reservoir, or in Washington Square. But I don't live near any of the parks or wooded areas. And I can't ever remember seeing a firefly in the postage-stamp piece of grass I call a yard."

She went quiet.

"What's all this about, Tyne?"

Still she didn't look at him. "Just thinking."

He didn't respond, figuring she'd elaborate in her own good time. Or not. Pressing her would only lead to trouble.

She picked up the bottle, took a long drink, and then set it back down on the table. "I've been trying to figure out where I went wrong. Was it that I raised Zach in the city? Could I have avoided all this—spray paint, police stations, court appearances, that god-awful dressing down by the judge—if I had brought him back home and raised him here?"

"Tyne, people live and raise their kids where they can find work. You've made a success of yourself living in Philly."

She muttered, "To my son's detriment."

"Don't be so hard on yourself."

She seemed stone deaf to his advice.

"Did he get into this trouble because I fed him too much sugar as a child? Or because I wasn't watching closely enough when he was three, and he stuck a bobby pin in that electric outlet? Or because I tried to do it all on my own? Because I left him with sitters? Because I put him in day care too early?"

Her large and beseeching eyes tore at his heart.

"Tyne, Zach is a good kid. You've done a good job. Okay, so he got into a little trouble. In the grand scheme of things, spray painting graffiti isn't all that serious. We'll get through this."

Her breath left her in a rush, and she turned to stare off at the horizon.

"You did the best you could. No one can ask more of you than that. I'm confident that you fed him right, took him to the doctor when he was sick, made sure he was inoculated against all manner of disease, made him do his homework. And I'm sure you only left him with people you trusted." He couldn't stop his grin. "Did he really stick a bobby pin in an outlet?"

She nodded miserably.

He wanted to laugh, but didn't. "Lots of teens go through a rebellious period. I know *I* did. This trouble Zach's in has nothing to do with where you chose to live, or that you're a single mom, or that he might have eaten one too many donuts."

She planted her elbow on the table, pressed her fist to her mouth.

"He probably would have experienced this defiant stage no matter where you raised him." Lucas rolled the bottom of the bottle against the wood of the tabletop, the foamy beer sloshing against the inside of the glass. "We can't even say that things would be different had I been in the picture from the beginning."

She rubbed her fingers against her temple. "Every mother wants a perfect family for her child."

"There's no such thing as a perfect family, Tyne. Every person—every parent—has quirks. No one is faultless. No family is perfectly ideal."

"But maybe if he'd had—"

"Stop." He paused and spoke her name, and then he waited several long seconds for her to look at him. "You grew up in the supposedly perfect, nuclear family. One dad. One mom. One daughter."

"Big house," she took up the litany, "big yard, and more *things* than any one little girl ever needed." She scooted her bottom against the bench. "And I was utterly miserable."

Lucas left the bottle next to hers so he could lift his leg over the bench to sit closer to her. "I never even met my mother. And my father died when I was really young. I don't remember a whole lot about him. But I still remember my childhood as being very happy. I'd put my uncle up against any mom-and-dad team out there."

Her mouth twisted wryly. "You were lucky."

The scent of wild roses drifted on the slight evening breeze.

His elbows on the table, Lucas laced his fingers and rested his chin on them. "It's not about who raises kids, Tyne. I mean, not that I know all that much about it. But logic tells me that what's more important is that the raising is done with love."

He knew in the light of day her eyes were a deep, clear blue, but the night turned them navy. Self-doubt shadowed them with vulnerability.

"It's obvious that you love Zach, Tyne. It's been impossible for me not to see it." He pressed his lips together, realizing he owed her an apology. "I regret questioning your parenting skills in front of the judge. I shouldn't have done that. And I'm truly sorry."

The tension in her expression eased, and at last she offered him the smallest of smiles. "Thanks, Lucas. That means a lot. A whole lot." Instantly, the corners of her mouth turned down. "I've spent hours and hours trying to figure out where I've gone wrong. I don't think I've been the best mother. It's worrisome, you know?" She sighed. "I always thought I was on the ball with this parenting thing. I always thought I knew my son and that I was sharp and quick in all the ways that mattered when you're raising a child. But I've just recognized over the past few days that I'm not all that sharp. And I'm certainly not quick. There have been things going on that I didn't even know about."

He lowered his hands into his lap and leaned forward enough so that he could see her face.

Her head tilted and her gaze connected with his. "I've just discovered that Zach is angry with me. He's spitting mad, Lucas. And I haven't a clue how long he's felt this way." She tucked a strand of her long hair behind her ear. "What's worse is I have no idea *why* the hell he's so mad."

She closed her eyes, her anguish unmistakable. Lucas didn't know what to do, what to say.

"Talk about being disillusioned." Her laughter was spiky and sardonic. "I've been bebopping along, as sanctimonious as anybody can be, thinking none of this is my fault. That I'd given him all I could. Offered him all I had. And now I'm realizing that my son has been trying to communicate"—she shook her head, groping for words—"*something*. His frustrations, maybe? Some need I didn't know about? I don't know. But I completely missed the boat. I didn't see it. I wasn't aware. I think he's angry that I haven't been there for him. That's got to be why he's snapping and snarling at me one minute and then ignoring me the next. He still wasn't getting my attention, so he went out and found a way to really wake me up. God, Lucas, I'm to blame for all of this."

"No one person is to blame, Tyne," he assured her. He was about to say more, but she turned her whole body to face him suddenly.

"Has he said anything? While the two of you have been out shooting and hiking, has he talked about how he's feeling?" She gave a small, frustrated shake of her head and her corn-silk hair rustled around her shoulders, radiant. "About me? About his life?"

Lucas shook his head. "Not really. We've spent a little of our time talking, getting to know one another. He told me a little about school. Some of his teachers. He's mentioned a couple of friends, what he likes to do, places he likes to hang out, that kind of thing. I've told him stories from my childhood, mostly. What it was like growing up here. He seemed really interested, and I just thought that was because my teen years were so different from his." He lifted one shoulder, one hand. "We're in the beginning stages of this thing. Zach and I need time to build up a little trust." She looked disappointed, and he slid his fingers over her forearm. "Hey, that's what this month is for, Tyne. Smoothing out the ruffles. Figuring out the problems and finding some answers. We don't have to solve everything in the first week, you know?"

The stiffness in her narrow shoulders relaxed, and she took a deep breath. She picked up her bottle of beer and held the cool glass first to her cheek, then to her forehead. Then she took a sip.

"Maybe you should spend some time alone with him," Lucas suggested. "Just the two of you. Take him for a drive. Or a long walk. Ask him if he's got any questions. Open yourself up to him. You can't find out what he's thinking if you don't talk to him."

Her head bobbed as she considered his suggestion. "You're probably right." She nodded again, this time more firmly. "I'm sure you are, actually. I think I'll make some plans for tomorrow. Maybe we could have lunch at the diner and then take a drive somewhere. Maybe the mall in Lancaster or something. I'll have to think about it."

The silence that settled between them wasn't the least bit awkward, which amazed Lucas. He watched the fireflies, listened to the peepers, dug his bare toes into the grass. Maybe they were all making strides where relationships were concerned.

"Lucas—"

She leaned her forearm against the corner of the table and turned her head, her long hair spilling over her lowered shoulder. He felt the urge to reach out and touch it. To see if it was as silky as he'd remembered. But he resisted.

"—what happened to your mother? I don't remember us talking about her."

"I don't know any details, really. I was never encouraged to talk about her." He reached for his bottle of beer only to realize it was empty. He set it back down. "I vaguely remember when I was very young—I can't even say what age I was—someone told me she'd died when I was born."

Tyne nodded; then she went still. Suddenly, her back straightened. "But she's not in the cemetery?"

Her pointed question startled him.

"When we took tokens to your father," she continued, "we never visited your mother's grave."

When Lucas had been a young man, his feelings for Tyne had taken on a whole new dimension when she'd agreed to visit the community cemetery with him to honor his father. She'd been amazed at the practice of leaving gifts to show respect and adulation for those who had passed on. During her first of many visits there, Tyne had spoken in hushed tones as she'd pointed out the small, weather-worn stuffed animals and the jewelry sitting on top of headstones, the cards and letters wedged into crevices, even money, bills faded and stiff with age weighted down with smooth river rocks on the grassy mounds. She'd been amazed that the graveyard hadn't been ransacked, and Lucas had explained that no one would dare touch the sacred favors that people had left for their loved ones.

"If we did, I sure don't remember it. And I'm sure I would."

"You're right. We never visited her grave." Lucas felt funny, light-headed, as if he had the alcohol content of four beers racing through his veins, rather than just the one. "Because she's not buried in the cemetery."

Tyne's unfinished beer sat on the table, forgotten. "So where is she? Do you know?" Her delicate brows arched high. "Haven't you ever asked?"

If he hadn't become so rattled by the unexpected change in the topic of the conversation, her questions would have brought a smile to his face. When they were teens, she would never have questioned him, would never have confronted him in such a bold manner. He studied her face, realizing what a stunningly beautiful woman she'd become.

"No," he finally admitted, his voice coming out sounding dry and grating. "I've never asked."

"Well, Lucas, don't you think you should?"

CHAPTER SEVEN

As it turned out, Tyne wasn't able to spend Wednesday afternoon with Zach. Jasper had shown up unexpectedly and asked her son to help him get ready for the youth meeting set for that evening at the Community Center. Caught up in the excitement of new people and places, Zach had been only too eager to become better acquainted with his great-uncle, and Tyne hadn't the heart to deny either of them some time together.

Zach had arrived home after the meeting last night full of excitement about all he'd learned. He'd met half a dozen kids his age, and he held his head a tiny bit higher when he'd told them how Jasper had complimented him on his sense of rhythm. Apparently, her son was adept at playing the water drum. Gourds, dried in the sun until their seeds rattled, were also used as musical instruments. Tyne had been surprised—shocked, actually—to hear that Zach had been enticed to also try learning a dance step or two.

Even this morning, as they sat around the kitchen table, Tyne and Lucas sipping coffee, Zach continued to recount his experiences between bites of crunchy breakfast cereal.

"I'm glad you had a good time," Lucas told him.

Zach nodded. "I can't wait until next week. Alice Johnson is going to teach us to make fry bread."

Tyne placed her palm under her cup, the ceramic warm against her skin. "I didn't know you were interested in cooking."

Her son swallowed a bite of cereal and scooped up another spoonful. A fat drop of milk hung on his bottom lip and he swiped it away with the back of his hand. "It's not the cooking I'm, like, interested in really. It's finding out, like, what kind of food my people like to eat." His gaze darted to Lucas. "It's okay to call them 'my people,' right?"

A smile flitted across Lucas's mouth. "Of course. You're part of the Lenape family."

"Some of the kids talked about getting together this weekend," Zach continued easily. "Maybe play some ball or something."

"You're making new friends." Tyne set her coffee on the table. "That's great, Zach." She went to the refrigerator and pulled out a carton of orange juice. "Listen, how about we spend the day together?"

Her son looked at Lucas. "Sure. What are we going to do?"

"No, not all of us, son," Tyne gently clarified. "Just us. You and me. Lucas said we can borrow his car."

Gray clouds seemed to roll in as Zach stopped, frowned, and stared down into his bowl of milky flakes. "I dunno."

Before he could outright refuse, she smiled brightly. "I'll take you anywhere you want to go. There's a mall in Lancaster. I'll buy you a new T-shirt. Or I'll take you to a movie. Maybe we could find a comic book shop. Music store. You name it."

He toyed with his spoon the whole time she talked, glancing up at her through hooded eyes, then just as quickly looking down again. "My shirts are fine. Don't really need anything."

"Oh, come on, Zach." The pleading she heard in her tone annoyed her. She'd never thought she'd have to beg her kid to spend some time with her. "We'll have fun."

Zach's gaze narrowed on her. "We can go anywhere? You mean it?"

She nodded emphatically. "Like I said, you name the place."

The last thing she wanted to do was have her nerves frayed to ribbons by two hours spent sitting through a loud, space-age movie that would surely bring on a headache, but if it meant she could have some alone time with Zach before and afterward, she'd just have to take two aspirin and suck it up.

"I want to see the high school where you guys, like, met. Where did you say it was? Broken Mills or something?"

"Oak Mills," Lucas supplied.

Tyne couldn't have been more stunned had Zach tossed his bowl into the air and splashed milk onto the ceiling.

Zach focused his attention on Lucas. "Didn't you say that's where Mom grew up?"

Lucas nodded slowly.

Zach nodded too, looking up at Tyne. "That's where I'd like to go."

Feeling as if all the blood had drained from her face, Tyne struggled to find words to express the thoughts zipping through her head. She took a moment, turning and setting the carton she held onto the Formica countertop. Then she opened a cabinet and took down a glass with deliberation. Orange juice gushed from the container into the glass, making a small mess, which she ignored. She picked up the glass and turned back to her son.

"Are you really sure that's what you want to do? There's really nothing to do in Oak Mills. I hadn't planned on going there."

Lancaster, in fact, was located in the opposite direction from her hometown.

The storm clouds returned, this time complete with flashing lightning and rolling thunder.

"See?" Zach shoved his way up from the table, his chair grating against the linoleum. "I knew you didn't mean it. It's just like always. You only want me to do what you want me to do." He stalked toward the kitchen door. "It doesn't matter what I want. You don't *care* what I want."

"Zach!"

"Zach."

Tyne and Lucas spoke in unison.

"Hold up." The light tone of Lucas's voice belied the sudden tension in his jaw, and when Zach stopped and begrudgingly turned back to face them, he said, "Can we just take a deep breath? Can we talk about this rather than shouting?"

"There's nothin' to talk about." Zach's shoulders were hunched, his fists clenched. "It's her way or no way. Don't you see that? That's how it always is."

Tyne tried to remain calm. "That's not true."

"*It is!* It is so true."

Her son was being a little snot, and she was just on the verge of pointing that out. She blinked a couple of times as it dawned on her; he was pushing her buttons as hard as he could push. Intentionally. If they ended up in a fight, he wouldn't have to go anywhere with her.

Going to the high school where she and Lucas had first met certainly wasn't on her "top ten" list of things to do. She couldn't imagine it even making her "top one hundred." Dealing with those memories would only lead to emotional upheaval. And tears, and crying, and...useless, emotional...crap. Who the hell needed that? But if going to the school meant she could spend the day with her son, she'd do it.

She found the calm she'd been striving for. "Zach, if you want to go see Oak Mills High, then we'll go see Oak Mills High. I'll show you the football field where Lucas was a running back, and the track where I sprinted a fifty-yard dash against the fastest girl on the team."

Zach seemed to turn down his contempt a notch or two. "The fastest girl on the team? You lost?"

Tyne grinned, shaking her head. "I won. Well...I won against her *once*." She chuckled. "And that girl was full of lame excuses, let me tell you; I jumped the gun, her shoe wasn't laced tight enough, she had dirt stuck in her cleats. She was a regular Tonya Harding, that one."

The tension in her son's gangly body melted a little. "Sore loser, huh?"

"You've got that right," Lucas said, his coffee cup poised close to his mouth. "Victoria Davis got her butt whipped, fair and square." Lucas grinned at Tyne, his voice softening. "I can remember that like it was yesterday."

She remembered too. She'd hung back when the rest of the team had jogged toward the locker room after practice, and she and Lucas had celebrated her win with a few passionate moments behind the brick concession stand, where anyone might have happened upon them. Oh, the risks they had taken when they'd been teens.

"Get yourself ready," she told Zach. "And we'll go."

Her smile faded the instant her son left the kitchen, but she didn't speak until she'd heard his bedroom door close.

"I was telling him the truth when I said I hadn't been planning to visit Oak Mills." She noticed her hand wasn't as steady as she'd have liked as she lifted the glass of orange juice to her lips. "There's no one there I want to see."

Questions shadowed Lucas's dark, searching gaze, and Tyne prayed that those questions would go unasked. But evidently no one up there in heaven was listening.

"Your parents," he probed hesitantly, "are they..."

"Alive and kicking." She set down the glass of juice. "And still living in the same house. At least, they were this past Christmas. That's when I last heard from them." She slid her hand onto her hip. "And it was an official 'mayoral' Christmas card. It simply would *not* do for the Whitlocks to give up their prominence in the community, you know."

Keeping the bitterness from coating her voice was impossible. The deep breath she took didn't alleviate any of her hard feelings.

Lucas scooted his chair an inch away from the table. "But if Zach doesn't know you're from Oak Mills, then—"

"He's never met them. That's right. And that's how I hope to keep it." She reached up and flipped her hair back behind her shoulder. "They have the address of a post office box I rent out on the Main Line. They don't know my home address or my phone number. They don't know where I work. I'm sure they could find us if they tried really hard, but I've done what I could to protect our privacy. Mine and Zach's. For his safety."

Zach's bedroom door opened, his sneakers clomping down the hallway.

Lucas's brows drew together. "His safety?"

"And his mental health," she murmured.

Her son appeared in the kitchen, his hair combed and a fleck of white toothpaste speckling the neckband of his gray T-shirt. "Ready," he pronounced.

Tyne pushed away from the kitchen counter and held her hand out to Lucas. "May I borrow your keys?"

∽

Nestled on the shores of the Susquehanna River, Oak Mills was a quaint town, picturesque, a perfect place for a child to grow up. Or rather, it would have been had Tyne been born into a different family.

The school parking lot was empty when she pulled into a space. The adjacent football field and the track surrounding it were vacant as well. Zach barely waited for the car to come to a halt before he barreled out and started jogging toward the open gate.

When Tyne caught up to him, he was out in the middle of the grassy field.

"He actually played ball here?" Zach turned in a circle, staring all around him.

"He did." She grinned. "No one could run like Lucas. Of course, the place didn't look like this back then." She shaded her eyes with one hand and pointed with the other.

"Those bleachers are new, and the lights. Back then the team could only play during daylight hours, and our bleachers were only half that size. Made of painted wood and rusty metal. You were lucky if all you got was a splinter." She laughed.

"Maybe I'll go out for football next year." There was a clear challenge in the tilt of her son's head.

"I didn't know you were interested in playing football." Avoiding an argument was enough motivation to keep her tone breezy. "If that's what you want, it's okay with me. But, Zach, you *do* realize that you'll have to keep your grades up?"

He ignored that. "I can run. I can block. I could make the varsity team." He tucked an imaginary football into the crook of his arm and feigned left, then right, then raced toward the goal posts. He ran thirty yards or so and then trotted back to where she'd settled on the home players' bench near the fifty-yard line.

"So...he was good, huh?"

"Lucas? Yes. He was good."

"Was he the star player?"

Tyne hoped her smile didn't reflect the sourness she felt. "No. Not the star."

Only because his skin was the wrong color, she wanted to add, but didn't. Instead, she said, "I notice you never refer to Lucas by name. You always say 'he' or 'him.'"

Zach shrugged. "Don't know what to call him. Can't call a stranger 'Dad.' Sounds freaky. And calling him by his first name would be"—again he shrugged—"*weird.*" Abruptly, he asked, "Were you a cheerleader?"

His question made her laugh. "For about five minutes. Didn't last long. I realized really fast that I wasn't one to stand on the sidelines. I ran track and played field hockey."

"All the cheerleaders in my school are snobby beeyotches. Won't give you the time of day." Zach scratched a spot on his shoulder. "If they do happen to look at you, they make a face that has you wantin' to, like, sniff your pits when nobody's lookin' to make sure you don't smell bad or something."

Tyne chuckled, slipping the strap of her purse off her shoulder. With her parents such important figures in the town, it had been impossible for her not to have been part of the popular crowd. And, yes, she'd have fit into the beeyotch category, she was sure. The superficiality of it all, the exclusive behavior, had bothered her. She'd often yearned for something deeper, more meaningful, although, as an adolescent, she hadn't been mature enough to use those words to describe the hollowness she'd felt. But she'd be lying if she said she hadn't enjoyed the status and the unending choice of sidekicks that the name Whitlock brought her growing up in Oak Mills. However, she'd learned that admiration and popularity—not to mention loyal friends—could be as fleeting as a puff of smoke...thick one minute, vanished the next.

"This is where you beat that Veronica girl?" Zach called.

While she'd been lost in thought, he'd made his way over to the track. She got up, snagged her purse strap, and went to the white starting line.

"Yep. Right here." She tucked her purse under her elbow. "But it wasn't paved or painted back then. It was covered in some kind of loose, gritty gray stuff. Covered your shoes with dust and turned your socks the color of lead."

She tapped the bottom of her sandal against the tartan surface. "This is nice." The silence that splayed over them was uncomfortable, like a scratchy wool blanket on a hot night. Tyne wanted to shove it off her as quickly as possible. "You could talk to him, you know. Talk to him about it."

Zach just looked at her.

"About what to call him, I mean."

She held her breath, uncertain if what she'd said would touch off his teenaged short fuse.

Finally, he only nodded, turning to glance up toward the school building that sat up on a small rise. "You guys go to dances and stuff like that?"

Her smile was lopsided, her attempt at humor failing. "Are you kidding? No way. We didn't go in for that kind of stuff."

Once they'd become friends, they avoided fellow classmates. After they'd started dating, they were careful not to be seen in public together. Dances, any school functions, really, were out of the question. Tensions grew quickly in mixed crowds.

"Sounds like you two were pretty boring."

The burst of laughter that shot from her was genuine. "Hardly." She realized he was looking for her to elaborate, but there was no way she could tell her son...Her whole body flushed with embarrassment as she muttered, "Well, maybe you're right."

After a moment or two, Zach must have realized that was all she was going to offer. He ran up the first three steps of the bleachers and back down again. "So what's next? I know you said there wasn't much here, but if this is where you grew up, there has to be more to see, right?"

They climbed back into the car, and Tyne drove him to the river, the steep road snaking downward to the rocky bank. The wide-open view was spectacular, full of cool, lush greenery and churning water. And she spent an hour teaching him to skip stones across the surface of the river. He caught on pretty quickly and seemed to understand the need to search for smooth, flat rocks, without having to be told.

"You're a natural," she told him when he'd made a rock skip several times before it plunked beneath the surface.

He scanned the ground for another stone, and when he found one, he smoothed his thumb across it. "This is a really big river."

"The Susquehanna is the largest river on the Eastern Shore. When I was in school, some of the kids tried to convince me that the name meant 'mile wide and foot deep,' and I even saw that listed in a visitor's brochure." She released a stone and it *ker-plopped* without making a single skip. "But Jasper told me it's an Algonquin word that means 'muddy current.'"

"Uncle Jasper's pretty cool, don't you think?"

She nodded. It seemed there was more her son wanted to say, but he only flung the stone he'd found and grinned when it hopped too many times to count.

"Show-off." She laughed.

"I'm thirsty," he told her, dusting his palms on his shorts. "Can we stop someplace for a soda?"

They headed back to the car, and when she jabbed the key into the ignition, she asked, "Are you hungry?"

Zach shook his head. "Nah. Not yet. Just thirsty."

They made their way to a convenience mart on the outskirts of town. Tyne had successfully evaded Main Street and the town square up until then. Zach hadn't asked about her childhood home, and she had no idea what she'd say or do if he did.

The store shelves were only chest high, so she could see her son standing at the glass door of a refrigerated section of teas, sodas, and juices. She'd brought him out today to talk about his anger toward her, but she had no idea how to broach the subject without just coming right out with it. It felt awkward, and because she couldn't begin to guess how he might react, she hadn't even tried to raise the subject.

Having paid for her bottle of water and his peach Snapple, she headed out the door. Zach paused by the stack of newspapers sitting by the door.

"Hey, Mom," he called out, jogging across the parking lot after her, "look at this."

She stopped at the driver's side door, her hand on the latch.

"The town paper. It's okay. I didn't steal it. Says right here it's free. But look."

Tyne slid behind the steering wheel, and Zach got in beside her.

"It's an article about the mayor." Excitement sparked his tone as he read, "*'Mayor Richard Whitlock cut the ribbon of the Sheer Elegance Hair Salon on Third Avenue this past Saturday.'* How cool is that? The mayor has our last name. You know him?"

CHAPTER EIGHT

Time. It's what she was in desperate need of. Time for her heart to stop pounding. Time to figure out what the hell to tell her son. She unscrewed the top of her bottle of water and tipped it up for a *very* long drink.

"Wow," she said at last, swiping the back of her hand across her mouth. "That's cold. And delicious. Just what I needed. I was thirstier than I realized. How's your tea?" Misdirection failure. Even as she asked the question, she knew he wasn't going to fall for it.

The bottle sat, unopened, where her son had tucked it between his thighs. Zach was too busy staring at the paper.

"Do you know this guy?"

His expression was curious, so guileless, in fact, that she was forced to look away. Her first instinct was to lie. Brazenly. But she couldn't. She respected her son too much to do that.

She looked him in the eye and said, "He's my father, Zach."

A tiny frown bit deep into the space between his brows. "Your father is the mayor of Oak Mills?" His voice had gone pliant.

"Yes. My parents live here, son. Lucas told you I grew up here."

He gazed down at the newspaper in his lap, then out the front window at the people coming and going through the door of the convenience store, back at her, then down at the paper.

"How come you never told me? How come you never brought me here? How come they never visited us?"

His tone intensified with each question until it seemed the last one was hurled at her rather than spoken. Her heart palpitated and she felt light-headed. She twisted the key and started the car, flipping on the air conditioner the instant the engine purred to life. Cold air blasted from the vent, and she pointed it directly at her face and chest.

"Zach, can we try to stay calm?" she began. "Can we try to talk about this without getting upset? I just don't think I could take it if you—"

"I have *grandparents*!"

There didn't seem to be an ounce of joy in the revelation. The words he fired off were crammed with angry accusation.

"I have grandparents I've never met." He shoved the paper, and the newsprint tumbled to the floor around his feet.

"Cut it out, Zach," she scolded. "You're going to smudge ink on Lucas's car seats."

"I don't give a shit about the car seats."

"Watch your mouth, young man."

"I won't." He glared at her. "I'll say whatever the hell I want." He shifted away from her, closer to the passenger-side door.

Tyne shoved the car into gear and glanced behind her before pulling out of the space, fearful that he might leave the car before she could get moving. Seeing the street was empty, she put her foot on the gas.

"That's what *you've* done for my *whole life*." The paper crinkled when he moved his leg. "Whatever the hell you want. You don't think of anyone but yourself."

"What are you talking about?" The interior of the car suddenly seemed too hot to support life, so she reached for the knob on the air conditioner and turned the fan up a notch. Logic and experience told her that defending herself by pointing out all the things she'd done for him, all the times she'd put his wants and needs before her own, wouldn't assuage his anger at this moment.

"Zach," she began, then whatever words she meant to say jammed in her throat along with a big knot.

He faced the passenger-side window, his body a tight ball of muscle. "Every year at school we had Grandparents Day. Everyone invited their family for lunch."

She wasn't going to let him go there. "Ms. Josephine went with you several years in a row, Zach."

"Ms. Jo," he spit out contemptuously. "She was my babysitter, Mom. My babysitter."

"She loved you very much. She was happy to stand in—"

He turned on her, his gaze fierce. "I'm just now learning that I didn't *need* a stand-in. I have the real thing. I just never knew it. Thanks to *you*."

Tyne's jaw clenched at the same time that her hands grew white-knuckled on the steering wheel, and her gaze latched onto the road ahead.

"I want to meet them. I want you to take me to their house. I want you to take me there right now."

"No." She didn't take her eyes off the road. "No, I can't do that."

She didn't have to look at him to know his coal-black eyes were staring a hole right through her skull.

"You have to trust me on this, Zach," she said. "When you've calmed down—when we've both calmed down—we'll talk about it."

The BMW flew fifty-five in a thirty-mile-per-hour zone, but she didn't ease up on the gas pedal one iota. She knew exactly what she was doing. Knew exactly where she was heading. To Wikweko. To Lucas. He was the only person on the face of this earth who could help her explain this to her son.

∾

Something was... off. Lucas's gut told him so. It wasn't anything his uncle had said or done. Intuition alone alerted Lucas that something wasn't quite right between him and Jasper.

Tyne had warned him of this, and he'd scoffed at the idea. But the strange electricity tingling along his arms and the back of his neck every time there was a short lull in the conversation made him realize he should have heeded Tyne's warning.

He'd come to the apartment over the gallery where his uncle lived this morning, looking for information, but this awkward air bothered him, so much so that the questions he'd wanted to ask about his mother went unasked.

The kettle had been heating on the stove when he'd arrived, so he accepted his uncle's offer of tea. Although Jasper's kitchenette was compact, it had all the necessary conveniences. The two men sat opposite each other at the small, round table, another silence stretching out long, tentacle-like fingers, and Lucas could barely resist the urge to rub his palm over the prickling sensation at his nape. He was just about to point out the huge elephant that seemed to be sharing the small space with them, when Jasper spoke.

"There was a fish," his uncle said, "that lived in a tiny cove."

Lucas went still. He knew that tone. It was the one Jasper used when he recounted Lenape myth. As a boy, Lucas had been mesmerized by the stories his uncle told, spending hours going over them in his head so he wouldn't miss a single nuance of wisdom they contained. However, today his Uncle's profundity was ill timed and less than welcome. He rolled his eyes, and under his breath he mumbled, "Here we go."

"The fish swam in a school with other fish just like him. Brothers. Sisters." There was a dramatic pause before he added, "*Family*. He grew and was happy. One day he heard about a place. A wondrous place called the ocean, and the fish decided he no longer wanted to live in the cove with his own kind." Jasper set down the mug of fragrant herbal tea. "He wanted to experience new things, to be amazed and astounded by those things he had not yet seen but had only heard of. So he left his family. He began a long journey to the ocean."

Even just half-listening, understanding dawned on Lucas, and he sat forward in his chair to focus on his Uncle's words. He'd moved away. He hadn't been home in years. He'd neglected his duties as a nephew. The path this story was taking was plain. He deserved a lecture; he'd sit here quietly and take it like a man. At least the cause of this stiffness between them would no longer be a mystery.

"The fish swam into deeper water, following the swift current." Jasper's gaze never wavered from Lucas's face. "The water became so deep the sunlight could not penetrate, so the fish had trouble seeing. He wondered if he should turn back, but ambition to see different things—to *be* different—urged him on. He was not used to the strong undercurrent. He was tossed and flipped and flung, the jagged rocks and brightly colored coral ripping at his tender flesh. The loss of scales made him weak."

Lucas frowned.

"A storm arose," Jasper continued, "and churned the water, capturing the fish in a dangerous eddy that tore at his fins. The fish rested by a pristine clam shell only to be nearly devoured by a barracuda."

"Stop." Lucas stood and took a couple of steps to stand at the kitchen's narrow window. The scent of smoky bacon wafted on the breeze. One of the other artists on the street must be having a late breakfast.

He turned to look at Jasper. "I thought I knew what was going on. Thought I'd figured out the moral of your story. But you've lost me." Lucas tugged on his earlobe and shook his head. Then he stood up straighter. "I'm not a kid, Uncle Jasper. If you have something you want to say to me, just say it."

Jasper listened and then looked down to study his mug. "You used to hang on my every word." The older man lifted his gaze. "But you are a man, and you want to be treated like a man. I understand."

The turn the story had taken had unsettled Lucas. He wasn't weak; he wasn't torn or tattered. He crossed his arms over his chest.

His uncle seemed to be measuring his thoughts. Finally, he said, "Ambition is a hungry master. It feeds on pieces of its servant until—"

"I *have* no master."

They stared at one another.

"I don't want you to lose sight of who you are, Lucas. Of where you came from."

"I know who I am. I am Lenape. And I know where I came from."

There was no judgment in Jasper's expression. So why did Lucas sense that his uncle was dubious of his claims?

Any lawyer with two brain cells to rub together knew not to argue a point without preparation. Well thought-out logic and reason must be used if one was to make a winning case. He decided it would be best to leave this argument for another day.

He went back to the table and sat down. "Uncle Jasper, I came here to ask you some questions."

Jasper's calm demeanor never changed.

"I want to know about my mother." He took a breath, licked his lips. "If she died when I was born, where is she buried? What was her name? Why are there no photos of her anywhere?"

The questions disrupted his uncle's peace. Jasper tried to hold Lucas's gaze, but he failed. Finally, he simply shifted in the chair so he was no longer facing his nephew.

"I need some answers," Lucas pressed. "I feel as if I have this gaping hole in my life. I'd like to fill it in. I need closure. I want to know who she was. I want to visit her grave. Honor her memory with a gift. Please. Tell me where I can find her."

Jasper issued a deep, soulful sigh.

"I'm sorry." A frown creased Lucas's brow. "I know it's a subject no one ever wanted to talk about. I felt that the whole time I was growing up. Sensed it. So much so, that I put her completely out of my mind. But not knowing who my mother was...well, it's just not normal. You have to see that."

His uncle's expression grew more troubled with each passing second.

"What?" Lucas was becoming agitated. "What is it? Is it something bad? Was *she* bad? Is that it?" Frustration got the better of him, and he conjured the worst scenario he could think of. "What? Was she a prostitute or something?"

Jasper barked his name sharply.

He lifted his hands, palms up, in a quick, short, jerky motion to emphasize his apology. "I didn't mean to speak ill of the dead."

"She isn't dead, Lucas."

He couldn't have been more stunned had his uncle swung out and cuffed him on the jaw.

Jasper shifted so they were face to face. "She didn't die giving birth to you."

"But someone told me that." His voice was barely a whisper. Somewhere in the back of his brain he registered that greasy smell of bacon. "Someone." He shook his head. "Told me."

"It wasn't me. And it wasn't your father." Jasper's chest expanded when he took a deep breath. "Ruth Yoder was alive the last time I saw her. And that was the day she placed you in your father's arms...and walked away. We knew we would never hear from her again. And we promised Ruth and her father we would never contact her."

His mother's name was Ruth. Lucas let the name echo in his head.

Jasper rested his elbows on the table, clasping his hands lightly below chin level. "Your father promised, Lucas. You should uphold the promise."

Lucas sat for moment, searching his uncle's face. "Traditions like that caused our people a world of hurt. Generations holding onto promises made *eons* ago."

Jasper's shoulders sagged and he looked away. With his eyes focused on something across the kitchen, he said, "Your mother was of the Plain People. Her father was a bishop in one of the religion's most conservative sects." He shook his head. "I don't remember the name of the church. Don't know that he ever told us.

"Bishop Yoder used to drive his horse and buggy here to Wikweko," his uncle continued. "He bought horse liniment from an herbalist here. And resold it to the Amish farmers."

Lucas was silent, taking it all in.

Jasper looked him in the eye. "You must leave things be."

He felt as if he were moving in slow motion, shaking his head, pursing his lips. "I don't know if I can do that."

Jasper sighed. "She'd be only a few years younger than me. She could have crossed over due to some illness or another. If she's still alive—" He shook his head, leaving the rest of his sentence unspoken. "You really need to think about this, Lucas. Your father made a promise."

"Don't worry." His stomach churned. "I will."

Birdsong floated in on the summer breeze, a chirpy, jarring noise.

"Lucas, I want you to remember that things are not always as they seem. *Lucas.*" Once their eyes met, Jasper continued, "I want you to remember that a Lenape always acts honorably."

His uncle closed his eyes, his throat convulsing with a difficult swallow. He looked down then, sliding his mug closer to him and lacing his fingers around the white ceramic.

"I would rather you leave this alone. But if you cannot…whatever you find, whatever you learn, you must never forget that you are enjoying life because this woman gave birth to you. Do not cause her harm."

Somewhere at the periphery of Lucas's consciousness, he heard his uncle's odd warning. But he couldn't take in any more, couldn't digest anything else; he was too overwhelmed with the idea that the woman who had abandoned him might still be alive.

Lucas pulled open the screen door and felt as if he'd entered a battleground.

"Then I'll call them myself!" Zach flung the words at his mother in a bellow.

"You will do no such thing. I mean it, Zachary Whitlock. You are not to—"

"And what are you goin' to do, Mom? Send me to my room? Take away my CD player? I think I can take it."

Clamping a firm hand on Zach's shoulder, Lucas said, "Lower your tone. You shouldn't talk to your mother that way."

Gratitude softened Tyne's blue eyes.

"But you don't know what she did!" The teen was so upset his voice cracked. "I have grandparents living in Oak Mills. I never knew about them. *She* never told me." The pronoun was spit out viciously. "For all I know, they don't know about me either." He narrowed his black gaze at his mother. "You're the most selfish person on the damned planet."

"Zach," Lucas warned, "I said stop."

But the boy didn't seem to hear, continuing to glare at Tyne. "I'm going to see my grandparents. And I'm *not* going back home with you. I'm staying here."

Tyne cocked her head. "Don't be ridiculous. You don't know—"

"I know enough."

Lucas couldn't believe Zach's behavior.

"I know everybody here looks like me. I fit in here. That's all I have to know. I'm stayin' and there's nothing you can do about it."

"You might want to stay," Lucas told him, "but would they want to have you?"

His son cast him a shocked sidelong glance.

"The Indians of Wikweko want residents to bring value to the community, Zach. How much value will you bring?" Lucas wasn't expecting an answer. "You disrespect your mother. You disrespect authority. You disrespect the property of others. You're a troublemaker. What did the judge call you? Ah, yes. I remember now. A delinquent."

Tyne stepped toward them. "There's no need to be hurtful, Lucas."

His bark of humorless laughter was sharp. "He doesn't seem too worried about hurting your feelings." He looked at Zach. "A Lenape doesn't insult his heritage by acting like a little shit. By demanding to have his way. By shouting whatever inane thoughts might float through his pea-brained head. And above all a Lenape respects his elders. I'd say you've failed on all counts, Zach."

The notion hit him that he might have gone too far. However, hearing Zach lash out at Tyne with such insolence had been too much.

The teen was nearly as tall as he was, and for a moment Lucas thought Zach might slug him with the fist he'd balled up knot-tight. But all Zach did was shrug his shoulder with enough force to free himself of Lucas's hand.

"What do you know about me?" he sneered, his lips barely moving. "You don't know me. You don't know nothin' about me."

Lucas should have let it go, but he couldn't. "The way you're acting now, I don't want to."

The firm, hard line of the teen's mouth told Lucas he'd hit a raw nerve.

Zach moved to the door, but before leaving he glanced at Tyne. "I'm going to Uncle Jasper's." Then he was gone.

The living room felt oddly quiet now that all the shouting had stopped.

"Well," Lucas said with a forced chuckle, "you have to admit there's been some improvement. The last time he left angry, he didn't tell us where he was going. And did you notice? He didn't slam the door."

Tyne sat down on the edge of the nearby easy chair. "This isn't funny, Lucas."

"I know." He sat down on the sofa, sliding his palms up and down his thighs. Their knees were mere inches apart, and he could feel the heat of her. Damn, if she wasn't gorgeous when her eyes were lit with anger. "I was only trying to make you smile. Lighten the tension a little."

"Oh, god, it was awful, wasn't it?" She smoothed her palms together absently. "I felt like I couldn't breathe there for a few minutes. I think I should find a counselor. Someone to help him deal with his anger."

Lucas nodded. "He does need to learn to control his tongue."

Her hands fell limp in her lap. "I want you to know he's never acted like this before. Never treated me like this, I mean."

Something outside the picture window drew her gaze, and he took the opportunity to study the delicate curve of her jaw.

"We were close, he and I," she said softly. "It's only natural that we would be, I guess. All we had was each other, really." Her gaze met his. "I told you before that things seemed to change a couple of years ago, and I put it down to teenage hormones. But he's never been disrespectful, Lucas. Not like this."

"I believe you." A faint citrus scent drifted on the air, and he realized it was coming from her skin or her hair. "If this behavior, this belligerence, is something new, I'd say you caught it early. Maybe a counselor would be a good idea."

Tyne nodded, but although she was looking at him, he got the distinct impression that she was miles away in thought. He noticed the navy flecks in her pensive blue eyes. She blinked a couple of times, and he knew immediately she was once again focused on the present.

"I don't dare take him to see them," she whispered.

Tyne didn't have to identify *them*; he knew of whom she spoke.

"I don't want to see them." Her voice grew stronger. "And I sure don't want them anywhere near Zach."

When Lucas told Tyne that they should focus their efforts on Zach, he'd meant every word he'd said. The past had a way of tangling everything in knots. Questions about the events that had taken place when they'd been teens had driven him nuts, but he'd done his best to follow the plan, focusing on the problems at hand, the problems in the present. Until now.

"How did all this happen, Tyne? *What* happened?" he asked. "How did you end up on your own? Raising Zach alone?"

Her whole body seemed to wilt, and she closed her eyes. "They were so disappointed. I had just started my first semester—"

She'd been accepted into Millersville University, while Lucas had been forced to work for a couple of years and save up funds for college.

"—and I showed up one day and announced, 'Hey, Mom and Dad, I'm pregnant.'" She pressed her fingertips to her mouth and shook her head. "They had such dreams for me, Lucas."

As the only child of the Whitlocks, Tyne was destined to shine, even if her parents had to hold her down and apply the shellac themselves. When they'd been dating, Lucas would listen as Tyne lamented all the favors her father had called in from his cronies just for her. Tedious obligations as she saw them. To an Indian living hand to mouth they'd have been huge breaks, golden opportunities, and he couldn't deny the slight pang of jealousy he'd felt. But he hadn't let envy keep him from encouraging her to take advantage of anything her father could offer. As a teen contemplating their futures, he'd come to the conclusion that hers had seemed as bright as the sun next to his flimsy flashlight.

"And they were determined," she continued, "that their dreams for me would come true." She sighed. "They insisted on an abortion. I flat out refused. They badgered me with their reasons: I was too young; I had my whole life ahead of me; a baby would destroy my chances to get an education. They were distraught and disillusioned. And, hell, so was I. They wouldn't leave me alone for two minutes, afraid that I'd contact you—which they had forbidden me to do. They threatened me with everything they could think of."

Tears glistened in her eyes and she glanced away; his heart wrenched.

"They were right, Lucas. I was too young. I couldn't imagine having a baby. I was a *teenager.*"

He noticed that she'd laced her fingers tightly in her lap.

"Then they suggested adoption." Her gaze remained fixed on the spot somewhere in the far corner of the room. "And I finally came to the conclusion that maybe they were probably right."

Her anguish was almost palpable. "Tyne—"

She cut him off with a shake of her head. "Let me finish. I need to tell you." She pressed the curled fingers of one hand to her chin. "I went to my aunt's in Florida for the duration of my pregnancy. By summer, I'd changed my mind all over again. I'd fallen in love with my child even though I hadn't set eyes on him yet. I couldn't give him up." Her hand lowered to her lap. "My parents were livid. They called me every day, arguing and pestering me. But I was adamant.

"I didn't go back to school," she said. "As a last resort, my mother begged me to come home. She said she would watch Zach while I attended classes." Tyne's mouth flattened momentarily. "But I wasn't going to do that. I wanted to break free. Make my own way. And I did. Well, mostly, anyway. They did help me at first. Sent me a little money and paid for a couple of Zach's doctor visits. But only for a while. I was determined to become independent." She lifted her gaze to Lucas's face. "I made the right choice, didn't I? Not going home? I couldn't subject Zach to that, you know? To *them*." She moistened her lips and swallowed.

He wanted to tell her she'd done the right thing, keeping Zach away from his grandparents, but instead he said, "I wish you would have called me."

She moved then, shifted from the easy chair to the couch, sitting close to him and gathering one of his hands into both of hers.

"I know I should have, Lucas." Her blue eyes pleaded. "I should have contacted you. I should have told you about the baby. You had a right to know. But I couldn't."

His blood froze. That wasn't what he'd meant…wasn't what he'd expected to hear. She didn't know. How the hell could she not know?

"That last time we were together you were so excited to have saved enough money for your first year's tuition. Then my father told me you'd been offered a full scholarship. I knew you must have been deliriously happy." She bit her bottom lip, her brow furrowing. "He said a baby would ruin your future just as much as it would mine. Dad wasn't right about much in this whole situation, but I believed with all my heart that he was right about that." She closed her eyes a moment. "After I'd decided to keep Zach, I was too ashamed to call you. I couldn't admit to you that I'd considered giving up our son."

She leaned in and hugged him then, resting her head on his shoulder. "I hope you can forgive me, Lucas."

He hadn't prayed in a very long time, but at that moment he thanked The Great One that she wasn't looking at him, because he knew without a shadow of a doubt that guilt was etched in every crevice of his stony expression.

Her arms drew him tighter to her, and he smoothed his hands up her back, her skin hot against his cold palms, his icicle-stiff fingers.

"What am I going to do?" Her breath was warm against his neck. "I've got to keep Zach away from my parents. How will I ever explain it to him, Lucas? He'll never understand. How can I tell my son that his grandfather is a bigot?"

CHAPTER NINE

A loud crack ruptured the air as the bat made solid contact with the ball. The crowd on one side of the field cheered for the batter, who raced toward first base, while the people on the opposite side shouted at the shortstop to throw the ball to the first baseman. Tyne loved the fact that the teams were co-ed. Everyone who wanted to play was invited. Boys and girls in a wide range of ages from tweens to teens, some even in their early twenties, had arrived late that Friday afternoon at the ball field.

Some of the players' families had turned up with lawn chairs, blankets to spread on the grass, picnic meals and drinks or snacks to share. A wonderful camaraderie danced among the laughing, chatting spectators, proof that the Friday ballgame was a popular community event.

Zach was barely speaking to her and Lucas. He'd spent another whole day with Jasper, but he'd come home for something to eat before the game. The air was tense as the two of them sat at the table together, and Tyne had been relieved that her son hadn't brought up the subject of her parents. When she asked him where he was going and found out he was off to the Community Center for "the big game," she'd expressed an interest in coming along to watch. He'd shrugged and told her it was a free country. So after he left, she'd slathered on some sunscreen, grabbed her sunglasses and an aluminum lawn chair from the shed in the backyard, and walked to the sports field behind the community building.

"And where's my nephew?"

Tyne smiled a hello at Jasper as he unfolded his chair and nestled it next to hers. "Lucas is meeting with a man who lives here. The guy called yesterday, looking for some legal advice, so Lucas went to his house today after lunch."

Jasper nodded his approval.

"I'm surprised he wasn't back before I left the house." Tyne adjusted her sunglasses. "I texted him, and when he didn't respond, I left a note at the house. Just in case there's something wrong with his cell. I'm hoping he'll show up here. Eventually."

"I'm sure he'll be along. Who wants to miss the big game?" Jasper scanned the field. "I wasn't able to close my shop until five thirty, and then I had to return a few phone calls and grab some dinner. What did I miss?"

"Not much. Bottom of the first. Zach is out in left field."

He gazed toward the outfield and lifted his hand to acknowledge Zach's wave.

"I want to thank you for spending so much time with him," Tyne said.

"No thanks necessary. He's family."

She brushed the toe of her sandal across the grass. "We've been having some...problems lately. Zach and I."

Jasper watched the young man who stepped up to the plate. "I know."

His reply surprised her. "He's told you?"

He shook his head. "Not outright. He's keeping secrets; an old man can see these things. I can also tell from what he has said that he's upset about something. Angry. Bitter, really. And worried." Jasper shrugged. "About something."

The smoke from a charcoal grill wafted toward them, carrying with it the scent of grilling hot dogs.

When she didn't speak, he continued, his eye riveted to the batter, who now had a strike against him. "I want to tell you that I like Zach. I like him a lot. He reminds me of Lucas when he was young. He's smart, and he's inquisitive. Those are fine traits for a young man to have."

A lump gathered in her throat and tears sprang to her eyes, and she was suddenly very grateful for the cover of her sunglasses. Her heart swelled hearing Jasper voice a positive opinion about Zach. She'd been sick with worry. She knew somewhere inside her son lurked the happy, considerate individual she'd raised, but she was at a loss about how to bring that out in him again.

Jasper went quiet when the batter hit a fly ball into left field. His hoot was unrestrained, and he clapped when Zach caught it and clinched the third out. A buzz of conversation stirred through the spectators as the teams switched places.

Giving Zach a thumb's up, Tyne tried not to be bothered when her son refused to acknowledge her. She crossed one leg over the other and sighed.

"I have noticed," Jasper said, "that Zach has—at the risk of using the current psychobabble of the day—some issues.

He can be moody. He's got a temper and a penchant to blame others when things go wrong."

Tyne fixed her gaze on the field, watching the opposing players take their positions. "You learned all that in the short time you've spent with him?"

Jasper chuckled. "You forget. I raised his father."

Tyne smiled.

Then he leaned toward her. "I haven't mentioned this to Zach; I wanted to ask you first. Would you allow me to take him camping? It would give us a chance to spend a few days together, one on one. I'll teach him to pitch a tent and build a proper fire. We'll do a little fishing, a little hunting, a little cooking on an open fire. And we'll have plenty of time to talk."

"Hunting? Oh, I don't know, Jasper." The idea of killing an animal made Tyne shiver. "We buy our chicken cutlets and ground beef at the local Acme. I don't know if Zach could handle something like that." And she wasn't sure she wanted him to.

"It's the middle of summer," he reminded her with a gentle smile. "We might have special permission from the state to hunt on our own land year round, but game is scarce in the heat. The animals tend to move up into the mountains where it's cooler." His grin made his chocolate-brown eyes twinkle. "I'll remember to pack a loaf of bread and a large jar of peanut butter. The truth is, Tyne, we will be hunting, but not for game. We're going to find Zach's manhood."

She just looked at him, uncertain what to say, and again her eyes welled. Her voice came out wobbly when she finally said, "I'd love for you to take him camping, Jasper. I trust you completely. I can only hope and pray that the hunt is successful. And I want you to know that I'll be grateful for anything you're able to do for him." She frowned then and glanced over to the bench where her son and his teammates were seated, Zach's broad back facing her. Then she looked at Jasper. "There are some things you should know—some things I should probably tell you."

He lifted his calloused palm. "Zach will tell me whatever I need to know."

An absolute assurance exuded from him, and she was pervaded with a strange and wondrous tranquility.

Jasper's gaze lifted to somewhere behind her. "Lucas is here." He lifted a hand in greeting.

Tyne turned too late to see if Lucas returned his uncle's wave. He made no move to join them.

"Excuse me," she murmured to Jasper. "I'm going to go say hello."

Passing the batter's box, she saw Zach was choosing a bat from among several that leaned up against the chain-link backstop.

"Smack one out of the park," she called. He didn't lift his head. In fact, he made no reaction whatsoever. She wasn't really surprised.

She smiled at Lucas when she reached him. "You got my text? I'm glad." Since he'd walked in on her and Zach's quarrel and she'd ended up telling him about the past, she'd experienced a sort of buoyancy, as though sharing her burden had somehow lightened it.

"Sorry it took me so long. Jim and I caught up a bit."

"You want to come sit down?" she asked.

"If you don't mind, I'd rather stand. I've been sitting all afternoon."

"That's fine." She smoothed her hands over the sun-warmed skin of her forearms. "Were you able to help him? Your friend?"

"I was." He nodded. "A communications company wants to install a tower on a corner of Jim's property, and he needed some help deciphering some of the legal jargon in the contract." He smiled. "He wanted to pay me, and when I refused his money, he made me take a pack of New York strip steaks. 'A fair barter,' he called it."

"Steaks for legal advice." She licked her lips animatedly and touched her tummy. "Yum!"

They both went quiet when Zach stepped up to the plate. He gave the bat a couple of practice swings, then settled into a tense stance. The ball sailed across home plate, Zach swung late, and the ball slapped into the catcher's mitt.

Lucas shouted, "It's okay, Zach. Relax. Plant your front foot."

"The next one's yours, Zach," Jasper called out.

The pitcher threw the ball, and again Zach swung just a fraction too late.

Tyne pressed her hand to her stomach, sucking in a breath with a hiss. "Strike two," she whispered.

Cupping his hands around his mouth, Lucas yelled, "Plant your front foot, son!"

Zach's attention wavered from the pitcher, his gaze swinging to Lucas. Tyne knew exactly what had taken her son aback. If Lucas realized what he'd done, he didn't show it. He was frantically pointing at the pitcher, an appeal for Zach to keep his head in the game.

This time, Zach swung the bat with perfect timing, his front foot firmly nailed to the ground. A satisfying *smack* resounded. He dropped the bat and raced toward first base. The crowd cheered, and Tyne jumped up and down until her son safely reached the base.

"Jeez," she muttered to Lucas. "This anxiety is enough to give me ulcers."

"Tell me about it." Lucas grinned and shook his head. "The way he kept looking at me rather than the pitcher, I was afraid he was going to give them an easy out."

"He was startled." When Lucas still didn't seem to understand, she explained, "You called him 'son.'"

Lucas frowned; then his brows arched. "I did, didn't I? You don't think I upset him, do you?"

"Don't worry." She reached out and tugged on the sleeve of his shirt. "I think he's been waiting for it, actually."

The next batter hit a fly pop, and Lucas shouted for Zach to wait. The outfielder missed the catch, and Lucas and everyone else yelled for Zach to run. Tyne's heart pounded, and she let out a breath when both runners safely made it to their bases.

"Lucas, Jasper wants to take Zach camping. I told him it would be okay." She looked at him, took in the curve of his ear, the corded muscles of his neck. "He said something about helping him become a man. Do you, um…"—she slid off her sunglasses and squinted up at him—"do you think it's okay that Zach goes?"

For an instant, she regretted the question. She slipped her sunglasses back onto her face and turned her gaze back to the ball field. Asking anyone's opinion about anything when it came to Zach felt foreign to her. She made all the decisions herself, had done so for fifteen long years. What would she do or say if he disagreed with her?

Luckily, though, he grinned.

"I think it's great. I don't know why I didn't think of it myself. There's definitely no need for an anger management counselor when we have a Lenape elder around." He chuckled. "Uncle Jasper and I went hunting for my manhood many times before we found it." Memories had his mouth twisting wryly. "Trouble is, no one told me what we were hunting. The hardest part for Zach is going to be figuring that out. And he might not, the first time out."

Tyne watched as the batter bunted and ran toward first. Zach advanced to third, but the batter was tagged out by the first baseman.

She wanted to ask if she should be worried, but she couldn't find the words. Instead, she murmured, "He's never been camping."

Lucas turned to face her then, and ever so gently he reached up and slid her sunglasses down her nose just enough so that he could look directly into her eyes. "Zach'll be perfectly safe." He paused a heartbeat before adding, "But he won't come home the same person."

The mild alarm that shot through her must have registered on her face, if only for an instant, because he placed his hands on her shoulders. "It's okay. It'll be a good thing, Tyne. You'll see." He turned back to the game, leaning his forearms on the top of the fence. "Jasper will work him hard, and talk to him a lot. There will be a lot of stories. Fables or parables, I guess you'd call them. Cryptic tales that are often difficult to understand but always have a lesson attached. Stories meant to make him think. This won't be like any other experience Zach has had, I'm sure."

She pushed her sunglasses back into place and settled next to him, resting her forearms on the fence too. They watched as the next batter struck out and the teams switched positions on the ball field again. Her son kicked the dirt, miffed that he wasn't given the opportunity to score.

"First off," Lucas said softly, "Jasper will have Zach collect enough dry, dead wood to feed a fire for a month. Then my uncle will have him cut it into uniform size. Zach will swing an ax until his biceps quiver. Then when it's time to cook dinner, Jasper will realize he's forgotten the matches at home. So Zach will spend an hour trying to light kindling with flint and steel. Have you ever done that?" He rolled his eyes and shook his head. "When Zach is so frustrated he's about to scream, Jasper will conveniently remember he has a piece of charred cloth in the tinder box, and they'll start a fire like magic. Making charred cloth is a lesson he'll learn another day." Lucas toed a clump of weeds at the foot of the fence.

"Zach will eat the trout he's caught and cleaned and cooked on a fire he started himself, and he'll fall asleep feeling proud as hell that he did it all on his own. Jasper has a real knack for making a boy feel as if he's accomplished something great. And Zach will sleep like a baby because he'll be more exhausted than he's ever been in his life." Lucas chuckled. "And he'll never realize he's been played like a tune by his great-uncle."

They were so close, the sleeve of Lucas's shirt tickled Tyne's bare shoulder. "Sounds like you've been played." She grinned.

He nodded. "Like one of those soulful country songs." The soft laughter they shared ended with a warm smile.

They watched the game for a few minutes; then Tyne smoothed her fingertips over the cool metal fencepost. "What have you decided? About your mother?"

He'd confided all that Jasper had told him about Ruth Yoder. She'd been astonished to learn that his mother hadn't died as he'd remembered being told.

"I don't know," he said, heaving a sigh. "I've thought about little else. I feel like I don't have a choice, really. I have to at least try to find her." He turned his head to look at her. "Don't I?"

She was quiet a moment. Then she reached up and took off her sunglasses, folding the earpieces with slow deliberation.

"If you don't," she quietly told him, "I'm afraid you'll regret it for the rest of your life. I know I would."

He didn't say a word, only searched her face.

Tyne moistened her lips. "I'll help you find her, Lucas. We can do it. Together."

His mouth curled into the smallest of smiles, and his eyes glittered in the bright sunlight. He reached over and captured her fingers in his, and something hitched in her chest. The pulse point of his wrist pressed firmly against her skin, and she felt his heartbeat, quick and hot.

The ball field was packed with spectators, but for the span of a few seconds the sounds of shouting, cheering, and applause faded, and Tyne felt as if she and Lucas were all alone under the beautiful blue sky, a halo of golden sunshine enveloping them.

She closed her eyes and sucked in a slow, deep breath. Rob's face appeared before her in her mind's eye, startling her with such force that she actually jerked. Awkwardly, she tugged her hand from Lucas's, slid her sunglasses onto her face, and focused on the baseball game.

CHAPTER TEN

"I'm sorry I couldn't help you." The man adjusted the flat-brimmed straw hat on his head.

Tyne and Lucas stood at the door of Jacob Yoder's barn. Unfortunately, it wasn't the Jacob Yoder they were searching for.

"I appreciate your taking the time to talk to us," Lucas told him.

Mr. Yoder hooked a thumb behind his black suspender. "Happy to. If you don't mind my saying, you've got your work cut out for you. There are over twenty-five different Amish, Mennonite, and Brethren church groups in this county alone. And all of them probably have a bishop or two named Yoder."

Lucas grimaced. "Tell me about it. We've spent the whole morning going from farm to farm." He released a weary exhale. "To farm. Feels like I'm on a wild goose chase."

"There are over ninety Yoders listed in the phone book," Tyne said. "And those are only Lancaster addresses. We haven't even looked in Millersville or Oak Mills or Mountville, or East or West Hempfield." Seems they'd set themselves up to tackle the impossible.

She and Lucas had stopped for lunch after spending hours talking to dozens of people, each and every one offering up suggestions on where to find a Bishop Yoder who had a daughter named Ruth. The list of possibilities was growing long.

Jacob Yoder tugged on his beard. "Many churches don't allow phones."

Tyne's mind reeled at the thought of trying to find Lucas's mother in what now seemed a sea of black hats and white bonnets.

"Is there anything else you can tell me about the man you're hoping to find?" Jacob tucked his hands into the pockets of his black trousers. "I really would like to help you."

That's one thing that had impressed Tyne; none of the Plain People had turned them away. Not a single person had been unfriendly. Everyone they had approached today had been willing to listen and had tried to help, even if it had been in some small way.

Lucas's posture was loose, his dark eyes glum. "I know that the Bishop Yoder I'm looking for drove a horse and buggy to Wikweko to buy horse liniment. He even tried to buy the recipe so he wouldn't have to deal with anyone outside his own community. But apparently, the recipe wasn't for sale, so he was forced to do business in Wikweko."

"Horse liniment," Jacob murmured.

Lucas nodded, and Tyne watched him hesitate.

Finally, Lucas said, "He brought his daughter along with him. Ruth Yoder had a baby." His Adam's apple dipped. "Out of wedlock."

The Amish man shifted his weight from one foot to the other. "I don't know anything about a baby. But there was a man who used to sell liniment. Years ago, mind you. South of Millersville. Near Slackwater. And I believe his name was Yoder." Jacob shook his head. "I couldn't say if he had a daughter. But the church down there follows the strictest Ordnung. A system of rules for, um, how to live your life. They're Old Order down there. That might be the Bishop Yoder you're looking for."

Hope had a way of stomping out frustration and fatigue; it also sparked a sizzling anticipation in both Lucas and Tyne. Their gazes met, and they shared a wide smile filled with renewed energy. Lucas pumped Jacob's hand with hearty appreciation, and after listening to some general directions, they headed back to Lucas's car.

Over two hours later, Lucas's hope hadn't diminished. They were both tired, yes, but they'd finally—*finally*—found someone who actually knew "Old Bishop Yoder" who'd once sold horse liniment and who had a daughter named Ruth. The people of the Old Order Amish were less inclined to associate with outsiders; the men refused to even look at Tyne, so Lucas had had difficulty obtaining the information. However, he'd prevailed by asking his questions politely but persistently—very persistently—and now they actually had a specific address in hand.

Tyne looked out the car window at the lush, green trees flanking the narrow country road.

"You know," she murmured, "I've been so focused today that I haven't thought about Zach. I wonder what he's doing."

Lucas glanced at the clock on the dashboard. "He's probably cleaning the fish they caught. Or stacking the firewood he collected." He grinned. "Or sitting in a hole trying to figure out how to get out."

"*What?*" She couldn't tell if he was serious or if he was teasing her. "What are you talking about?"

"Uncle Jasper put me in a hole once."

Tyne couldn't believe her ears. "Lucas. Come on. Don't tease me."

"I'm serious." He lifted one hand off the steering wheel. "First, he made me dig the hole. I spent a whole day with a shovel in my hands. 'Deeper,' he kept saying. 'Deeper.' And he made me go to sleep next to it that night, not knowing what the danged thing was for. 'That is for tomorrow,' was all he'd tell me before sliding into his sleeping bag."

Lucas's smile never faltered. "The next morning he told me to jump down into the hole. Which I did, no questions asked. He told me I could have breakfast as soon as I'd climbed out, and then he walked away."

She was quiet, her mind taken up with the idea of Zach out in the woods with Jasper…maybe standing in a hole he'd been forced to dig.

"Nearly three hours later and I was still standing there. Filthy from trying to scale the walls, frustrated as hell that I couldn't."

"Your tone is telling me this is a good memory," she said, "but for the life of me, I don't understand."

He laughed. "Neither did I. And that was precisely the point of why I was in the hole for hours."

She frowned.

"Little did I know, but my uncle was busy in the night. While I slept, he'd angled the sides of the hole so the opening was smaller than the base. It would have been impossible for me to climb out. It'll be impossible for Zach to climb out too."

"Lucas! You are not making me feel any better. Get to the good part, please."

"I just hope he figures it out quicker than I did," Lucas continued easily. "You see, many of those camping tasks will emphasize independence. They're about learning self-reliance. But the hole? The hole is designed to make a man realize there are times when he can't go it alone. He needs others."

Tyne nestled into the seat, crossing her arms tightly over her chest. "My son's out in the woods somewhere, digging a hole," she muttered. Her tone lowered. "*Trapped* in a hole." She heaved a sigh and shook her head. "Wonderful."

He chuckled at her, the sound of it not at all unpleasant.

"Physical exercise is good for him, Tyne." His voice went soft and serious. "You know it is. Shoveling dirt or carrying wood, it doesn't matter. He's out in the sunshine with someone whose only wish is to teach him the things he needs to know to get through life unscathed. Zach will benefit by learning to think for himself. Learning to scope things out, decipher situations, anticipate the consequences of his actions."

She took in everything he said, her shoulder and arm muscles relaxing. Thinking about the trouble Zach had gotten himself in back in Philly, she had to agree that her son needed some practice in all of those things.

"Oh, wait. Slow down. There it is," she said, pointing to the road sign they'd been watching for. "Jasmine Way." She leaned forward a little as he made the turn. "Now to find the house."

Lucas slowed the car, pulling to a stop on the wide shoulder of the road.

"I don't know if I can do this." Tension laced the edges of his words.

Her heart ached for him as she took in his ridged jaw and his tight grip on the steering wheel.

"That hole in the ground I told you that Uncle Jasper had me dig…" He paused long enough to swipe the back of his hand across his mouth. "It wasn't just an opening in the dirt. It was meant to represent predicaments. Life's difficulties. I spent hours down there, excited and determined. If my uncle told me to climb out, then there most certainly was a way for me to climb out. I just had to find it. But after a while, I was forced to look at the sides—*all the sides*—of the problem." His eyes narrowed.

"Once again, I've focused all my energy on my own excitement. My own determination to solve the problem." Absently, his thumb worried the leather covering of the steering wheel. "What if she's not interested in meeting me?" he murmured. "What if she's never given me a second thought? What if my showing up on her doorstep only causes her grief?"

She heard no self-pity, only matter-of-fact inquiry. Tyne sat motionless. When she did speak, her tone was just as soft as his. "I'm a mother, Lucas, and I can't imagine that she hasn't thought of you. That she hasn't wondered. A person would have to be heartless…" She let the rest of the thought fade. He didn't seem to be listening to her anyway.

His eyes remained riveted to a spot somewhere on the distant horizon. "What if she married someone, you know, from her own religion? What if her husband knows nothing about me? What if she has other children? And all they know is that their mother is perfect in every way? I could ruin everything for her. I could cause this woman a whole world of—" His mouth thinned, and his shoulders dropped a full inch. "That's what he meant."

"What? Who?" A car passed by; Tyne gave it little notice.

"Uncle Jasper. He told me not to cause Ruth Yoder harm. I thought he meant I shouldn't say anything mean to her. Or, you know, blame her." Doubt shadowed his gaze. "But I realize now he meant so much more. Just by showing up on her doorstep, I could end up hurting her."

The air conditioner hummed, blowing a cool draft into her face. She reached out and flicked the lever, redirecting the air upward.

"What do you want to do, Lucas?" she asked softly. "Do you want to just let this be? We could turn around and go home."

That wasn't the best choice, in her mind. But coercing him wouldn't be the right thing to do.

"I meant it when I said I'd help you with this. I'll support you in whatever you decide to do." The instant the words left her mouth, heat flushed through her, and something profound tugged in the pit of her belly. Her mouth went dry, and she was relieved to find him distracted, deep in thought.

"I don't have to introduce myself," he said finally. "I mean, I don't have to go there and announce my relationship to her. I could just, well," his gaze lifted to hers— "keep that to myself, right?"

Tyne could see how desperately he wanted to meet his mother. "Of course, you could." She smiled lightly. "You look like your father, Lucas. No one would ever mistake you for being Amish. I can't imagine anyone suspecting a thing.

We could stop under the guise of asking for directions." She lifted her hands, palms up. "To Wikweko. That would work. You've got relatives there. That's not even a lie."

"Directions," he murmured. "To Wikweko."

He nodded. The smile he offered reflected immense gratitude, and Tyne felt another tight pull deep in her stomach. She didn't even try to analyze it—didn't want to, really—as he steered the car back onto the winding country road.

After several more miles, she said, "There. Could that be the place?"

Lucas slowed the car.

The small, white clapboard house sat back from the road. A sturdy split-rail fence surrounded the tidy yard. A large vegetable garden thrived along the south side of the house, and a woman stood among the plants, bent at the waist, pulling weeds. The old man sitting in a wheelchair on the concrete porch had Tyne nodding.

"This has to be it, Lucas." Her heart thudded an erratic beat against her ribcage.

He pulled to a stop on the shoulder of the road, and with slow, deliberate motions, he put the car in park and shut off the engine. They both got out and met at the mailbox at the end of the narrow sidewalk near the front of the car. The woman in the garden straightened, looking at them while reaching to wipe her hands on the white apron tied around her waist. She started toward them, the skirt of her shin-length black dress brushing the thick vegetation.

Tyne stood beside Lucas, waiting for him to take that first step. The Amish woman was halfway to the gate, and still he hadn't moved. Tyne turned to him. He looked frozen in place. It was difficult to watch such a commanding figure become overwhelmed with apprehension. She slid her hand in his, and the trembling of his chilled fingers had her whispering, "It's okay, Lucas. This is going to be just fine. Come on."

She took a step, giving his rigid arm a gentle tug, and he followed.

The three of them met at the gate, and when no one spoke, Tyne asked, "Ruth Yoder?"

Lucas and the woman hadn't stopped staring at each other. The awe on Ruth Yoder's face was answer enough, but she nodded. "I am."

Mother and son stood, face to face, for the first time in thirty-five years, the gate standing between them an uncanny yet solid symbol of the emotions holding them at bay. Tyne's breath caught as she waited to see if it would swing open wide or remain closed.

Finally, Lucas said, "I'm...I'm..." He stopped suddenly and swallowed, emotion glistening in his eyes.

The woman smiled. "I know who you are."

The strings of her bonnet hung loose, one trailing down her chest, the other draped back over her shoulder. By no means an unattractive woman, Ruth, with her natural glow, looked much younger than the early to mid-fifties Tyne had calculated her age to be.

"You look so much like your father. Tall like him too." The woman spoke softly. She gave Tyne the barest of glances, then asked Lucas, "Your wife?"

He shook his head. "I'm not married. But you have a grandson. Zach is fifteen."

Ruth's smile tightened and tears sprang to her hazel eyes. "I wish I could invite you in." She turned her head as if to look toward the house. Her voice caught as she added, "But that's impossible."

The man on the porch called, "Ruth? Who is it?"

The transformation in the woman's face was painful to see. Her smooth features contracted and her eyes darkened. When he didn't receive an immediate answer, the old man barked out her name a second time.

Coming to her senses quickly, Tyne offered, "We're here asking for directions, sir."

"Just some lost tourists," Ruth told him. She offered Tyne a grateful smile. "He can't see. He went blind years ago." Lifting her gaze to Lucas, she said, "He's very sick."

"I need to go inside," the old man demanded. "Come and take me inside."

A gentle breeze blew a tendril of Ruth's brown hair across her face. She automatically swiped it aside and tucked it under her bonnet, smudging dirt across her forehead in the process. Tyne noticed the rich, black soil caked under the woman's short nails, evidence of her work in the garden.

Tyne had never seen regret expressed so clearly on anyone's face before, and her heart twisted into a painful knot.

"I should go," Ruth told Lucas. The sad, painful smile she offered them seemed to strain her lips.

"Wait." He reached out and placed his hand on top of hers on the gatepost in an effort to hold her there, if only for a moment longer. "Just a second."

They stood in the open, summer sunshine raining down on them, a floral-scented breeze rustling the leaves of a nearby tree, yet Tyne felt there wasn't air enough for her to take a breath.

"Are you happy?" he asked.

The old man chose that moment to call her name once again.

Ruth's expression never changed. She searched Lucas's face and finally whispered, "I'm content." She blinked once and went very still. "I want you to know that I've prayed for you every day, Lucas."

For several seconds he didn't move, the look in his eyes intense but inscrutable. There was no way to tell whether hearing his mother speak his name for the first time triggered pleasure or distress. His jaw muscle jumped, and Tyne feared he might tell her exactly what she could do with her prayers. Finally, he released her hand, reached around, pulled his wallet from his back pocket, and slid out a business card. He offered it to her. She accepted the card in silence, tucking it beneath the waistband of her apron without looking at it, and after a final long glance at his face, she turned away.

Now it was Tyne being tugged along by Lucas toward the car. That couldn't be it. That couldn't be all they were going to say to one another. They had years to catch up on, memories to share, regrets to express.

Before she could think of a polite way to articulate her thoughts, they were in the car and driving away from the house. Tyne glanced behind her, stricken with sadness by the sight of that closed gate.

CHAPTER ELEVEN

"I just don't understand."
Besides ordering coffee from the waitress in the café, this was the first thing Lucas had said since leaving Ruth Yoder's house.

Tyne had tried to get him to talk, but not knowing what he was thinking or how he was feeling, she couldn't gauge how to best be supportive. Should she compliment the woman? Rail against her? Lucas's mother had been neither warm and welcoming nor unreceptive. So Tyne waited for Lucas to take the lead. But he hadn't. He'd uttered not a word. He'd just driven.

Even though the car was headed in the wrong direction, she'd kept quiet, figuring he needed time to think. After about twenty minutes or so, he'd pulled into the parking lot of the coffee shop.

"I mean," he continued, absently swirling the spoon around in the heavy ceramic mug, "I realize religion is important to some people." He tilted his head. "But more important than raising your kid?"

Memories from her own past floated up to haunt her. She glanced out the window toward the parking lot.

There must be millions of different reasons why people give up their babies.

Tyne had been young and unmarried and scared when she'd considered giving Zach up for adoption. In the end, she'd made the right decision. A rush of relief hit her just as it had a thousand times over the years.

Gazing across the table at Lucas, she couldn't deny the affinity she felt for Ruth Yoder. Surely, the woman had experienced the same deep desperation Tyne had. She couldn't imagine any woman facing that dilemma without doing a huge amount of soul searching.

"She's the one who made the mistake." His tone went hard. "Why did I have to suffer? Why did I have to grow up without a mother because she wasn't smart enough to insist on a condom?"

Tyne reached out and touched his arm. "Stop talking nonsense. If she'd used birth control, you wouldn't be here."

"And *him*," he said.

Instinctively, she knew he was referring to the old man. Ruth Yoder's father.

"How can a man ignore his own grandson for nearly half a lifetime?" Lucas shook his head. "The good bishop probably saw me as evil." His lips twisted as he mocked, "The spawn of his daughter's sin."

"Oh, stop, Lucas. I mean it. This isn't helping." His arm felt warm beneath her fingertips. He was being so ridiculous she wanted to laugh at him, but she didn't dare risk hurting his feelings. "You could spend the rest of your life making dire speculations, and all you're doing is torturing yourself. You don't know anything about the circumstances your mother and father were facing."

He captured her fingers in his, nodding. "You're right." He took a deep breath, and when he released it, the tension in his shoulders eased. "You're absolutely right." The hint of a smile he offered was rueful. "I can always count on you to set me straight, can't I?"

The smile she shot back was broad. "You betcha."

He sipped his coffee and set the mug on the table. "She seemed afraid of her father, didn't she?"

Tyne only nodded.

"I guess she just couldn't find the strength to go against him, her church, her beliefs"—he shrugged—"her community. They're a tight-knit bunch. And since her name's still Yoder, I guess she never married. Unless she divorced and took back her name. Do the Amish believe in divorce? Do they allow it?" Lucas heaved a sigh. "I know almost nothing about them. Who knows what repercussions she's had to deal with all these years?"

His grip on her didn't lessen.

"Focus on the good," she told him, ignoring the tiny frown that marred his brow. "She thought about you every day. You heard her say it."

He didn't react immediately, but then his head slowly bobbed. He lifted her hand a few inches.

"Thank you," he murmured. "For urging me to do this. For going with me. For letting me vent." He kissed the valley between her first and second knuckles and then pressed them to his chin. "For everything."

Excitement trilled in her stomach, and her body flushed with heat. When he set her fingers free, she tucked her hand in her lap to hide its trembling.

"Things might not have turned out as I'd imagined, and the whole meeting was over almost before it started, but I am glad I went." He grasped the mug. "Listen, all this had me thinking. I, um, I want to thank you for having the strength to go against everyone and raise Zach on your own. If you hadn't, he wouldn't know us." He paused. "Can you imagine that?"

She couldn't.

"You were brave, Tyne," he said.

The compliment made her uncomfortable. "I don't know about that. But I *was* naïve and inexperienced, and there were times when I felt extremely ill-equipped as a parent. That's for sure."

Lucas chuckled. "You have to stop regretting that bobby-pin incident."

"It wasn't only that." She balled up her paper napkin. "There were times—" Closing her eyes for an instant, she shook her head. There was no easy way to sum up those infant and toddler years full of motherly mishaps. "I think the worst was dealing with the grief of losing his stepfather."

His eyebrows arched and he blinked twice. "You were married?"

"I guess I should have mentioned it before, but..." She looked across the café where several other customers enjoyed a late afternoon snack. "It happened so long ago that—" She stopped abruptly and lifted a shoulder. "I met David when I catered a party for his construction company. It wasn't *his* company. He was a cabinetmaker for the company. He made beautiful furniture." She slid back on the Naugahyde bench. "He was older than I was by quite a few years, and we were just friends at first. Because of him, I started my first savings account. And he looked over a used car I wanted to buy. Things like that." Memories made her smile. "When he suggested marriage, I actually laughed at him. His feelings were terribly hurt.

"Anyway, he knew I was struggling financially. Knew I was raising Zach by myself. Zach was two then. Just a toddler." She smiled. "David doted on him." A powerful sadness swept through her, and she paused long enough to rein it in. "David presented a very logical argument; he didn't have anyone to depend on, and Zach and I didn't either. He thought we made a great team. We did get along well. So I agreed to marry him." She looked Lucas in the eye. "It wasn't a love match by any means. We both knew that. We were a team. It was a partnership."

She felt an odd reprieve to be able to tell Lucas that, and she refused to stop and wonder why that would be. "But we were happy together. David was good to me. And he loved Zach." The napkin was a tight ball in the palm of her hand. "We were together just three years, though."

It had taken a long time for her to talk about this without tears coming to her eyes. "There was an accident on the site. They were never able to tell me if he lost his grip on the bank of cabinets he was installing because he had a heart attack, or if he had a heart attack after the cabinets fell on him. He died on the way to the hospital."

She swallowed around the lump in her throat, determined to finish her story. "Do you have any idea how hard it is to explain death to a five-year-old?" Tyne focused on breathing, slow and steady. "That child cried himself to sleep for weeks."

Lucas waved the waitress away when she came offering a refill.

"I'm forever indebted to David. Because of the insurance payout, I could stop worrying so much about money. Oh, things remained tight. But I had the funds for a down payment on the house. And I was able to buy a partnership in Easy Feasts when the opportunity arose." She ran the pad of her middle finger around the rim of her mug. "I'm sorry. This certainly wasn't the best time for me to unload all that on you."

Lucas slid his coffee mug toward the end of the table. "I'm glad you did. I've been wondering, you know. How you and Zach have fared over the years. Where you lived; how you got along. I thought about you from time to time. Wondered if you got married. If you were happy." He waited until she looked at him, before adding, "I'm really glad that Zach had you, Tyne. I'm happy you raised him."

His gaze slid away from her, and the air chilled a degree or two. Then he offered her a synthetic smile. "So, um, you and Rob. I guess this is the love match you've been waiting for?"

She just sat there, startled as much by his odd and suddenly artificial demeanor as by his question. He had gone from warm and appreciative to cool and measuring in mere seconds. It threw her off kilter.

Focus.

Love match? Rob and me? She let the phrase sink in.

If Rob was her love match, why had she reacted to that tiny kiss Lucas planted on her hand just now? Then again, had she ever thought of Rob as the man of her dreams? The questions made her stomach go queasy. She was engaged to him. Had promised to become his wife. Shouldn't she answer Lucas with a resounding *yes*?

Why had she only thought of Rob a handful of times since leaving Philly? They'd talked on the phone several times, but now that she was truly conscious of the exchanges, she realized that Rob had initiated all three conversations. The notion to call him hadn't even entered Tyne's head. Had she been that consumed with Zach and his problems? She looked at Lucas and frowned. Then she swallowed, pushing her coffee cup away, fearful of putting another sip of the stuff in her unsettled belly.

Lucas's chuckle sounded forced. "I'm sorry. Really, Tyne. Forgive my questions. Your love life is none of my business." He shook his head, his words picking up speed. "That would be as bad as you asking me about mine. Love life, that is. Not that you *would*." His gaze skidded from his coffee cup, to the condiment basket, to her face, and back to his cup. "And not that there'd be anything to tell." He grasped and released the handle of his mug several times. "I've dated, sure." He shook his head again, his brows rising slightly. "But I've never expected to find 'the real thing,' if you know what I mean. I learned the truth about *that* myth long ago."

Their eyes met again, and his face went hot before he scanned the café for the waitress.

Tyne's heart thudded so hard against her ribs, she was certain he must hear it. She'd been the one who had taught him the truth about "the real thing." She'd taught him the futility of looking for true love. That was all too clear.

The conversation turned as sticky as the humid August day.

"We should probably go, don't you think?" Clamping her hand firmly on her purse, she slid out of the booth.

"Yeah." He pulled out his wallet and tossed several bills on the table, clearly relieved that she'd changed the subject. "You're right. We should head on home."

∼

Lucas had kept himself busy all day Sunday. After cleaning the carburetor on the ancient lawn mower, he'd mowed the lawn. He'd trimmed back the overgrown bushes on the property and called to have the piles of branches removed. He'd washed his car and cleaned out the shed in the backyard.

Tyne didn't know if he was avoiding her because he needed some time to think about his meeting with his mother or if it was because he was feeling embarrassed about having tread on the prickly ground of their love lives.

Here it was Monday morning, and they'd barely finished their coffee and the cinnamon buns she'd baked, when there had been a knock at the front door. Another Wikweko resident had come looking for legal advice from Lucas. The man and woman had both looked troubled as they had settled onto the couch in the living room, so Tyne had slipped on a pair of sneakers and walked into town to give Lucas the quiet he needed to consult on the couple's problem.

Although the people had left by the time Tyne returned home in the afternoon, Lucas continued to work, spending several hours making notes and telephone calls, she assumed, to his office in the city. He'd stopped to eat the simple dinner of Cobb salad she'd fixed them. And while their conversation was a little awkward, that's when she'd learned that a fraudulent financial planner had swindled the couple out of their life savings and they were hoping Lucas could somehow find a way to help them recoup their losses.

"Wikweko doesn't have a law firm in town?" she'd asked him.

He'd shaken his head. "They'd have to drive into Oak Mills or Millersville or Lancaster. Martin and Patricia have been lied to. They were taken advantage of. It's difficult for them to trust anyone's advice. They weren't sure where to turn. I'm like family, I guess. Someone to rely on without making them feel stupid for handing some stranger all that money. I'm happy that they came to me for help. Otherwise, they might have just given up. Taken the loss."

The idea had been disturbing.

Lucas had gone back to work after dinner so Tyne had taken her book out into the backyard. But it became difficult to read in the twilight, and she'd decided to take a walk.

Since Lucas had coupled the "love match" phrase with Rob's name Saturday afternoon, Tyne had thought of little else.

Did she love Rob? That one small question continued to torment her.

Before Lucas had asked her point-blank, forcing her to really and truly think it out, she'd have said she did. She cared about Rob. That much she knew. The two of them got along well enough, rarely arguing unless it was over something disrespectful Zach had said or done. Rob had no experience with teens and didn't understand the idea that all adolescents go through a rebellious stage. He seemed understanding when it came to her job; a lot of men wouldn't like or put up with her work schedule. He didn't mind that she wasn't overtly social, and that her idea of nice date was a quiet dinner and a movie at home. But were those small positives enough to base a marriage on? Would *getting along* offer a firm foundation for a life together?

Was there really such a thing as true love? Or soul mates, for that matter?

True, Rob didn't stir in her that dizzying titillation one usually associated with the head-over-heels kind of love. But then, David never had either. She'd gone into her first marriage with her eyes wide open, and she'd thought she was facing her future with Rob the same way. The practicality of it felt... right. She'd come to the conclusion that that hot and needy kind of fervor didn't really exist. Feverish passion was something Hollywood moviemakers had created. It was a myth. A fantasy. Just as Lucas had said.

But Lucas made you feel it.

She exhaled an exasperated sigh. That had happened years ago. And it had been nothing more than raging teenage hormones. She had wanted him so badly back then she'd thought she'd be completely consumed by her urges. Talk about feverish passion! She'd been frantic for him. *Insane* for him. She closed her eyes, an irrepressible smile curling her mouth. Even now, her skin burned when she thought of their fiery, frenzied lovemaking.

She blinked her way out of the heated memory and gazed up at the inky sky with its thick mantle of glittering stars. The wide swath of the Milky Way was clearly visible.

Realizing she'd come farther than she'd meant to, she turned toward home.

They might have been young and awkward, but what she and Lucas lacked in experience, they'd made up for in eagerness. One particular memory floated to the surface; in the back seat of his car, they had struggled out of their shirts, leaning forward at the same time and smacking their skulls together painfully. She chuckled out loud and was happy that she was alone with her thoughts. But her smile faded when she realized Lucas had made her feel that same intense giddiness several times since they'd come to Wikweko. A look here; a touch there. And most electrifying, that kiss he'd pressed to her hand at the café. He'd merely been thanking her, yet his lips had roused a firestorm inside her. She'd felt—

"No," she firmly told the silky darkness. That had been nothing more than remnants from the past rising from the deep. Slivers of steamy memory that just happened to churn to the surface when he was simply showing his gratitude for her support.

Slivers from the past. Yes. That was it, exactly. Tyne lifted her left hand, the hard, cold diamond mocking her as it winked in the moonlight.

Movement on the shoulder of the roadway ahead had her squinting into the night. The large pack and bedroll the man lugged on his back made her smile. Jasper. She quickened her pace to meet him.

"You're back," she said, giving him a hug and a kiss on the cheek. "Where's my son?" She pulled back enough that she could look into his face. "You didn't leave him in a hole somewhere in the woods, did you?"

Jasper laughed. "You've been talking to Lucas, I see."

"Yes, I have."

"You tell my nephew that Zach figured out the solution to *that* problem in half the time Lucas did."

She clapped her hands together, her smile growing wide. "That's great. I can't wait to rub it in."

He shifted the strap of his backpack. "We're not far from my house. Come have a glass of iced tea with me. I want to talk to you about Zach."

Walking a few blocks out of her way into town was a small inconvenience if it meant hearing how her son's weekend went.

"He's amazing," Jasper told her. "Even before we pitched our tent, that kid understood there was more to our camping trip than merely having some family time. He's smart, Tyne. And he's confident enough to speak up about what's on his mind."

Smoothing her hands over her upper arms, she arched her brows. "Usually, his 'confidence' comes through sounding suspiciously like rebellion and disrespect."

The elderly man nodded in response. "Well, don't be surprised if he begins to temper that."

"Oh?" She let her hands drop to her sides in a natural swing as she walked along beside him. "What did you do? Perform some sort of miracle out there in those woods?"

He chuckled. "No, no. Not me. Zach was the one doing the work."

They made a right onto Water Street, the moon casting shadows over the paved sidewalk.

"He easily grasped the meaning of every tale I told him. He understood the broad themes, but he also picked out the fine details that many people miss the first time around." The sole of Jasper's hiking boot scuffed against the concrete. "He realized we were there on serious business, and he embraced the opportunity to grow." The overhead street lamp made his dark eyes shine. "It didn't hurt that he really wanted to impress me. I have to say I was—and still am—amazed by how mature he acted."

Tyne listened, teetering between feeling proud of her son and wanting to ask if he was sure he was talking about Zach.

"He's been ready for this for some time, I suspect," Jasper said quietly. "I think what he needed was someone from outside his small circle to look him square in the eye and tell him it's time to grow up. Time to take responsibility for himself. Time to think about his actions beforehand, rather than dealing with the disaster afterward."

They turned down the alley that ran behind the row of galleries.

"Don't be surprised if he's pensive for a few days. He'll probably want to spend time on his own." Jasper let himself into the back door of his shop and flipped on the light switch. "We laughed a lot. Had a lot of fun. But we talked even more. About some very serious topics. I gave him a lot to think about, Tyne."

She lifted one shoulder. "Considering the trouble he got himself in, someone had to." She sucked in a sharp breath. "Oh, crap. Jasper, I promised him I wouldn't say anything."

He let his backpack slide to the floor. "Not to worry. He told me all about his legal troubles."

She couldn't believe it. "He did? But he didn't want you to know."

"Yes, but adults don't keep secrets."

They looked at each other and Tyne grinned. "You really got him to believe that?"

His onyx eyes flashed. "Let me put it another way. Keeping secrets gets a person into trouble."

"Now *that* I believe."

They went upstairs to Jasper's apartment, and while he went to wash his face and hands and change into some clean clothes, Tyne made herself at home, pulling out glasses, filling them with ice, pouring the tea, and settling at the cozy kitchen table.

Jasper returned to the kitchen looking refreshed and fastening the bottom button on his shirt. "So where were we? Ah, yes, we were talking about your extraordinary son."

She beamed. "Thanks for spending time with him, Jasper. It means more to me than you'll ever know."

"Zach is the closest thing to a grandson I'll ever have. Growing up is hard. Making a conscious decision to act in a more mature manner is even more difficult. Every kid has to do it in his or her own time. But if I can ease the process, I'm happy to do it." He sat down across from her. "Oh, boy, that feels good. Sitting and sleeping on the ground is hard on these old bones."

Tyne sipped her lemon-laced tea. "Growing up *is* hard, isn't it? I thought it would be the end of me, Jasper. I honestly didn't think I'd make it through." The glass felt cold against her fingertips. "But I did."

Jasper nodded. "I remember. It was a bad time, Tyne. For everyone." He went quiet a moment. "I almost think losing you was harder on Lucas than losing his father." He rested his arm on the table. "You see, when my brother died,

I was there to step into his shoes. Not that I was able to fill them like he would have, mind you. But at least Lucas had someone to see him through. When you left, he was absolutely bereft. He hurt so bad I didn't think he could hold it all in." His mouth flattened. "I'd never seen him like that." The memory made him sigh. "Never. And I hope it's something I never see again."

They sat in silence, both caught up in the past.

When she'd left town for her Aunt Wanda's, she had known Lucas would be hurt, but she'd been too focused on the fact that her whole life had turned upside down. The pressure from her parents. The decisions about the baby that needed to be made. The prospect of her bleak future. It had all been too much.

"The thing I regret most," she said, her voice going husky, "is that I didn't tell him. I left town without telling him I was pregnant with his child." She blinked back sudden tears. "That's the least I could have done, Jasper. But, no, I show up in his office sixteen years later and say, 'Surprise! You're the father of a troubled teen.'"

Leaning her elbows on the table, she covered her face with her hands, worrying her fingertips up and down her temples. "I feel sick every time I think about how I've kept them apart for so many years."

Jasper allowed her to wallow in her misery for a long moment. Then he reached across the table and gave her shoulder a gentle pat.

"I told Zach many Lenape stories this past weekend," he said, the words soft with a smile. "Now I've got one for you."

Tyne lifted her head, sitting up straight.

"Wolf went to the Creator," Jasper began, "to complain about humans. 'They terrorize the animals,' Wolf charged. 'They take more than they need. They plant their crops without replenishing the soil. They move from place to place, leaving behind their trash and debris.' Wolf paced back and forth. 'Why do you put up with them? Why don't you just destroy them?'

"The Great One's voice sounded as big as the wind. 'It is not for you to judge my handiwork. You need to learn appreciation.' So the Creator sent Wolf out on a mission to find the greatest human attribute."

Jasper slid his chair closer to the table. "Wolf searched the earth, far and wide, until he found a man standing by a raging river. The man cut and carved many logs. He toiled in the hot sun, working every day, to build a bridge across the river. When he was nearly finished, Brother River rose and washed away all his work. But the man didn't give up. He gathered more logs and continued his chore for many days until he'd completed the bridge. So Wolf gathered a drop of sweat from the man's brow and took it to the Creator.

"'Perseverance is a wonderful quality of humans,' the Great One told Wolf. 'But it's not the greatest. Keep searching.'"

Tyne rested her hands on the table, listening intently.

"Wolf sprinted east and west, north and south, until he found a woman hiking in a forest. The woman came upon a child who was facing an angry bear. Without even thinking about it, the woman waved her arms and drew Sister Bear's attention. The animal attacked the woman while the child ran to safety." Jasper paused to drink from his glass of tea.

"Wolf had never seen anything like it. He gathered a drop of blood from the woman's battered body and raced back to the Great One.

"The Great One smiled. 'Sacrifice is an excellent human quality, but it isn't the greatest. Try again.'"

Tyne realized her breathing had slowed and calm cloaked her like a promise.

Jasper leaned forward a fraction. "Wolf traveled to the ends of the earth and back, finally finding himself back in his very own forest. He came upon a man running through the woods, his bare back laced with oozing wounds from the whip. The man had been judged a thief by the town baker, and his punishment had been a public lashing. Furious at having suffered another's penalty, the man aimed to exact revenge on the real criminal."

Silence hung in the air during Jasper's long pause. Tyne's heart skittered. Surely, there was more to the story.

"Well?" she asked. "Did he find the culprit?"

Jasper nodded. "Wolf followed the man to a cabin, watched from the trees as he peered through the window. The man's face crumpled and his eyes welled with tears. He turned away, his shoulders round, all thought of revenge gone. Wolf couldn't stand it. He had to see what had made such a change in the man. Wolf trotted to the cabin window and saw the real thief doling out bits of bread to five sunken-cheeked children. Wolf's heart ached at the sight."

Tyne felt her own chest paining.

"Wolf captured one of the whipped man's tears and carefully carried to it to the Creator. 'Forgiveness,' Wolf proclaimed. 'Forgiveness is the greatest human quality.'

"The Great One was pleased. 'You have done well. And you are correct. Forgiveness is what sets humans apart from all the rest of creation, and it is what fills their future with hope.'"

She knew the story had come to an end by the expression on his face. Jasper reclined against the chair back and gulped down his tea like a man dying of thirst. The ice cubes *thunked* against the bottom of the glass when he set it on the table.

"Ah, that was delicious," Jasper pronounced.

"That was a beautiful story." Tyne spoke out of politeness, really, since the story had left her a little confused.

Yes, the point of the fable had been forgiveness. But whom was she meant to forgive?

Zach? Had her son said something to Jasper about her being angry with him?

Lucas? But he hadn't done anything that needed forgiving.

Then it dawned on her. The last thing she'd said before Jasper had launched into his tale.

I feel sick every time I think about how I've kept them apart for so many years.

Then another correlation in the story clicked. Like the forgiven thief, she'd had honorable motivation for her behavior. If she thought about it a while longer, she'd be willing to bet there were other lessons to be found in the story.

The smile she offered Jasper was bright. "A really beautiful story."

CHAPTER TWELVE

With a basketball tucked between his elbow and hip, Lucas answered the knock at the door. He never expected to see Rob Henderson on his doorstep.

After welcoming the man with a handshake, Lucas said, "Tyne's in the kitchen."

Zach came into the living room from the hallway, surprise making him stop short. "Hey," he said to Rob, lifting his hand.

"Hi, Zach. How are you?" Rob looked at Lucas. "Could you tell Tyne I'm here?"

"Sure. Hang on." But Lucas had only taken a step toward the kitchen when Tyne appeared in the doorway, a tea towel in hand.

"Rob," she greeted, and Lucas couldn't help but notice that she didn't smile.

"This is the quickest I could get here," Rob said to her.

She dried her hands on the towel. "I thought you might come at the weekend. I didn't expect you to just drop everything and race out here."

He shrugged. "You sounded pretty serious on the phone. Like...well, like something might be wrong."

It got quiet, and the silence swiftly grew uncomfortable. Lucas wasn't sure who to address, Tyne or Rob, so he tossed out, "Zach and I were going to shoot some hoops, but if you'd rather he stuck around to visit…"

"No, no." A lock of Tyne's blond hair slid over her shoulder when she shook her head. "You guys go ahead. Rob and I need to talk."

When a woman used those words, it rarely meant something good was about to happen. Suddenly, he was reluctant to leave the house, but Zach tapped him on the shoulder.

"Let's go," his son said, and Lucas followed out the front door.

Lucas paused at the edge of the yard. "Instead of going to the Center, let's head over to the church."

"But there's only a half court there."

He lifted a shoulder as he tossed the ball to Zach. "We're practicing some shots. Half court is all we need."

Holding the ball at chest level between both hands, Zach turned his head to gaze up at the house. He looked at Lucas. "She'll be all right, you know. It did feel a little tense in there, but I've never seen 'em fight before. I've never even heard Rob raise his voice. Do you know what's going on? Did you know he was coming?" He stepped out into the street as he talked, bounced the ball once, then tossed it to Lucas and started walking toward the church.

Lucas fell into step beside him, and rather than answer his question, he asked one of his own. "So they get along well?"

The instant he asked, he regretted it. Zach was savvy enough to figure out when he was being pumped for information. Tyne and Rob's relationship was none of his business.

"I dunno." Zach shrugged. "They get along okay, I guess. I try to avoid 'em as much as possible." Zach reached over and stole the ball Lucas was bouncing. "They go out to dinner and stuff. Just the two of them. And when they're at the house, I make myself scarce. Go to my room. Or down the street to hang with a friend."

Before Lucas could ask why, Zach explained, "Nobody likes feelin' like a third wheel."

Lucas wondered if Tyne knew how Zach felt. If they were going to marry, if Rob was going to become Zach's stepfather—

Some dark emotion congealed deep in Lucas's gut. He was just starting to deal with the new experience of being a father, and now he had to contend with the idea of sharing his son with a stepfather.

"Do you like Rob, Zach?" He shouldn't press, but he couldn't help it.

Zach kept his gaze directed straight ahead. "I don't really know 'im. We've watched a few games on ESPN when Mom's running late at work, but…" He shook his head, letting the rest of his thought trail.

"Well, they're getting married. How do you feel about that? Has your mom ever asked you?"

He shook his head. "Nah. But why should she? It's her life. And I won't be living at home forever. I don't care what they do."

The tick in his jaw said differently.

Lucas let the subject drop. For now. It upset him to think that Tyne hadn't talked with Zach about her upcoming marriage. It bothered him even more that her fiancé wasn't more concerned with Zach. Granted, he'd only seen Rob Henderson twice. In the courtroom and just now at the house, but the man didn't give Zach much attention either time. And after hearing his son's point of view, Lucas could only conclude that Henderson wasn't interested in forming any kind of real relationship with Zach. The situation troubled him. Should he try to talk to Tyne about it?

A group of teens were shooting baskets in the church parking lot when he and Zach crossed the grass, and they were happy to have more players join the game. Lucas tugged off his T-shirt and tossed it onto the ground.

"Nice tat." Zach gave him a thumbs up.

Lucas automatically smoothed a palm over the dream catcher that covered his biceps.

Zach said, "I'd love to get a tattoo." Then he snickered. "Something a little less girly than that, though."

A good-natured chuckle erupted from Lucas. "Let's just say I thought it was a good idea at the time." Then he admitted, "Your mom picked it out."

"She did?"

Lucas nodded. "I would have had a yellow ducky tattooed on my forehead if she'd have wanted it." The look on Zach's face made him grin. "She was going to get one too. On her eighteenth birthday, we were going to get matching tattoos." He grinned. "But when she saw how much grimacing I did, she chickened out." Again, he slid his fingers over the dream catcher. "Let's just say I've done my best to wear this like a man."

Zach laughed.

"You guys playing, or what?" one of the boys on the court called.

There were seven of them once Zach and Lucas joined in, so the group played two on two and swapped out after a set number of points had been made.

Competition was fierce from the get-go. Although Lucas had several inches of height on all the boys, he lacked the stamina that came with their youth. He was further handicapped by the fact that he was trying to keep one eye on the road that ran alongside the church. The road that Tyne's fiancé would have to take on his way out of town. Twenty minutes later, he begged a time out and plopped on the grass to rest. The boys continued trying to hog the ball and outshoot each other. No other group of humans had honed the fine art of jeering at each other as well as male teens.

Lucas stood, swiping his palms down the thighs of his shorts, and caught sight of Rob Henderson's pale green sedan. The men's gazes met. Henderson didn't smile, didn't lift his hand, didn't slow the car. If anything, he gunned the engine as if he couldn't get out of Wikweko fast enough.

Lucas ground his back teeth together. Henderson's treatment of Zach was unacceptable, damn it. Even if he and Tyne were arguing, it wasn't Zach's fault. Henderson shouldn't breeze into town with barely a hello to Zach and then leave without at least saying goodbye. It was plain wrong.

"Zach," Lucas called toward the tussling players, "I'm going home for a bottle of water. You want one?"

Zach faked right, spun a full turn, and jumped, stuffing the ball into the net with a grunt. He let out a yell, bumping sweaty shoulders with one of the boys. Then he turned to Lucas. "Water would be great. Thanks." He moved toward the player who had possession of the ball. "I'll hang out here 'til you get back."

As he walked back to his house, Lucas marveled that he could feel both irritated with and concerned for Tyne at the same time.

The fact that she allowed her boyfriend to ignore Zach annoyed him. Why would she want to marry a man who didn't seem to want anything to do with her son? It just didn't make sense.

Henderson's demeanor when he'd arrived had made Lucas uneasy, and the way he'd left town had only bugged him further. The knot in Lucas's gut told him Tyne and her fiancé had fought about something. If that bastard hurt Tyne, Lucas would—

Would what?

Hell, what happened between Tyne and her lover was no business of his, damn it.

With the perfectly logical thought still ringing in his head, he jogged the last fifty yards to the house.

"Tyne," he called. The living room was empty. So was the kitchen. He paused by the stove. Muffled sniffs and jerky breaths came from behind her closed bedroom door. He rapped twice on the jamb, turned the knob, and pushed open the door.

"Tyne?" He went to the bed where she sat, her back to him. "What is it? What happened?"

He knelt beside her, and when she didn't respond to his questions, he scooped up her hand in his.

"Tyne, talk to me. Whatever he said, he probably didn't mean it. Guys can be jerks, honey. We just can't help it. You gotta know that."

Lucas was talking off the top of his head. The sound of her crying was ripping his heart to shreds. He'd say anything, *do* anything, to dry her tears and make her smile.

Finally, he reached up, touched his index finger to her chin, and gently guided her face so he could look into her eyes.

Her nose was red and runny, and tears clung to her eyelashes, streaking wet trails of mascara down her cheeks. He remembered a time when they were teens and her father had found them together. The man had called him a slew of derogatory names. Tyne had been mortified. She'd cried bitterly and apologized at least a dozen times for the hurtful things her father had said. Lucas had thought no woman could ever be more beautiful, even with her red eyes and splotchy cheeks. All these years later, he still thought the same.

He snatched a couple of tissues from the box on the bedside table and tucked them into her hand.

She wiped her nose and wadded the tissues in her palm. "I was the jerk, Lucas. I mean, I—I'm"—emotion hitched her voice—"sure he th-thought I was, anyway. But I just couldn't do it. I had to tell him that I just couldn't do it."

Sobs wracked her slender body, and a lump rose in his throat.

Just ten minutes ago, he'd been as irritated as hell, and he'd intended to tell her exactly what he thought of her lousy choice of husbands, or future husbands, or what-the-hell-ever. But all of that had dissolved into nothing in an instant, and the only thing he could think about was hugging away all of her sadness.

But then the strangest thought seeped into his brain. Although his shirt was dry now, he'd been sweaty out on the basketball court. He probably smelled to high heaven. As inconspicuously as possible, he turned his head and sniffed.

He looked up and realized he'd been caught in the act. Her chin trembled with upset at the same time her mouth quirked with a helpless smile.

"What are you doing?" she asked, suddenly chuckling and crying at the same time.

His brow furrowed and he lifted a shoulder. "I've been playing ball with the boys. Keeping up with them made me all sweaty." Resting his hand on her bare knee felt like the most natural thing in the world to do. "I probably smell like a wet hound."

"You're fine," she told him. "Come up here."

She pinched the sleeve of his T-shirt between her fingers and gave a little tug. He rose, sliding to sit beside her on the mattress. Her inhalation was deep; then she shook out the tissues and blew her nose. She sat a moment, taking a couple more full, slow breaths. "Believe it or not, I think I was crying because I'm relieved."

He kept quiet even though he still didn't understand what the heck had happened between her and Henderson.

"There must be something wrong with me." Still clutching the damp tissues, she lifted her hands, palms up, staring at the far wall of the bedroom. "*What is the matter with me?*"

Her tone told him she wasn't expecting an answer. Not from him, anyway. Even if she was, he wouldn't dare say a word.

She took another deep breath and then leaned over and plucked a fresh tissue from the box. After folding it in half, she dabbed at the outside corners of her eyes.

"He picked me up in the grocery store. Rob, I mean." She darted a quick look at Lucas, her mouth twisting. "In the produce department."

"You're kidding?" A chuckle slipped out before he could catch it. "I thought that kind of thing only happened in deodorant commercials on television."

Her eyes were still moist when she grinned, but at least she'd stopped crying. "And you have body odor on the brain."

All he could do was nod in silent agreement. The questions running through his mind were distracting, but he thought it best to wait her out.

"I was choosing avocadoes for guacamole, and he asked me how to tell when they were ripe." Her gaze slid to the battered mahogany dresser a few feet away. "Rob and I started dating and"—she lifted her hands again—"it was... easy. He didn't ask more of me than I could give. He didn't seem to mind that my job required that I work nights and weekends. It isn't easy dating someone who works every Saturday night. He didn't bat an eye when I told him that I had a son."

Yeah, he all but ignores that little fact. Lucas clamped his jaw tight.

"I wasn't expecting him to ask me to marry him," she continued. "And when he did, I don't really know why I said yes. It just seemed... the next logical step?"

Her blue eyes welled with tears again, and she ran her hands anxiously up and down her thighs—and that's when he noticed her left hand. Her ring finger was bare.

"You don't marry someone because it's easy, right?" Her chin trembled again. "What the hell is *wrong* with me?"

She looked him directly in the eye, and there was nothing vague about the query this time. Clearly, she wanted an answer, but he thought it wise to keep his lip zipped.

The old alarm clock on the bedside table ticked loudly in the quiet that fell around them. He'd never known silence between two people could become so jarring.

Finally, he murmured, "There's nothing wrong with you, Tyne."

She rolled her eyes.

"I'd never thought about it, you know?" Her voice hiked an octave. "If I loved him, I mean. How could I not have thought about it? Oh, I'd have said I loved him just because...well, I did agree to marry him." Her chin dipped in an effort to hide her wince, but then she lifted her gaze to his. "But until you asked me about it this weekend, Lucas, I never really sat down and reasoned it all out." Softly, she added, "That just sounds so crazy to me. That I hadn't put any real thought into why I was planning to get married."

When he'd asked her about Henderson at the café, he'd thought her shocked expression had been in response to his ballsy, bad manners.

"I'd never call myself the most intelligent woman in the world, but I'm sure not stupid. I don't live with my head in the clouds. I'm not a ditzy blonde." She looked up at him. "Am I?"

Ready to assure her she was not, he only had a chance to smile before she barreled ahead.

"Granted, I took on a great deal of responsibility when I bought a partnership in the business. We expanded operations and took on more clients." She moistened her lips and reached out to toss the tissues into the wicker basket near the bed. "But I couldn't possibly have been so busy that I could blindly walk into this whole marriage thing... turn it into such a horrible mess."

Once again, she looked up at him. This time she blinked, her lashes brushing against pale cheeks as she whispered, "Could I?"

Lucas wasn't really sure what she was asking or exactly how she expected him to respond. She'd said her tears were because she was relieved. He had some of that running through him, as well. But she seemed confused and filled with such doubt that he knew in his heart his conscience would never be completely clear if he failed to point out the obvious.

"Tyne, maybe he left too soon. Maybe you should be discussing all this with him."

The shake of her head was emphatic. So was her frown. "No. No." She raked her teeth over her bottom lip. "I'm sure I did the right thing." Pain flashed in her eyes, and her voice sounded squeezed off as she whispered, "He didn't like Zach."

Lucas straightened. So she had noticed.

"Not that he *dis*liked him," she clarified. "But he didn't seem... interested. One way or the other. At first, I thought it was Zach. I thought it might be because he was at an awkward age, that he could be prickly, standoffish. I thought maybe he was jealous of Rob. I thought the problem would resolve itself. I thought he'd come around once they got to know each other. But, little by little, I realized that Rob was just as indifferent to Zach as Zach was to Rob. I didn't know what to think. Or do. Was it some kind of game they were playing? Was the testosterone level so high they were seeing who would break first? Should I confront them? Ignore them?" She sighed. "It was just easier to let it ride. But when Zach was picked up by the police, Rob's apathy became absolutely unmistakable. This was no game. He just didn't care. But I was too focused on solving Zach's problem to deal with it."

Her shoulder muscles eased. "Breaking it off was the right thing to do. I never should have accepted the ring in the first place."

She reached over and plucked another tissue from the box. Lucas sensed that she'd done so simply because she needed something to do with her hands.

"Rob wanted to know if it was because of you." She blurted out the words so swiftly that they came out sounding husky. "If I broke our engagement because of you. I told him no, but... I've been feeling so strange since we got here." She twisted the tissue between her fingers. "You said you believed that true love was some kind of fantasy. I guess I'd come to the same conclusion. Why else would I get so involved with Rob? And David? When both were men I didn't love? It's got to be a myth, right?"

Tiny pieces of the ragged tissue scattered across her lap, some on her shorts, some on her bare thighs. White fluff against creamy skin. Lucas swallowed, his mouth going dry.

"But I think we're both wrong about that, you and I. Because we had it."

The words exploded from her like an accusation, a charge she couldn't prove.

He realized suddenly she was no longer sitting next to him, and when he looked up at her, her face bloomed with a rosy blush.

"I'm sorry," she said, brushing at the bits of fiber that clung to her shorts. "I shouldn't have said that. I didn't mean it. I'm upset. I've been delving into the past. I thought I had things straight in my head, but Rob's visit...I broke off the engagement. Gave him his ring. It's got me all discombobulated." Her laugh was too loud, and she continued wiping at her tears, even though every speck of tissue was gone. "You shouldn't be listening to me babble on and on."

She narrowed her gaze on him. "What are you doing here, anyway? You're supposed to be with Zach. Where is Zach?" The short questions were fired off with precision.

"We were thirsty," he told her. "I came home for water."

"Zach is waiting for you?"

She latched onto that excuse to end their conversation as if it were some sort of life-saving device, shooing him off the bed and out of the bedroom with fluttering hands. And he let her because he was just as eager to end this discussion that had clearly bowled them both over.

"He's probably dying," she said. "There's filtered water in the fridge." She stayed at the bedroom door while he went into the hall toward the kitchen. "I've got a thousand things to do. That potato salad won't make itself. And I need to run to the store. We're out of milk."

She talked as if he were keeping her from her vital tasks. Lucas smiled despite the whirlwind of thoughts and questions rolling through his mind. She'd have made a good lawyer.

He ducked into the refrigerator and grabbed the steel gym bottles filled with cold water, and when he glanced down the hall toward her room, she'd already disappeared from the doorway.

Lucas pushed his way out into the bright sunshine, those thoughts and questions still churning like mad in his head. He'd learned a lot about Tyne over the course of the last ten minutes. Hell, he'd learned loads. However, there was one thing he'd discovered, one thing she'd said, that intrigued him more than anything else. She'd said Henderson had asked her if she had broken their engagement because of Lucas.

I told him no, but...

But. It was a small word. Infinitesimal, really. Most people thought it to be quite insignificant. On the contrary, Lucas knew that thinking was flawed.

But. It could be major. Hell, it could be momentous. Any attorney would agree. Lawyers in every courtroom kept their ears perked for such a juicy plum presenting itself for plucking. The whole of the legal world knew that precedent-setting cases had been won and lost—all on account of that one tiny word.

CHAPTER THIRTEEN

Teens and cliques seemed to go hand in hand. Back when Tyne went to high school, there were the "rah-rahs" and the jocks, cheerleaders and athletes who lived in a world all their own and would rather die than be caught next to a punkster, those kids who bragged about cutting class and smoking cigarettes or weed behind the gym. There were the techs, those kids who boarded a bus each afternoon that took them to a school where they learned to rat hair or tune carburetors and who should never be confused with the techies who loved computers and gadgets and who couldn't be confused with Trekkies who dreamed of visiting galaxies far, far away with Captain James T. Kirk.

There were subgroups within groups, insiders who snickered at outsiders, for the sole purpose of power, exclusion, and control—coping mechanisms to combat pubescent insecurity.

But as the dusky, pink twilight fell over the birthday gathering, Tyne couldn't help noticing how well the Lenape teens got along. Sure, there was some teasing, but there was nothing mean-spirited in it. There could have been some underlying tensions going on; these *were* normal teens, but from what Tyne witnessed, these kids were amazingly friendly toward one another. It could be that the inequitable treatment these young men and women received from outside their close community impelled them to be more open to their own, more embracing of individual differences.

The change in Zach was unbelievable. Just as Jasper had predicted, her son had been contemplative for days following his camping trip. When he communicated, it was in quiet tones and measured words. He did what he was told without argument. He pitched in around the house. He hadn't asked about visiting his grandparents, hadn't mentioned Oak Mills even once. If Tyne hadn't witnessed his dark eyes shine with anger earlier today, she might have suspected that Jasper left her son out in the woods and brought her back a "Stepford" child.

The incident had been sparked when a group of teens had arrived at the house that morning, planning to drive to Millersville to swim at the home of a friend of one of the girls. Tyne didn't know the driver of the car and didn't know the other teens, and the way they'd hemmed and hawed answering her questions about adult supervision had made her uncomfortable. She'd finally told Zach he couldn't go, and he'd been furious. She'd braced herself for a tirade.

He'd wrestled with his emotions; then he'd grown quiet, taken a couple of deep breaths, and walked away. The other teens left with shouted promises of seeing Zach at the birthday party later on in the evening. Although her son hadn't spoken to her for a couple of hours after that, Tyne couldn't really call his behavior sulking. He'd agreed to help Lucas replace the handle on the shed in the backyard, and once they had returned from the hardware store, she'd heard them laughing together as each took a turn trying to pry off the old, rusted latch.

If Jasper could find a way to bottle whatever techniques he'd used to transform her son, the man would be a millionaire.

"I brought you some water." Lucas handed her the bottle and then sat down beside her on the old quilt they'd brought to the party.

"Thanks." Tyne unscrewed the top and took a drink.

He looked over to where Dorothy Johnson was being fawned over. A little boy was perching a paper tiara on the old woman's head.

"She looks happy, doesn't she?" Lowering his voice, he added. "And she doesn't look a day over ninety-eight."

"Lucas!" Tyne laughed. "I can't imagine living a hundred years, can you?"

He grinned at her. "A better question is, would we want to?"

Tyne casually lowered her chin, studying the cap of the bottle she'd just opened, a bright spot of white against the green cotton cloth. All he had to do was flash those dark eyes at her and her body reacted erratically.

Over by the cake table, Dorothy laughed and clapped at something the child said to her.

"Not that you wouldn't make a beautiful centenarian," he murmured.

Again, Tyne laughed. "Do you care much about beauty at that age?"

He shrugged and then stretched his long legs out in front of him, resting his weight on his elbows. The blue jeans he wore only seemed to accentuate his muscular thighs, and it was easy for Tyne to remember smoothing her hands over them even though she hadn't touched him intimately in what felt like an entire lifetime.

"The chicken's delicious," he told her. "I snatched a piece. You should have something to eat."

She nodded. "Later. I'm too busy watching all these people. There's so much going on."

A group of toddlers kicked a ball not too far away. Women shuffled bowls and platters of food on the long row of tables in order to make more room as people arrived with their potluck offerings. Further out on the field, a dozen or so adults played a game that looked a little like football, but the rules were obviously different. It was men versus women. The men couldn't run the ball but could only pass it from one player to another in their attempt to cross the goal line. The women could run, pass, and punt, and they became inordinately physical with the men in order to steal the ball. One woman jumped on a man's back, tugged on his ears, then covered his eyes with one hand and smacked the ball from his grasp with the other. Her teammate scooped the ball off the ground and raced like the wind. When they'd arrived for the party, Lucas had told her the game was called *pahsahëman*. The players were having a good time, but the game looked too rough for Tyne to give it a try.

"I've missed this." He tapped his thumbs on the blanket as if he were keeping the beat of some rhythm playing in his head. "The food. The family and friends. It's really nice." His thumbs stilled, and he sank a little lower. "It feels homey. Comfortable. Right."

The way his voice had gone all soft around the edges made her belly tense. The bottle of water she held was slick with condensation. She reached up and brushed her moist fingers across her forehead. "You ever think about moving back?"

Without hesitation, he said, "I couldn't make any money here." He sat there looking at her and then tilted his head slightly as some inscrutable emotion passed over his face. Then in one effortless motion he sat up, bent his legs, and palmed his knees. "Well, I'll be damned if he wasn't right."

Tyne tucked her feet beneath her. "Who was right? What are you talking about?"

"Uncle Jasper." Once again, his thumbs started drumming but this time on his knees. "A couple weeks ago, we had words." His palms lifted up in the air for an instant. "Well, as much as anyone can argue with Jasper, anyway. The man's never raised his voice in his life, I don't believe. Doesn't have to. He chooses just the right thing to say to make you feel about this tall." He held his index finger and thumb less than an inch apart.

Tyne had known something was going on between the two men.

Lucas rubbed his palms back and forth across his knees, gazing out at the field.

"So," she gently prodded, "what'd he say?"

Lucas was so deep in thought, she doubted he was even aware she'd spoken. She busied herself taking a sip of water and then putting the cap back onto the bottle. A little boy shouted in triumph when he caught the ball tossed to him by his mother. Dorothy admired a necklace made of dyed pasta strung on bright yellow yarn, a gift from a girl who looked about six or seven. The child's eyes glowed as Dorothy leaned forward and kissed her on the cheek.

"He told me a story. About a fish, making its way to the ocean."

Lucas's tone was almost a whisper. "Jasper feels that my ambition has caused me to lose sight of Lenape values. Giving up pieces of myself. That's what he insinuated." He balled his hands and propped his elbows on his knees. "I thought I was reaching for success." He tapped his knuckles against his chin. "I've got a four-bedroom house in the city. Two new cars. A walk-in closet full of designer suits. A timeshare in Fort Lauderdale. Another in Vale I've never even seen." The sound he emitted was harsh. "I've only been to the one in Florida once. Couldn't stand all that heat and solitude. I give away my vacation weeks. Or lose them in the Wednesday night poker games." He shook his head, his stark gaze turning full on her face. "How extravagant can one person be?"

Tyne thought of how she'd struggled and done without in order to provide for Zach. If it hadn't been for David's life insurance and the subsidy she'd qualified for because she was both a first-time home buyer and a single mother, she never would have achieved the dream of owning a house. Her two-bedroom row home was cozy, but it was enough. Her battered Toyota wasn't totally reliable, but that was the next big-ticket item on her list to replace just as soon as her savings account was padded enough to take the hit. She thought of all the times Zach had asked for things—ridiculously expensive sneakers, an iPad, a skateboard that cost more than three months worth of electric bills—and she'd had to say no simply because she couldn't afford them.

"From the time I was a kid," Lucas said, "I was taught that taking and giving was necessary. As normal as breathing. We inhale the oxygen we need and exhale the carbon dioxide that's crucial to every plant and flower and tree on earth. Give and take. Every elder I ever talked to lectured that taking more than what's needed upsets the balance of nature."

Half a dozen questions sprouted in her mind about how he'd been raised compared to his current extravagant lifestyle, but she held her tongue. The concentration etched on his brow and the set of his jaw told her he was doing plenty of self-examining all on his own.

Tyne watched as Jasper and four other men helped the teens wheel a flatbed cart from the rear door of the Community Center. A large drum sat securely on the cart. A group of teens, Zach included, lifted the drum and gingerly set it on the grass near the small fire that crackled and flickered against the growing darkness. The game of *pahsahëman* broke up, the adults laughing and talking as they made their way over to the bonfire.

Five young men formed a tight semicircle, shoulder to shoulder, and began to pound a beat on the drum while Jasper sang. Two other elders made their way toward the drumming and took up the chant. The strong harmony carried on the hot summer air, haunting and powerful.

A couple of the teens looked self-conscious, but not Zach. His smile was as broad as his puffed chest, his dark head bobbing with each synchronized strike on the drum.

"He really does fit in up there, you know?" Lucas murmured. "He's loving it."

Tyne only nodded silently, thinking the same thing. She'd never seen her son enjoying himself so thoroughly.

The strains of the first song had barely ended when the second began. This one was livelier than the last. One of the drummers waved at a man in the crowd to join him; Zach invited Lucas with a short jerk of his head. Lucas jumped to his feet and jogged over; his shoulder pressed against Zach's as he took up a knobby stick and thumped the ancient beat.

It was a good scene, a happy scene. But watching father and son bonding around the ceremonial drum filled her with sadness. It also made her doubt every decision she'd ever made as Zach's mother.

∽

Later that evening, Tyne helped herself to strawberry shortcake, smiling when the young woman at the table scooped a dollop of freshly whipped cream on top. The fruit was sweet on her tongue; the cake, buttery; the thick cream, delectably rich.

The teens had taken a break from drumming, and a trio of flautists was entertaining the crowd, the wooden instruments producing an orphic melody that flowed like a lazy river.

The small hairs on the back of her neck stood on end when someone approached her from behind.

"Come with me," Lucas whispered close to her ear. "I want to show you something."

Ever since he'd drummed with their son, his gaze kept seeking her out and finding her. When she'd gone to give

Dorothy her birthday gift, she'd felt him watching. And during a conversation with Jasper, she again caught Lucas staring.

He slipped the plate from her fingers and set it on the table; then he took her hand and led her away from the gathering.

Before he'd taken his first step, instinct told her where he was headed. Vivid memories skimmed across her skin like fairy dust, raising goose flesh and making it difficult to breathe.

He rounded the corner of the building and headed for the large oak that stood sentry at the edge of the thick forest.

It was under that very tree, on a clear evening just like tonight, at a gathering much like this one, that he'd kissed her for the first time. He'd been a senior and she, a sophomore. She'd been a member of the popular crowd and had a ton of friends. He'd been a loner with a rebellious reputation. A troublemaker in tight jeans, a bad boy who had intrigued her beyond reason—from afar, of course. She'd have never extended her friendship to him; doing so would have broken every single unwritten rule and would have resulted in social suicide. But once they'd had a chance to talk, it hadn't taken her long to sort out fact from mean-spirited gossip.

They'd met at a football game; he'd made a phenomenal catch and had run the ball across the goal line. Later on, she would learn what a rare occurrence it was for Lucas to be involved in a play. She had stopped him after that game to compliment him. She'd merely meant to be polite. He'd looked at her as if she were from another planet. But just as the feeling of insult began to set in and she turned to walk away, he'd called to her. He'd thanked her for her compliment, and then he'd invited her to a movie. There had been something in his confident stare that excited her. The sharp angles and hollows of his face, the dusky tone of his skin, made him seem almost exotic to her.

Not allowing herself to consider the consequences, she'd agreed to meet him at the theater. For weeks they arranged rendezvous at various places around Oak Mills: a diner out on the main road, a stand of pines on the more remote side of the park, the old Dairy Freeze. She'd thought they'd been careful, but she'd lost friends faster than she'd ever thought possible. That hadn't mattered; she'd been too captivated by the boy with the sable eyes and the long, sexy hair.

Vivid dreams of heated kisses and tentative touches had shocked her awake each night, but three excruciating weeks went by, and he hadn't even held her hand. All he'd done was talk, and he seemed to want to know everything about her. Of course, she was happy to oblige, but being with him was torment. A voice in her head whispered that he was all wrong for her, but her more sensual urges made her desperate to discover the taste of his lips on hers.

Then in late September, he'd invited her to the Lenape Harvest Festival.

Lucas had acted so nervous once she'd arrived that he'd set *her* on edge. She had known something was going to happen, but for the life of her she couldn't figure out if he was garnering the courage to finally kiss her or tell her their budding relationship had all been a mistake.

She'd trembled when he'd finally taken her hand and led her into the darkness, just as he was doing now. Her knees had grown quivery back then—she could still remember the feeling as if it had happened yesterday—and she'd been thankful for the support of the solid tree trunk at her back. He hadn't said a word. Had only studied her face for the longest time. She had feared she would drown in the black depths of his gaze. And then he'd kissed her, gently, softly, over and over again.

It had been the most romantic moment of her life.

He'd turned bold, looking directly into her eyes as he'd skimmed his hand over her shoulder, her waist, her hip. She'd let him touch her, never breaking eye contact, as kaleidoscopic feelings shivered and pulsed through her body. And then he'd kissed her again, this time rougher and deeper, but not rough or deep enough to satisfy the new and burgeoning need radiating in her belly and between her thighs. Then he pulled her to him and wrapped his arms around her. The solid mass of him made her sigh.

Lucas had whispered against her neck, "You're beautiful," and she'd thought she would dissolve into a pale, liquescent pool right at the base of that oak tree.

She'd have given herself to him, then and there, on the grassy ground. She'd have surrendered her heart, her virginity, and anything else he might have wanted.

And here they were again all these years later, the massive tree at her back, those black, piercing eyes boring into hers.

"Do you remember?" he whispered.

She didn't have to speak. Her answer radiated from her like a humming current of energy.

Sounds of faint laughter and happy voices carried on the still air just as they had all those years ago.

"I've been thinking about this spot all evening." He smoothed his thumb along her jaw. "About that night. That kiss."

And she'd been trying hard all evening not to.

CHAPTER FOURTEEN

The entrancing strains of that magical music quavered with the rhythm of her heart and threatened to whisk her away. Lucas's penetrating gaze searched hers. He leaned toward her, and she was hit with a heady adrenalin rush.

"Sorry," he murmured, "but I've just got to do this."

The apology made her frown, but his lips brushed hers, once, twice, featherlight, kick-starting her pulse into a staccato beat that clashed with the dreamy, melodious harmony of flutes. He deepened the kiss, and her whole world became focused on the corporal; the hardness of his chest beneath her palms, the heated scent of him filling her nostrils, lulling all thought. His fingers skimmed over her shoulders and down her arms, settling on her waist, his touch sure, unhurried, deliberate. He slid his hands upward toward her ribcage and breasts, and she bent her elbows and tucked them tight against her, blocking him with her forearms.

"Whoa," she whispered. "Hold on."

He pulled back a few inches, a question in his eyes.

She smiled, shaking her head, uncertain if embarrassment and simple apprehension were making her feel so overheated or if it was he, his kiss, his touch. "We're not teenagers anymore, Lucas."

He grinned. "Yeah, ain't it great? I know just what to do and how to do it."

His eyelids drooped subtly and he leaned in, his bottom lip glistening from their kiss, and she nearly surrendered and let him take her wherever it was he wanted to go. But logic snapped on like a glaring light.

She lifted her hand, touching her index and middle fingers to his moist, hot mouth. "Wait." Indecision forced her gaze to dip, but then she looked him in the eye. "Lucas, what are you doing?"

Deadpan serious, he told her, "I think that's obvious. I'm kissing you."

The passion hazing his gaze, roughening his voice, caused the muscles low in her gut to constrict.

"Lucas." She tried to elevate the volume of her voice but failed. "We can't do this." She'd lowered her hand a little, but it remained, hovering between them. The heat of him was intoxicating. It would be so easy to surrender.

"Sure, we can. Let me show you how." He pressed his body against hers.

Her small exhalation was short, forceful. "You know what I mean. We *shouldn't* do this." But even as she said the words, she had to resist the urge to release a low groan. This felt so good. So very good.

Now he smiled, the intensity in his handsome face relaxing. "Well, that's another whole issue, now isn't it?"

But he stayed close. Too close.

"This will only complicate things," she told him. "And things are complicated enough, don't you think?" He didn't respond, and he didn't step back. Struck with the overwhelming need to temper her argument, she quickly added, "Besides that, we're not the same people, you and I. We can't be, with all the time that's gone by, you know?"

Nerves tickled at her and every inch of her skin became hypersensitive. Recognizing the hard length of his penis bearing against her hip should have forced her gaze from his, should have had her elbowing her way out of his heady embrace, but that's not what happened at all. In fact, her own desire flared, white-hot, and when she spoke, it was as if someone else were forming the words.

"We don't know each other, Lucas."

Her little speech cleared his dark eyes and he backed away. And even as she was flooded with relief, she was also glutted with disappointment. His hands slid from her waist, and even with the hot summer heat, she felt suddenly chilled. He didn't agree or disagree with what she'd said, but he did take her hand. And as he led her back to the birthday party, she heard him say, "Guess we'll have to rectify that."

∼

"Hey, Mom." Zach plopped down on the ground beside her and the small pile of weeds she'd plucked from the flowerbed.

Shaded from the sun by the eves of the house, Tyne sat on the cool, green grass, turning the soil to get it ready for the flats of marigolds Lucas had bought, the only flower hardy enough to survive the sizzling summer heat.

"Hi," she said, smiling. "I thought you and Lucas and Jasper were doing something this afternoon."

He nodded, a shank of dark hair falling into his eyes. "We had burgers for lunch and then hung out in town for a while. Uncle Jasper had some great stories about, well,"—Zach's gaze darted to his hands—"you know, about him."

"Lucas?"

"Yeah."

Evidently, her son was still trying to figure out what to call his father. Tyne smacked a clump of earth with her hand trowel, crumbling the dirt. "I'm sorry I missed that."

"Then some guy stopped him"—again he stumbled—"you know, Lucas, on the street. He was, you know, the guy was, like, real upset. Said something about changes in a new contract he got in the mail, like, yesterday or something."

She set the shovel aside. "A contract for a communications tower?"

"Yeah. That's it."

"Lucas has talked to him before." An errant weed, now shriveled by the sun, marred the black soil, and Tyne reached over, pulled it, and dropped it onto the pile. "But I'm surprised Lucas interrupted his afternoon with you and Jasper for—"

"Oh, he didn't." Zach started tugging at a dandelion that was growing between the grass and the bricks that bordered the flowerbed. "We were on our way back to Uncle Jasper's, anyway. The guy was, like, really angry, so I told him, you know, Lucas, that I'd, like, walk home."

She tugged off one glove and looked at her son. "That was nice of you."

Zach shrugged. He focused on the large weed. "Listen, Mom, I've been wanting to..." He cleared his throat, reached out and plucked a green leaf. "I've been, like, thinking."

Announcing the need to talk was a rarity, a near impossibility, for a teenaged boy. At least, she'd found that to be true for her son.

Tyne pulled off her other gardening glove. "I'm listening."

He didn't look up from the dandelion. "I want to apologize. For the way I've been acting. For the trouble I got into back home. I didn't act like—well, you know, like I should have."

Staring at her son, she was astounded. Unexpected tears scalded the backs of her eyelids, and the knot rising in her throat choked her. But she took a breath and willed the emotion aside. "Zach—"

He looked up and immediately narrowed his gaze. "Now, don't make a big deal about this."

Her gaze darted to the pile of weeds she'd created, and she did her best to blink away the tears. "Why would I do that?" The gloves slid back on with ease, and she tackled the flowerbed with renewed gusto, just to have something to keep her hands busy.

The dandelion popped free of the ground, and Zach tossed it aside. "Uncle Jasper says that, like, the only thing a man really has is his honor. Every decision

I make, every word I speak, every action I take reflects on, like, my integrity. And the kind of person I am has an impact on, like, you know, the whole family. Uncle Jasper called it a clan. 'Cause I'm...one of 'em." Zach picked up the trowel and stabbed at the dirt. "What I did before, Uncle Jasper says, isn't, like, as important as how I act now. I mean, now that I've been told. Now that I know how important honor is to a man—to a *person*— to their family, and their whole clan. But even though Uncle Jasper is willing to let me off the hook, it's bothering me. I mean, like, my behavior. You know, the trouble I got into." He sighed in frustration. "I'm not explaining this very well."

Sentiment softened her smile, and she cast him a quick glance. "You're explaining it perfectly."

"Anyway, I can't blame other people for my decisions." He jabbed at a vine-like weed, picked it up, and shook the soil from the roots. "I can't, like, blame you or Rob or, ah, Lucas, and—and not even those kids I was with that night I got arrested. I got in trouble because of the choices I made."

Tyne smoothed her gloved hand over the ground, leveling out the area of the flowerbed she'd been fussing over. Zach would be horrified if she were to grab him and plant a big kiss on his cheek, so she continued working the earth between her fingers.

"Uncle Jasper says becoming an adult means, like, taking responsibility for your actions. The things you do, the things you say. Even the things you think."

That was a lesson she hadn't learned until she'd become a mother. While staying at her Aunt Wanda's home in Florida, waiting for her baby to be born, Tyne had accepted all the help her parents and her aunt had offered. It wasn't until she'd held Zach in her arms, saw the child her actions had produced, that she'd finally put all the pieces together and realized the seriousness of her situation.

She was responsible for this baby. She was the one who had to grow up and start making mature, sensible decisions.

Now here she was, seeing her son learning the same lesson... only he was learning it at an earlier age than she had.

Zach tapped the tip of the metal trowel against the brick-lined border. "I guess I, like, knew that. I should have, anyway. But the way Uncle Jasper explained it, I *really* understood, you know?"

Tyne couldn't stand it any longer. She jerked off her gloves and swiveled her feet under her so that she was propped up on her knees, sitting back on her heels. She turned to Zach. "I don't want you to make a big deal about this, but would it be okay if I gave you a hug?"

It was obviously the last thing he wanted, but he suffered through her embrace. She pressed a kiss to his hair, hoping he didn't feel it.

"I'm proud of you," she whispered. Then she slid along the flowerbed a foot or so and went back to weeding, afraid her emotions would overwhelm her.

"I'm going to go get a soda," he told her, rising to his feet.

The screen creaked open, but it didn't close.

"Mom," he called from up on the concrete stoop.

She lifted her face.

"I am going to try to do better. I promise."

Again, her smile was tight; it was necessary to keep her chin from trembling.

"I don't want you to be ashamed of me ever again."

She gasped. "Zachary, I have never been ashamed of you."

Skepticism planted itself between his brows. "The truth is important, Mom. I can handle it."

Her eyes never wavered from his. "That *is* the truth."

The crease on his forehead only deepened. "So why didn't you tell him about me?"

Guilt jarred through her like a bolt of summer heat lightning.

"And why don't you want your parents to know about me?"

She'd rather have been stripped of her clothes and forced to run down the street stark naked than answer those two innocent questions.

Abortion. Adoption. Bigotry.

The vileness of her teen years made her head swim. Taking responsibility for your actions was one thing. Hurting someone you loved with the painful truth was quite another.

Her son deserved answers. But she wasn't willing to wound him by supplying them.

"Honey," she said softly, "you're going to have to trust me. I want you to know that I'm only doing what's best for you. That has always been my only motivation."

Her son's face went slack. This wasn't the response he'd hoped for.

He stepped inside and she called his name. He paused and then slowly turned to face her, his disappointment only slightly obscured by the web of screening.

"I want you to know something important. It's not you I'm ashamed of."

Her son looked at her for a moment longer, unasked questions clouding dark eyes that were too much like his father's. Then he disappeared into the house, and with shaky fingers she continued yanking weeds from the flowerbed.

CHAPTER FIFTEEN

Tyne's hand moved to her belt buckle, and then she smoothed her palm down her short, twill skirt as she looked around at the other diners. "I'm not dressed appropriately."

Years ago, Reflections used to be a family restaurant, but the owners had obviously elevated their status several notches above the upscale casual attire she was wearing.

"You look great." Lucas's hand was tucked securely at the small of her back, and the two of them followed the hostess to their table.

The outfit was the dressiest she'd brought with her from Philly. Spending an evening at an elegant restaurant in Lancaster hadn't entered her head when she'd packed. Wikweko was a laidback place, homey, comfortable, easy, so she'd only brought shorts and jeans and cotton tops. The skirt had been tossed in as an afterthought.

Thank goodness for afterthoughts.

Lucas looked good enough to serve as first course in his charcoal suit, crisp dress shirt, and black tie. He scooted in Tyne's chair and then took a seat across from her. A harpist plucked out a jaunty melody, and soft light glowed from the candle centered on the small, round table.

"I hope Zach has a good time tonight," she said.

"Are you kidding?" Lucas tucked the crimson linen napkin onto his lap. "They popped six gallons of popcorn and rented four horror flicks. He's going to be at the Community Center until the wee hours. Our kid is in slasher-movie paradise right now."

She grinned. "I wonder how Jasper's feeling about this."

Lucas chuckled. "Don't ask. But he was the one who offered the kids a free night to do what they wanted." Again, he laughed. "I think he expected them to choose an activity that was a little more...cultural."

Tyne shook her head. "He works with teens all the time. Shouldn't he know better?"

The grin on Lucas's face had to suffice for an answer when the sommelier approached, introducing herself as Christy. He chatted with the young, smiling brunette, and Tyne took in the woman's short, edgy haircut. Her black eyeliner and heavy mascara made her eyes look large on her delicate, pale-skinned face. The sophisticated, knee-length skirt and silk bolero jacket hugged her rail-thin body. Tyne slipped her hand beneath the table to give the hem of her skirt an awkward tug, her bare toes curling in her casual sandals.

Once Christy sauntered off to fetch the wine Lucas ordered, Tyne said, "She's cute."

Lifting one shoulder just a bit, Lucas tilted his head. "Never noticed. I only have eyes for one woman tonight." His tone grew hushed. "The one I brought."

She laughed and shook her head. "Lucas. *Really?*"

He leaned his elbows on the edge of the table. "What do I have to do to get you to take me seriously?"

Saturday night had changed everything between them. The few heady moments they had spent under the oak tree had made them overly conscious of each other. For the last four days, every word, every glance, every inadvertent touch seemed to hold extraordinary meaning. Tyne had tried, but ignoring the awareness that shivered between them had become impossible.

Her gaze lowered to the crystal water goblet sitting in front of her.

"Tyne, what you said this weekend is true," he told her. "We're not teenagers anymore. We should be able to talk about what's going on between us."

"But that's just it." She strained for levity. "There's nothing going on."

Without a word, he fisted his hands and rested his chin on his knuckles. Although he didn't speak, his obsidian eyes disagreed with her completely. The air went so taut it nearly vibrated in tune with the harpist's melody.

"Okay, okay," she finally relented. "We need to talk."

A faint smile curled his mouth. "Thank you for not making me come over there and wrestle that out of you."

The glint he offered her held enough sexual innuendo that her pulse quickened. She only rolled her eyes at his teasing.

"You said that we're not the same people. That time has changed us. And I'd have to agree with that theory. We don't know each other." He shrugged. "So the first thing we have to do is fix that, right? We spend time together.

We talk. We laugh. We fill in the gaps of all those missing years." The candlelight made his eyes glimmer. "Who knows where all that talking and laughing and filling in will lead?"

Her mind went blank, and she did her best to disregard the distinct tightening in her groin. If she weren't careful, she might do something she'd end up regretting.

"You were also worried that if we were to explore a relationship, it would complicate our circumstances." Again he shrugged and this time accompanied it with a small shake of his head. "We're mature adults. We can handle 'complicated.'"

She picked up her napkin simply to have something to do with her hands. "But what if the problems become too difficult to deal with?"

His lips quirked and he shook his head. "There you go, focusing on the negative. I think we should concentrate on the positives. And there are many." He leaned forward. "All I can think about is that kiss. And how you tasted. And how your skin felt warm and soft under my fingers. And how all I wanted to do was—"

She twisted one corner of the napkin in her lap. "Lucas, there's more to a relationship than sex."

His deep chuckle sent a tingle down her spine strong enough to make her want to arch her back like a cat lazing in sunshine, and the throbbing in her vagina intensified.

"Yeah, but," he murmured, "we gotta start somewhere."

Rosy buds of heat blotched her cheeks, and perspiration prickled the back of her neck.

"Now, *that* is what I call cute."

Her face flamed hotter. "Lucas, stop." He continued to stare, and she shot him a half-hearted grimace. "You're making me feel...strange."

Lightheaded, happy... *desired.*

He grinned. "Strange wasn't what I was going for at all."

The raw eroticism in his voice was unreal, and she knew his intention was to knock her off balance.

She smoothed out the wrinkles she'd creased in the square of linen. "Lucas, if you're serious about talking—"

"I love it when your face goes pink like that."

She crossed her arms, leaned against the chair's back, and went quiet.

He chuckled. "Pushed you as far as I can, huh?"

The man was handsome when he smiled, but he was orgasmically gorgeous when his sharp-angled features shifted into that "let's get down to business" expression. Tyne pinched the corner of the napkin again and started coiling.

"Let's hear it," he said. "I can see from the look on your face that you've got reservations."

She nodded. "I do. I—I really do." She stopped long enough to take a sip from her water glass. "I mean, I will admit that there's something there." Her gaze dipped for an instant as she muttered, "An attraction or whatever."

"Good." A smile hid just beneath the surface of the short response. "At least we do agree on that much."

"But don't you see the past as a problem?" She'd twisted the napkin into such tight coils that, when she released the fabric, it squirmed like a snake in her lap. Thank goodness the draped tablecloth covered her nervous handiwork.

"I do. I see it as an obstacle. A huge obstacle. Too big for us to climb. Too big for us to overcome."

He reached across the table, opening his hand in invitation. When she lifted hers from her lap, she was vaguely aware that her napkin slithered to the floor. His palm was warm against her fingers.

"Stop looking for trouble," he told her. "We had a son together. And because you were brave enough to raise Zach alone, I have the opportunity to know him." His eyes warmed. "Personally, I think that's something to celebrate."

"But..." *What about the ugly details?* she wanted to ask, but couldn't get her tongue to form the words.

"Tyne? It *is* you. Tyne Whitlock!"

The high-pitched female voice made Tyne wince. The bosomy woman approaching their table looked vaguely familiar. Her stone-gray hair spiked outward behind her ears, and she'd gained a considerable amount of weight, but when Tyne placed her, remembering her name, the blood drained from her face.

"Mrs. Denver?"

The elderly woman waved her hands in a "come, come" motion, and Tyne slipped her fingers from Lucas's and stood without giving it a thought. Good Southern manners prohibited any other choice. Vera Denver's Chanel No. 5 hit Tyne like a solid wall when they hugged.

"I just knew that was you. I told Earl, but he didn't believe me." Vera shifted her shoulder so her husband could nod hello.

Tyne raised her hand to him in greeting, but dread had her face too numb to smile.

"I saw your mother in church on Sunday," Vera said. "And she didn't say a word about your being home."

"She doesn't know."

"Oh!" The woman clapped her fleshy hands together. "I can't wait to call her—"

"Please, don't." Tyne's throat constricted so tightly that she could barely squeeze out air, let alone words.

Vera nodded, the ends of her spikes bobbing at her neckline. "Ah, I see. A surprise, is it? Lovely!" She glanced at the table and then Lucas before looking at Tyne. Vera blinked, then let her gaze fall down the length of Tyne's body, evidently taking in her casual attire for the first time. The delight in her voice withered when she hesitantly murmured, "I came over to invite you to join us."

The prospect had Tyne flattening her palm against her stomach. "Oh, thank you for the offer, but—"

"Excuse me, Tyne, but we have to go."

Both the women turned to Lucas who was already standing with his wallet in hand, pulling out several bills, and dropping them onto the table.

"Mrs. Denver, this is Lucas Silver Hawk," Tyne introduced. "Lucas, Vera Denver. She's a good friend of my parents."

"Lifelong friends. Why, I changed Tyne's diapers," Vera supplied.

Lucas smiled politely at the woman, murmuring, "A pleasure," and then gave Tyne a sad look. "I just got a text. I'm needed. I hope you don't mind, but we have to leave now."

The man was a quick thinking and skilled liar. She could have kissed him.

"No, no. I don't mind." She reached for her purse and looked at Vera. "Enjoy your evening. It was lovely to see you." The fib snagged in her throat like a barbed fishing hook.

Christy arrived at the table with their open bottle of pinot grigio.

"Ah, I'm terribly sorry," Lucas told the woman, "but there's been an emergency." He pointed to the money. "That should take care of things, though."

The young woman's gaze darted to the bills on the white tablecloth, and then she offered him a wide smile. "Yes, sir. Don't worry about a thing."

He took Tyne by the elbow and guided her toward the front door.

Once they were in the car, the engine idling, the air conditioner blasting, Tyne took a deep breath. "Thank you."

He just smiled. "I thought we'd better get out of there before you threw up all over dear Vera's pretty, pink dress. In fact, you still look a little green." He waved his hand in front of his face. "And you smell like an old-ladies' perfume factory."

She groaned. "Of all the people to meet. My mom is going to know I'm here before the night's out. I just know it. Vera's probably in there dialing her number now."

"You asked her not to say anything. Maybe she won't."

Tyne only sighed.

Traffic was heavy for a Wednesday evening. Lucas maneuvered the car onto the highway.

"Maybe you should go see them," he suggested. "Get it over with, and then you don't have to worry about it anymore."

She stared hard at his profile. "You're kidding, right?"

His silence told her he wasn't.

The ugly details of how she'd left town reared up in her mind like the hissing snakes on Medusa's head. He wouldn't understand until she described them for him, fangs and scales and venom and all.

The leather seat felt cool against the backs of her arms and thighs when she settled herself. Softly, she confessed, "I'm angry with them, Lucas. I've been angry with them for a long time."

Tyne was only vaguely aware of the bright lights of the businesses they passed along the way.

"My mother betrayed me," she said, her voice flat. "I went to her for help, and she ran right to my father with the news of my pregnancy. I was so young. And they shut me off from everyone. Lectured me. Hounded me. They hashed out the options, planned my life and my future like I wasn't even sitting there. Abortion, they finally decided." Her stomach clenched sickeningly. "That was the best answer. We would slip away in the night, so no one would see. We would make this problem go away. And I wasn't allowed to have an opinion.

"That exam room was cold." The memory made her shiver. "And stark. And scary as hell with all those instruments lined up on that stainless steel tray." She swallowed. "They left me there on that table, practically naked, and all alone." She could still feel the rough paper gown grazing her skin. "I can't adequately describe the rage and resentment that filled me while I waited for the doctor who was going to come and abort my baby."

Too angry to cry, that's when she decided she could no longer be the good little girl, the obedient daughter. "I slid off that table and got myself dressed and walked out of that room. Mom went completely crazy. She was yelling like a banshee." Tyne swept weary fingers across her forehead. "I'll never forget the last thing I heard her say before I pushed my way out of that clinic. *'What am I supposed to tell your father?'*"

The question rang in her head, and it roused her fury even after all this time.

"There was a second round of lectures—god, I thought they would never shut up—and when I didn't budge on the abortion idea, they started harping on adoption. They were like some tag team. Dad would go a few rounds, shouting about how he refused to let me ruin my life, and Mom would start spewing out propaganda about making the dreams of some childless couple come true."

She covered her face with her hands. "I was so damn confused. I knew I had disappointed them. Knew I had messed up. I only wanted to make things right. I am so sorry, Lucas,"—she glanced at him before burying her face in her hands again—"and I never wanted you to know this, but I came to the conclusion that adoption was something I could at least live with."

His stony silence tensed her gut into anxious knots.

"They put me on a plane to Palm Beach," she said. "Aunt Wanda was very gentle and compassionate." Her voice went all fuzzy as she added, "I'll always be grateful to her for that."

She shrugged. "But I disappointed everyone once again. I just couldn't, Lucas. I thought I could. I even met the people. The prospective parents. The couple who wanted my baby. They were very nice. They fawned all over me, but I guess that's natural. I was the teenaged genie who came to grant their wish."

The bright cluster of city lights had faded into more widely spaced suburban street lamps and strip malls.

Tyne sighed. "I took one look at those beautiful, dark eyes and that head full of black hair, and knew I was keeping my son. He was perfect, Lucas. His skin was so transparent, I could see the little blue veins in his cheeks. His nose, his fingers, his toes. Everything about him was—"

You, she'd nearly said. She watched the passing scenery for a few minutes, wondering what all those people were doing inside all those houses. Were any of them desperately explaining their decisions of the past? Were any of them nervous as hell because their justification was receiving no reaction whatsoever?

"I never talked to my parents directly again. Aunt Wanda became my go between." The muscles in her shoulders and neck began to ache from the tension. "Dad was adamant that the only way I could come home was alone. Mom phoned her sister with promises to work it out. That she'd talk to Dad. That she'd make him come around. That she wanted me home even if it meant 'that child' had to come too."

She reached over and turned down the setting of the air conditioner's fan. Lucas gripped the steering wheel with both hands. She'd tried to warn him that the past was unpleasant.

"I'm sure she tried," Tyne said. "But...I didn't...things just..." She exhaled and closed her eyes, searching for the right words that would make him understand. "I was so mixed up. I hated them for how they treated me. But I wanted their love. Was desperate for their approval." She raked her fingernails over her scalp. "It sounds so twisted, doesn't it?"

Tipping up her chin, she looked up. The leather lining the roof was smooth and taut and unblemished.

"Aunt Wanda came to me one day," she continued, directing her gaze forward out the windshield. "She was smiling. Happy. She said my mother had called, that she was nearly there. My dad would agree to let me and the baby come home any day now." Her throat swelled and tears stung her eyes. "I was breastfeeding Zach out on the sun porch. I looked into his big eyes, smoothed my fingers over his chubby cheek, and I remembered how my father had treated you. The terrible names he'd called you. And that's when I realized the awful truth. My father would never accept my son. Never."

She moistened her lips. "And that's when I decided I wasn't going home."

The headlights of the car glared against the Wikweko sign. Talking had worn her out.

The car bumped up onto the driveway and came to a halt. Lucas shut off the engine but didn't pull the key from the ignition.

He shifted in his seat, turning toward her, and she saw the single tear trailing down the hollow of his cheek for only an instant before he dashed it away. He swallowed and frowned.

"I'm sorry." His words where thick and rusty sounding.

The silence stretched out like a yawn.

"It would have been easier for you to give him up, I think."

Every ounce of tension left her when she heard no anger in his voice, saw no judgment in his eyes. Relief flooded through her, the impact of it making her feel almost woozy-headed.

"I couldn't do that, Lucas," she whispered. "He was all I had left of you."

CHAPTER SIXTEEN

The empty darkness was a perfect cloak for someone hiding a shameful secret. The clock's orange numbers glowed 2:47 on the stove. Guilt, like a jolt of caffeine, kept him wide awake.

Lucas stared out the kitchen's wide bay window. Dim light cast by the thin crescent moon shrouded the yard in shadows. Tonight would have been the perfect opportunity to unload his oppressive burden. She'd opened herself up completely, exposed all she had gone through when she'd been eighteen and pregnant. He could so easily have followed suit.

But after she had divulged her experiences, when he'd learned of the agony her parents had put her through, he simply hadn't been able to confess the truth.

He'd spent a lot of years harboring anger and bitterness about how Tyne had handled things back then... or rather, how he'd *thought* she'd handled things. For a long time, he'd done his best to remember her as a spoiled brat.

Their first arguments as teens had been when he'd voiced that very opinion. She'd wanted a new dress for some event or other, and she'd been spitting nails over the fact that her mother had refused.

"If I'm bringing you as my date," Tyne had wailed, "she said I couldn't have a new outfit. Can you believe that?"

The concept had been an easy one for Lucas to understand. Her parents were doing what they could to deter their daughter's relationship with an Indian. Tyne had ranted on, ad nauseam, about the sorry state of her life, until Lucas couldn't take another minute of her whining. He'd asked her what was wrong with the clothes she was wearing, and then he'd called her a snot-nosed baby. Somehow, he'd fit in the spoiled brat moniker, as well.

He grinned in the darkness, remembering her fury. She'd slugged him in the arm with a loosely closed fist and had jammed her finger in the process.

Later on, he'd learned that she'd run away from Oak Mills—from *him*—and planned to give up their baby for adoption; his first thought had been of the fleeing girl. Taking the easy way out was just what he'd expect of an overindulged princess.

The powerful resentment he'd clutched so tightly had allowed him a certain amount of haughty self-righteousness. Enough, at least, so that he could live with what he'd done, how he had gone about attaining success.

But after these weeks of living with her, of hearing all she'd endured, what she'd sacrificed and suffered in order to raise their son on her own, all he felt was awed. Her strength amazed him; her determination stunned him. Single parenthood would have bested him.

It hadn't defeated his father. Lucas rubbed a hand over his jaw. His dad would also have been in his late teens when Ruth Yoder had handed over their newborn son and walked away. Lucas had great memories of his dad. As a kid, Lucas had felt loved and wanted and worthwhile. He'd like to think he'd have risen to the task too, if he'd been presented with the opportunity. But he had serious doubts.

Richard Whitlock's smug face swam in his head, a bad memory that made him scowl. But it was Lucas's own behavior that absolutely sickened him. He'd been unconscionably quick to snatch the money and run.

He'd meant it when he'd told Tyne that her life would have been easier had she simply gone along with her parents' plan. However, because of her unyielding resolve he was now enjoying the blessing of being a father, he was getting the chance to play a real role in his son's life. He owed her a hell of a lot. He imagined telling her the whole truth, pictured the pain and disillusionment that would surely distort her beautiful face and shatter her heart into a thousand pieces.

A light touch on his bare back made him start.

"Sorry," Tyne whispered. Once he turned to face her, she slid her fingers up his bare chest and rested her palms on his shoulders. "I thought for sure you must have heard my door open. Those hinges need oiling."

Soft moonlight glowed against her creamy skin and made her pale eyes glisten with a mysterious iridescence. Something in her gaze sent a rippling, liquid heat flowing through his body.

Her palms skimmed to his neck, and he marveled that she didn't seem to notice the fire smoldering just under his skin.

"Thanks," she murmured, "for listening to me tonight."

She lifted up on tiptoe, pulled him toward her, and kissed his mouth, gently but fully. Lucas thought he might lose his mind.

"Thanks for not judging me."

Her voice was as feathery as her second kiss. Her fingers slipped up to his jaw.

"Thanks for not being angry with me."

She kissed him again, and he wrapped his arms around her, pulling her body up tightly against him.

"You were a kid." The words grated roughly in his throat. "A scared kid who was only weighing all her options. I can't be angry about that."

She pressed her open mouth to his. Her hair spilled between his fingers like fine silk as he cradled the back of her head in his hand. She tasted like heaven. Her full bottom lip shined in the silvery light that slanted through the windowpane, and knowing the wetness was his had him growing rock-hard.

She stepped away from him and took his hand in hers. "Come on. Let's go to my room."

"Whoa. Hold on now." He resisted, and she turned to look into his face, her hungry eyes eating him up. "Should we really be doing this?"

His heart hammered while he awaited her response.

"You're not sleeping," she pointed out softly. "I'm not sleeping. Besides that, I'm horny as hell. Come on."

He was utterly amazed that her smile could turn brazen and coy at the same time. Now he was sure he'd completely lost his senses, but still he hesitated.

"Yes, Lucas." She nodded, sliding her free hand over his erection. Then she kissed him on the jaw. "We should be doing this."

Her silky top felt cool to the touch as he slid his hands under her arms and across her back. He crushed his mouth to hers, and in one swift move, he picked her up, turned, and perched her on the edge of the granite countertop. Her fingers threaded through his hair, pulling him so close; his teeth raked her lips. A whispery apology rang in his head, but the need thrumming through his veins wiped it out before it had a chance to fully form.

Her legs wrapped around him, her ankles locking at the small of his back. She tightened her thigh muscles, and he found himself pressed up tight against her crotch. The searing heat of her made his already explosive desire intensify.

Lucas slid his hands up over her flat belly, gently urging her away from him. She followed his lead and reclined against the window. The pale light from the moon seemed to magnify as it reflected off her long, blond hair. Her eyelids slid closed, and the sigh she emitted was the sexiest sound he'd ever heard. One of the corded straps of her top slid over her shoulder, revealing her milky skin to his voracious gaze. The sill that braced the middle of her back forced her breasts into an upward thrust. The erotic sight made him salivate. The dark circles of her nipples were visible through the cream-colored fabric, the twin taut, sharp points added a tactility that stole away all thought. From where he stood, moonlight gilded her hair, her face, her shoulders, her torso. He wanted to touch her. Smell the scent of her. Taste her sweetness. Hear her breath quicken and know he had caused the reaction in her.

He slid both his palms up over her breasts and couldn't help but notice that they were larger, fuller, riper than he remembered. Lucas kneaded, more roughly than he'd intended. But to his surprise, not only did she not stop him, she moaned softly as if urging him on. He couldn't fight the overwhelming desire to taste her.

Bending forward, he cupped one lush breast and laved it right through the silk. Her heart thundered beneath his palm, and her chest rose and fell just a little faster. He straightened and took a moment to savor the wet stain he'd left on her top. The fabric clinging to her skin had gone nearly translucent, her nut-brown areola as visible as if she were naked.

Lucas's fingertips traced their way down to her waist, her hips, and slid beneath the hem of her flimsy top. The lace of her panties was gossamer soft. She lifted one hip, then the other, and he quickly tugged them off her body.

The mound of light-colored curls yielded as he brushed the backs of his fingers across it. The fleshy folds were hot. And supple. And damp.

She rested her heels on his hips, parted her knees, and arched the small of her back. Lucas took his time, smoothing and teasing. The sounds of pleasure—murmurs, groans, sighs—that grated from her throat lit a fire in his groin that one thing and one thing only would extinguish. But they had all night, and rushing this was the last thing he wanted to do.

His massaging became more steady, more rhythmic, and progressed to light tugs and pulls. Without thought, he lifted one hand and inhaled. The musky scent of her was enough to drive him over the edge of reason.

Reaching up, she planted a palm on the window glass, splayed her fingers, and strained to raise herself up to him. He knew what she wanted, knew what she silently pleaded for, and he didn't disappoint her. Lucas shifted her feet to his shoulders, and then he kissed and nuzzled, licked and teased.

Her orgasm was quick. And fierce. He watched the glorious tension in her face, and he smiled. His crystal-clear memories of their lovemaking told him she wasn't finished, that she wouldn't be satiated for a while yet.

Tyne panted, dragged her eyes open. Her gaze met his, and she grinned at him. She elbowed herself away from the windowsill, wincing and muttering, her legs now dangling on either side of him. "That was wonderful, but I'm too old for this kind of acrobatics."

"Oh, no, you're not," he whispered. "No, no, no." Each tiny word was emphasized with a kiss.

"I'm going to be sore tomorrow." She nibbled on his neck and her lips spread as she added, "But this is worth a few achy muscles."

Tyne hugged him, caressed his shoulders, his back. "Lucas, this place smells like sex."

He couldn't contain his grin. "Yeah, it does."

"What if Zach wakes up? What if he needs a drink of water or something?"

Lucas chuckled, and then he kissed her, deeply, thoroughly. Damn, if he didn't feel her naked body against his soon, he would go absolutely nuts.

"Let's fix that," he told her. "Let's go to bed."

He lifted her knees and she automatically wrapped her legs around him again. Lucas freed himself from his sleep pants, scooted her off the counter, and slid himself into her as deep as he could go. Her eyes went wide with surprise. She fit him like a tight, wet glove, and Lucas feared he might lose all control. He gritted his jaw, determined to rein in his need. At least for the moment.

Desire smoldered in her gaze, and soon she was wiggling and shifting against him. Her brazen kiss scorched his mouth, her tongue inviting him to do as he wanted. "Yes," she pleaded. "Let's."

Lucas carried her into her bedroom and closed the door.

~

Fresh, hand-pitted cherries sat in a bowl on the countertop, macerating in kirsch that had been diluted with an equal part of water. In a second bowl, a mixture of flour, ground almonds, baking powder, and cocoa had been thoroughly blended. The whites of six eggs were in a third bowl. Tyne crooned a wordless melody as she used a wire whisk to beat the egg yolks together with a couple ounces of powdered sugar in a fourth bowl, watching closely for the ingredients to reach that perfect pale fluffiness.

Although she loved preparing any type of food, everything from vegetables, meats, and fish to grains, pastas, fruits, and nuts by any method of cooking, roasting, steaming, smoking, broiling, braising, simmering, or sautéing, she had to admit that baking was her true forte. Bread was fun to make, and nothing beat the luscious smell of a fresh loaf browning in the oven, but baking sweets made her hum with pure happiness.

When the yolks were a light lemon yellow, she mixed in melted butter and vanilla, then reached for a rubber spatula and folded in the dry ingredients. The alarm on the stove sounded, letting her know the oven was preheated.

She liked to work alone in the kitchen. There was something about measuring and stirring, whipping and folding, that calmed her. And after waking up in Lucas's arms at sunrise and remembering how intense, how carnal, their lovemaking had been the night before, she'd felt the need to find some way to compose herself. She was waiting at the market when the shop owner unlocked the doors for business, and as soon as she'd returned home, she'd shooed Lucas and Zach out of the house with a promise of something sweet and spectacular.

Zach had peeked into the grocery bag, his eyes lighting up when he spied the cherries, the cocoa, and flour. "Black Forest cake," he'd exclaimed. The confection had long been his favorite.

She'd playfully smacked his fingers away from the ripe fruit and told him to get lost for the rest of the morning.

With the batter nicely mixed, she started whipping the egg whites.

Her thoughts turned, yet again, to Lucas. Her behavior last night had been overly aggressive. She wasn't sure if that was because she feared he would reject her or what, but once they were in her bedroom, she'd pulled off his pajama bottoms, nudged him down onto the bed, and then slipped out of the silk cami she usually slept in. She'd touched him, kissed him, straddled him, fitted him inside her... and rode him. Slowly at first, and then with increasing swiftness, as if something or someone were chasing her.

The whisk clattered against the rim of the bowl, and she saw that the egg whites were stiff and glossy. She began folding them into the cake batter.

Nerves chirruped in the pit of her stomach as she tried to figure out why she'd been so bold with Lucas, so unreserved. He hadn't seemed to mind; in fact, judging from his response, he'd enjoyed himself.

Their ruined evening at Reflections interrupted her sensuous musings, and quickly following were thoughts of Vera and Earl Denver. Maybe Vera wouldn't blab to her mother about seeing her at the restaurant. Maybe.

The mere thought of seeing her parents caused her hands to tremble. They'd browbeaten her to the point that they'd wrung every ounce of self-worth out of her; by the time she'd left for Florida, she'd felt like an old cleaning rag, floppy and completely used up. But despite all her hurt and anger, she still felt guilty that she'd disappointed them, and that triggered a strong annoyance at herself for allowing them to manipulate her. God, what a vicious cycle of negative emotion. She released her hold on the bowl and the spatula, rested her palms on the countertop, and gulped in a deep breath.

She *was* being chased. By the past. And it was surely going to catch her.

A couple of hours later, that's exactly what happened.

She had pulled the three round layer cakes from the oven and set them on the counter to cool. Then, with the rich scent of warm chocolate hanging heavy in the air, she'd taken a long soak in the tub, with a good paperback, and realized what a luxury a mid-morning bath could be. She'd gotten dressed, dried her hair, reapplied her makeup, and was pulling out the whipping cream to make the filling for the cake, when the doorbell rang.

The screen in the door obscured the man who stood on the front step, but before she had a chance to voice a greeting, her brain kicked in.

"Daddy."

Funny how a single word could make her feel twelve years old again.

"Tyne, honey. It's so good to see you."

Shock froze her muscles, solid as ice. His hair was still thick and wavy, but instead of the rich chestnut she remembered, it had gone granite gray. And his smile pressed deep grooves all over his fleshy face. He must have put on forty pounds or more since she'd last seen him.

"Earl called me last night, honey." Her father lifted his hand to shield his eyes from the sun. "He said he and Vera had run into you."

So Vera had kept her word. Sort of. But she got her husband to rat her out. Damn it.

"Tyne?"

The timidity she heard in his voice sounded utterly foreign to her. Her father had always been assured to the point of being imposing. Frighteningly so.

"Honey?" He blinked, waited, and when she said nothing, he asked, "Will you invite me to come in for a minute?"

He looked so...old. So...unsure. All of a sudden, she felt the same.

The metal handle of the screen door was cool against her fingers when she pushed it open. Her dad stepped over the threshold, but didn't move any farther.

She feared he meant to wrap his arms around her, but she didn't think she was ready for that. Physically, he was close, awkwardly close, as he gazed into her face, yet the accusations and blame and disappointment jarring her insides were as spiky and dividing as a barbed wire fence.

There was no graceful way to move away from the door, away from him, but that didn't stop her from trundling backward a few feet. She couldn't miss the flash of dejection that clouded his gaze.

"Can I offer you something to drink?" she asked. The question had enough sharp edges to cut the most calloused of skin. So she tried hard to soften her tone when she added, "Tea, fruit juice, ice water?"

"No. Thank you. I can't stay long. Have to get back to my office." He rubbed his hands together, then let them fall to his sides. "I have a meeting with Mike Masters, the town treasurer, in an hour." There was more palm rubbing as he shuffled from one foot to the other. "I would have been here earlier, but I had a breakfast meeting I couldn't get out of." His chuckle was forced. "It seemed to go on forever."

Many people share a common misconception; they attempt to crowd out the uneasiness in a room by filling the air with words.

He tipped up his chin and inhaled. "Something smells awfully good."

Ambivalent about responding, she waited a moment or two. She'd developed her cooking skills to the point that she earned her living using them, with little help and absolutely no encouragement from this man. But it seemed absolutely rude not to make some kind of reply to his comment. Finally, she told him, "I baked a cake."

He nodded, and silence settled over them.

"You look good, honey," he said. "You're a beautiful woman." Pride shined in his smile. "The image of your mother."

His eyes went misty.

When Tyne had been exiled to Florida for the duration of her pregnancy, she'd considered hacking off her hair and dying it flaming red or sable brown just so she wouldn't be reminded of her mother every time she looked into the bathroom mirror, but she feared the chemicals might harm the baby, and once Zach had been born and she'd decided to go it on her own, food and lodging took priority over those things that became trivial matters, like vanity in her appearance.

It seemed that someone had flipped her politeness autopilot switch, because she heard herself asking, "How is Mom?"

"She's well. Still busy with her groups—bridge, garden club, tennis. She's always out and about." He smiled. "She's been busy in the backyard. Had a pool put in. A pool house built. You wouldn't recognize the place. She coordinated the whole project herself. Oh, and she joined the Red Hat Society."

Tyne found it difficult to imagine her mother sporting a floppy red hat.

"She's healthy. Fit and trim as ever," her father said. Rubbing his paunch, he added, "Unlike me."

A frown bit into her brow. "You've got health problems?"

Her silence for the past sixteen years might have revoked her right to even ask such a question.

"Oh, nothing serious, honey. A touch of arthritis, achy joints. The normal problems of aging, I guess you could say." His grin went lopsided. "All those extra desserts I sneak don't help, I'm sure."

Her dad always had a voracious sweet tooth.

"How have *you* been, Tyne?"

The concern tugging his brows closer together seemed utterly sincere, and that touched her heart.

"I've been okay..." *Daddy*, a little girl's voice inside her head nearly succeeded in adding. "I've been fine," she amended. "Great, actually."

His wide shoulders dropped, and the corners of his mouth pulled back. "I'm so glad to hear it." He toyed with the button on his suit jacket. "Your mother really wanted to come with me. But I made her stay home. I didn't know how things would go. Didn't know how you'd feel. How you'd be. If you'd even talk to me. I didn't want her feelings to be hurt."

Those same fears had made her break out in a sweat whenever she imagined running into her parents.

"Now," he murmured, "I wish I'd brought her. She'd love to see you, sweetheart."

Unable to think of a reply, she blurted, "How did you know where to find me?"

He just looked at her, then his gaze slid off her face as he said, "I've been here before. Years ago. During...you know." He stuffed his hands into the pockets of his trousers. "I came to talk with the uncle."

Just one more strategy in his plan to drive a wedge between her and Lucas back then. The anger that flared in her must have shown in her expression.

"Besides that," he added, "these days, between the online property records and Google, you can find anything... or anyone."

She offered a vague nod.

"Look, honey," her father said, "I'm not proud of how I acted when—" He stopped short, then started again. "All of us could have made better decisions."

"I made the best decisions for *me*," she said tightly.

But she knew in her heart he was right. She could have kept the channels of communication open. She could have accepted the help they were willing to offer rather than letting her pride get in the way.

"I'm sure you did, honey. I didn't come here to fight. Honestly, I didn't." He pulled his hands from his pockets, laced his fingers, and steepled his thumbs at the apex of his diaphragm, close to his heart. "I came to tell you that your mother and I love you. That we're sorry. That we've missed you terribly, Tyne. And we want to know if there's anything we can do to be invited back into your life. Anything."

For an instant, she forgot how to breathe while tears threatened to spill, and before she knew what was happening, she was in his arms. He smelled of familiar, spicy aftershave and happy memories.

Yes, there had been good times, plenty of them, when she'd been a child growing up in Oak Mills. Their annual summer Saturday at Dutch Wonderland, even after she'd grown too old for the theme park. The hours her dad had spent pushing her on the tree swing he'd put up for her.

The drives into the Pocono Mountains to see the autumn leaves. The picnics with fried chicken, creamy coleslaw, and, of course, some scrumptious sweet her mother would make for them.

The laughter. The warmth. The love. She'd been so focused on the bad over the years that she'd forgotten all about the good times. And all it had taken to open the floodgates of her memory had been two tiny words.

We're sorry.

"I've missed you too, Dad," she whispered against his neck. Tears squeezed out of her closed eyes, but she brushed them away before he released his hold on her.

He was as choked by emotion as she. He cleared his throat, his smile unsteady.

"Come to dinner tonight, honey," he said. "Your mother would be so happy to see you."

Tyne's smile slipped and then disappeared altogether. "I'm not here alone. Zachary is with me. My son."

"Bring him along. We want to meet our grandson."

"And Lucas," she added. "I'm here with Lucas."

"Bring him along too." There was no hesitation in his voice as he merrily added, "It'll be a family reunion."

She paused, waiting for logic or instinct or some random sign of nature to tell her she'd be foolish to accept her dad's invitation. But she felt nothing, heard nothing, and finally she smiled.

"Okay. We'll come." She remembered the cake sitting on the counter waiting to be filled and frosted. "I'll bring dessert."

Hours after her father had left, she whipped the heavy cream and sweetened it, filled the cake layers with cherries and was just smoothing the last of the chocolate butter cream frosting on top when she heard Zach and Lucas come into the house.

"Ma!" Zach shouted. "Is that chocolate cake I smell?"

"It sure is," she called back.

He barreled into the kitchen, smiling. He clutched his bow in one hand and held the other out for her inspection. "Will chocolate and cherries cure a blister?"

"Another one?" She took his hand in hers for a closer look.

"Two," he said proudly.

"He's getting better with that thing." Lucas came into the kitchen on Zach's heels. "He's hitting the bull's eye more times than not."

Her son's fingers were grubby, but she could see small white blisters that had formed on the tips of his middle and ring fingers. She studied them longer than was necessary on purpose. When she finally looked up at Lucas, she floundered for words.

She lifted her eyes to her son's face.

"Chocolate heals whatever ails you," she told him, grinning.

"Mmmm. Can I have a piece now?" he asked.

"Oh, no. It's for later."

"But I'm wounded."

"Don't touch that cake." She reached for a towel. "We've been invited to dinner," she told them, striving to keep her voice cheery. "And I accepted. We're taking that with us."

"Where're we going?" Zach asked, eyeing the leftover sweetened whipped cream in the bowl on the counter.

"Wash your hands first," Tyne ordered. "You don't want those blisters getting infected." She dried her fingers on the dishtowel while Zach moved to the kitchen sink and turned on the water.

Lucas moved closer to her.

"Did you have a good time?" she asked him.

He nodded, and then said, "So?"

"So...what?"

Lucas didn't speak, just looked at her peculiarly.

"You never said where we're going to dinner, Mom." Zach lathered liquid soap in his hands.

"Oh," she said, as if she'd completely forgotten. She avoided Lucas's eyes because she knew he was aware that she hadn't.

"My father stopped by. We're going to my parents' for dinner."

"Really?" Awe painted her son's tone in bright shades of delight.

"Really?" Lucas's reply was flat.

She had known Zach would be thrilled to meet his grandparents. And she'd guessed that Lucas wouldn't relish the idea, even though he'd suggested contacting her mom and dad some time ago. She'd been right...on both counts.

Looking from one to the other, she firmly pronounced, "*Really.*"

CHAPTER SEVENTEEN

"Take a left at the light." Tyne pointed, even though Lucas was watching the road and couldn't possibly have missed seeing the turn.

"I remember. Believe me."

He'd been testy all afternoon. Visiting her parents wasn't high on his "wanna do" list. He hadn't come right out and voiced that opinion, but his temperamental behavior had told her all she needed to know. She shouldn't have sprung the news on him like she had; everyone wanted the courtesy of being asked rather than being told that plans had been made for them. She'd have to find some way to make it up to him.

"Hey, Mom," Zach said. "I've been thinking. I'd like to get a tat."

Surprise had Tyne blinking.

When she didn't respond, he offered, "A tattoo."

"I know what a tat is, Zach."

"Not anything huge," he breezed ahead. "Just something small. A feather maybe, or a—"

"No."

"No?" he complained. "Just like that? But you didn't even think about it."

"I don't need to think about it. You're fifteen years old. You don't need to be marking up your body with—"

"Tyne." Lucas glanced at her.

Something in Lucas's black gaze made her pause, but she was too deep into her mother-lecture mode to stop now. "Zach, a tattoo is forever. What if you change your mind later on? And besides that, it's a well-known fact that employers frown on hiring people with tattoos."

"But *he's* got one," Zach said, the words coming out almost as an accusation. "And he's got a *great* job."

Tyne should have focused on the conversation, but in a flash she was back in that tattoo parlor with Lucas. She had been so damned excited, and she'd thought the idea of matching tattoos had been more romantic than anything on the face of the earth. Lucas had let her choose the design. She'd loved the dream catcher, a symbol of unity and protection, and Lucas hadn't hesitated. He would have one put on his arm, and she would have a smaller version tattooed on her shoulder blade.

That had been the plan, anyway. Once she'd seen how he'd clenched his jaw against the pain of the buzzing needles, she couldn't go through with it. But she'd loved his tat. Loved the intricate design, the sacred beads woven into the delicate webbing, the regal feathers trailing down his arm beneath the circle. She remembered tracing her fingers over it every time they made love.

Zach leaned forward. "And *besides that*, he says *you* were gonna get one too."

Tyne gasped. "Lucas! Why would you tell him that?"

Lucas didn't take his eyes off the road. "I didn't know it was a secret."

She sighed in complete exasperation and then sat there trying to decide what to say to her son.

"Look, Zach," she told him, "can we talk about this later? We have plenty of time to discuss the pros and cons of tattoos."

Now it was her son's turn to heave a sigh, but his was filled with frustration. "Whatever."

"Yeah," Lucas murmured, "we have enough to worry about tonight."

Balancing the Black Forest cake on her lap, she softly said, "Dad apologized, Lucas."

She'd told him this several times already. Lucas tossed her a swift glance.

"Look, I'm nervous enough," she pleaded. "Your attitude isn't helping matters. You were the one who suggested we go see them and get it over with, remember?"

A metallic click resounded, and for the third time Zach scooted to the edge of the rear seat and poked his head into the space between the two front bucket seats. "What'd he do?" The question was thick with curiosity. "My grandfather—what'd he do that he needed to apologize for?"

Tyne twisted around, sticking the tip of her thumb into the cake's creamy frosting. "Zach! Now look what you made me do. If you take that seatbelt off one more time..."

She didn't have to finish the threat. Zach slid back into the seat, tugged on the belt, and secured it across his chest and lap.

Refusing to be put off, Zach repeated, "So what'd he do, Mom?"

Tyne glanced at Lucas, then faced forward, slipping her thumb into her mouth. The buttery frosting melted on her tongue.

How much should she tell her son? She wanted to caution him about what kind of people he was about to meet; it would have been irresponsible of her not to give him at least some warning. But she didn't want to taint what could very well be an important evening for him. He was meeting his grandparents for the first time. Everyone should have pleasant memories of their parent's parents, shouldn't they?

Her father had apologized. He'd expressed his love for her. Said they'd missed her. Wanted back into her life. Maybe...just maybe they had both changed.

"Your grandparents," Lucas said, zeroing in on Zach's image in the rearview mirror, "were very unhappy with your mother when she became pregnant with you."

Shifting in her seat, she saw that Zach had blanched. She glared at Lucas.

"So they did know about me?" Her son sounded upset. "You guys haven't seen each other all these years because of me?"

"This has nothing to do with you," she assured him as quickly and calmly as she could. "What happened back then was between them and me. I was very young. They had lots of plans for me. They wanted me to go to college. They wanted me to—"

"I can't believe," Lucas said, his tone heavy with incredulity, "you're making excuses for how they acted."

"I will say it again." Her teeth were clenched. "You are not helping matters, Lucas."

He looked at her. "He needs to know."

Everything, his sharp gaze advised.

Surrendering to her anger and blowing up at Lucas would have given her great satisfaction, but it would only deflect from what she already knew as fact. He was absolutely right. But how did you tell your son, who happened to be half Native American, that his grandparents were prejudiced?

She hadn't a clue exactly what to say; she only knew she had to prepare him. Just in case her mom or dad ended up saying something insulting.

"I need to know what?"

Tyne turned, careful of the cake she balanced on her thighs. "Honey, there are things you should know about my mom and dad. They can be very... opinionated."

The soft sound Lucas let loose sounded suspiciously like a snort. "That's putting it mildly."

"Lucas, I'm trying to ease him into this, okay?" She glanced over her shoulder at Zach. "Honey, you know that station on TV? The one that advertises their news programs to be fair and balanced?"

"Yeah."

"Well, your grandparents would never be interviewed by that network."

Zach sat a moment, chewing over the information. "So, what you're saying is they're unfair and unbalanced?"

Lucas chuckled despite his ill humor. "Two for two. Way to go, Zach."

Tyne struggled to hold back a smile. "Lucas, these are my parents we're talking about," she reminded him.

He shrugged, still smiling broadly. "If you don't laugh at life, all you'd do is cry."

"Whatever," she intoned. "What I'm trying to explain, Zach, is that your grandparents aren't very open-minded people, and—"

Her son's gaze left her face to stare, his mouth parting, his eyes widening. "Whoa! Would you look at that!"

Lucas turned the steering wheel, the car bumping slightly onto the asphalt driveway. Tyne looked up the hill at the house she'd been raised in. A lovely, old Victorian, the house sat on a rise that afforded a beautiful view of the town, rolling hills, the wide, winding river. Lush vegetation, deliberately placed to offer a variety of texture and color, decorated the vast lawn.

"They could charge admission to this place." Zach was taking it all in, glancing left and right as his father eased along the wide, curving driveway. "This looks like that place we visited. That botanist's house. Remember?"

"Bartram's Garden," Tyne supplied.

"Yeah. That was it."

As a single mother on a limited income, she'd become an expert at sniffing out inexpensive outings, places of interest to take her son to while away on a long summer day.

An in-ground pool and pool house sat off to one side, the building sporting the same lacy gingerbread trim as the main house.

Lucas motioned to the pool house with a slight jerk of his head and murmured, "We could have used that when we were dating."

She clamped her lips together to keep from grinning, but it was a failed attempt. Since they'd made love, there had been a deliciously playful air between the two of them. Even though Lucas was annoyed that she had obligated him by accepting her father's invitation to dinner without asking him, it obviously hadn't dampened the lively energy that danced between them.

"Zach," Tyne tried again, "what I've been trying to tell you—"

"There they are," Zach said, cutting her off.

Tyne shifted to face forward. Her parents stood waiting on the side porch, and the instant Lucas brought the car to a halt, they hurried down the steps toward them.

With her blond hair cut in a short, fashionable style; her tailored capris; and trendy blouse, Patricia Whitlock looked at least ten years younger than her husband. However, Tyne knew there was just a couple of years' difference in their ages. Her mom's eyes glittered with unadulterated excitement, and Tyne's heart swelled with bittersweet pain.

"Zach," Lucas said as he put the transmission into park, "I want you to try hard this evening not to react to anything you might hear or see." He twisted around. "Son, I want you to keep a tight rein on your anger." He glanced out the passenger-side window at Tyne's approaching parents. "We can talk about anything that bothers you on the way home. Understood?"

Although Zach's brow knitted with confusion, he nodded silently.

Smiles could convey many different sentiments; the one she offered Lucas expressed her gratitude for his ability to tackle the bottom line with their son when she hadn't been able to.

When Tyne stepped out of the car, her father smiled a greeting, kissed her cheek, and took the cake plate from her hands; and then, for the first time in almost sixteen years, she found herself in her mother's arms. A child waking on Christmas morning couldn't have been happier than she was at this moment. Sure, her inside churned with conflicting emotions and a heady sense of doubt, but this was her mom. *Her mom.*

Patricia pulled back to wordlessly gaze into her daughter's eyes, pressing her palms against Tyne's cheeks. The moment stretched out for an eternity.

Her mother has always had a tendency to teeter close to the line of kind, caring intimacy, sometimes crossing over into an odd realm of intrusion. With her mom's hands still pressed to her face, Tyne was reminded of the strange sense of invasiveness and claustrophobia her mother's officious affection caused her. It had only gotten worse when she'd become a teen. She remembered once complaining that her mother meant to bleed the life out of her with those long, yearning looks.

Annoyed with herself for finding fault before she'd even had a chance to say a word to her mother, Tyne smiled and pulled away from the loving but clingy touch. "Hi, Mom. You look wonderful."

"Oh, Tyne." Her mother pressed her palm on her heart. "I can't tell you how happy I am to see you. I just can't. There aren't words."

"Mom, Dad," she said, turning and motioning Zach forward, "I'd like for you to meet my son, Zachary. Zach, these are your grandparents."

The teen shook his grandfather's hand. "Nice to meet you, sir."

"Now, what's all this 'sir' stuff?" Richard Whitlock asked. "I'd be happy if you'd call me 'Granddad.'" His brow furrowed. "If you want to, that is."

Zach only nodded, his whole face transformed by the offer as he continued to shake the man's hand.

Patricia gave her grandson a big hug, and when she lifted her hands toward his face, Tyne quickly attracted her attention by touching her shoulder. Zach looked relieved.

"Mom, Dad," Tyne said, shifting herself a quarter turn, "I'm sure you remember Lucas."

"Of *course*." Her mother hugged Lucas as if all that nasty name-calling and animosity of the past had never happened. "It's so good to see you again."

Lucas caught Tyne's eye over the woman's shoulder, sending a silent message of disbelief. He murmured, "Hello, Mrs. Whitlock." Before Patricia could get her hands on his face, he took a quick sidestep and thrust his hand out toward Tyne's father. "Mr. Whitlock."

The wave of relief that hit Tyne was strong enough to make her lightheaded. Lucas intended to be civil. No one would have blamed him for acting otherwise.

"Mom, the place looks beautiful." She let her gaze wander over the yard. "Dad told me you were busy with your gardening, but this is just amazing." She lifted her hands and her eyes scanned from one corner of the property to the other. "Zach said you could charge an entry fee."

Patricia beamed at the teen, then looked at her daughter. "I couldn't handle this yard on my own. I have Martin's Landscaping come in. You remember Mr. Martin. You went to school with his son, Mark."

Indeed, Tyne remembered. Poor guy had environmental allergies and was always sporting some sort of angry rash that had him scratching his skin raw. His condition wasn't excuse enough to keep his father from pressing him into service on weekends, school holidays, and summer breaks.

"Mark went to chiropractic school," Patricia said. "He's got an office in Lancaster."

Tyne nodded, happy to hear he'd found a way to change his career path.

"Mr. Martin comes himself to supervise the crew, and I appreciate that so much." Patricia wrinkled her nose. "His workers are mostly Mexican or Cuban or Guatemalan. Puerto Rican?" She shook her head, lifting her shoulders dismissively. "Something like that."

"Hispanic?" Tyne supplied.

"Yes." Her mom nodded. "But they do a great job."

But?

Tyne shook her head, wanting to press the issue; however, she thought it best to bite her tongue.

"I'll take this inside," Richard said, lifting the cake he held in his hands. "It looks delicious, Tyne. There's fresh lemonade over by the gazebo."

Lucas, Zach, Tyne, and Patricia headed toward the pool. Next to the ornate gazebo there was an outside kitchen complete with a sink, granite countertop, and a massive grill.

"Do you like lemonade, Zach?" Patricia wrapped her fingers around the handle of the large glass pitcher.

"Yes, ma'am." The teen finger-combed his hair and then scrubbed his palms on the thighs of his shorts, eyeing the patio furniture, the kitchen, the pool.

His grandmother poured him a tall glass and set it on the bar. "You should come swimming while you're here. You could bring some friends. It would be fun. I'd like to meet your friends."

"His new friends live in Wikweko." Tyne heard the warning in her tone.

Patricia looked clueless.

"Mom, Zach's friends are Native American."

Her mom clicked her tongue, her breath leaving her in a huff. "I *realize* that, Tyne. What are you trying to say? That I don't want Zach's friends in my pool?" She crossed her arms. "I'll have you know I have a pool party for all of Mr. Martin's Mexicans—"

She stopped, then raced to correct herself.

"—*Hispanics* and their families, at the end of every season. Just to thank them for all the work they do."

Snatching up the ice bucket, Patricia rounded the granite bar. "Don't be difficult, Tyne. I'd wanted this to be...I'd hoped—" Her fuchsia-tinted lips pressed into a tight, thin line. "I'm going to the house for more ice." She glanced at Lucas and Zach. "I'm sorry. Excuse me for just a moment."

Tyne watched her mother storm across the lawn. "I'll be right back," she muttered over her shoulder.

Her father came out of the house just as her mother entered. He paused to talk to his wife, but Patricia swept by him, disappearing inside.

"What happened?" he asked Tyne, just feet from the back door.

"I'll fix this, Dad," was all she said.

She followed her mother into the house.

The mudroom looked like something from the pages of Martha Stewart's *Living* magazine. Wainscoting covered the bottom half of the walls and was painted a pristine white. The small, square window Tyne remembered in her youth had been replaced with a larger, bay window that let in loads of light. The gleaming washer and dryer were surrounded by white cabinets sporting shiny, porcelain knobs. Even the flooring was different, wide oak planks having replaced the old linoleum she remembered.

In the next room, she could hear her mother rummaging in the freezer, several chunks of ice thumping into the bucket that hadn't really needed filling.

Stepping over the threshold into the kitchen, Tyne said, "Mom, I'm sorry."

Her mother's anger was spent. Now her shoulders were rounded and the muscles in her face had gone slack.

Patricia closed the freezer door. "I can't tell you how often I've dreamed about this day. About you coming home. About meeting my grandson." She ran the tip of her tongue over her top lip and inhaled deeply. "When your father came home and told me he'd seen you and that you were coming to dinner, I thought I'd have a coronary. My heart was racing to beat the band. I wanted everything to be perfect. Just like I'd dreamed."

She set the ice bucket on the counter. "But I realized...just now...that it could never be perfect. Because—well, because, although I've always seen you as perfect in every way, as being amazingly talented and so intelligent, you were bound to succeed at whatever you chose to do"—she lifted her hand to her throat, her gaze drifting—"you've only seen me as...as..." She struggled for a moment, then shrugged. "Something ugly. Something stupid. And flawed."

Tyne chuckled in an attempt to lighten the mood. "Mom, I'm far from perfect. And when I left here the last time, perfect wasn't at all how you'd have described me, I'm sure." But her mother didn't react.

Patricia went to the cabinet over the dishwasher and opened the door. Then she shut it and turned around. "No matter what we did for you, it was never quite good enough."

"Oh, now, Mom, that's not true. I—"

"*We* were not quite good enough. We were an embarrassment to you."

Tyne went quiet, unable to dispute her mother's statement. Parents who shot off racist remarks like an unpredictable, misfiring automatic weapon mortified their teenaged children.

"Your father has a wonderful reputation in this town," Patricia said. "He's well respected. And I have more friends than I can count. The people in Oak Mills like us, Tyne." She frowned. "Do you know how it hurts to know your own daughter doesn't?"

"I love you, Mom." Tyne took a step forward and then stopped. "I might have been angry for a while."

"A long while," her mother pointed out.

And she was forced to agree with a small nod. "But I do love you."

"And we love you." Patricia reached up and tugged at a short lock of her hair. "We love you so much. Everything we ever did or said or planned was because we love you, Tyne."

Without being told, Tyne knew her mother was trying to explain their actions of the past.

"You have a son," Patricia continued, "a teenaged son. Surely, now that you're a parent you can understand our feelings. Our motives. We only meant to do what was best for you. You might not have been able to appreciate that then, but you have to be able to now."

There must have been a thousand things she'd done over the years that were in Zach's best interest: early bed times, the teeth brushing routine, controlling what he watched on TV. The list was endless. And as he'd gotten older, the parental choices had gotten harder because her son had discovered his voice. Despite his complaining, his anger, his complete displeasure, Tyne continued to do what she thought was best for her son. Keeping him from going swimming with his friends last week was a prime example.

She found herself nodding slowly at her mother. "I do understand," she admitted.

The frown creasing her mother's forehead smoothed a bit. "Now if I can just get you to see that I didn't mean anything bad before. When I mentioned Mr. Martin's Mexicans." She closed her eyes and frowned, her chin jutting forward. "*Hispanics.* Because I didn't, you know."

Tyne sighed. Keeping her words as gentle as possible, she said, "Mom, do you hear yourself? You talk as if Mr. Martin owns his employees."

Patricia gasped. "I did no such thing."

"Come on, Mom. 'Mr. Martin's Hispanics.' Don't you hear the inference?"

"No, I don't," Patricia countered. "They're *his* crew."

"Why is it necessary to mention their nationality at all?" she asked civilly.

Once again, her mother's hands lifted in exasperation. "Because *that's* what they *are.* Tyne, you don't understand. I am sure that they are very proud of who and what they are. I'm sure they have no problem with me calling them 'Mr. Martin's Hispanics.' I complimented their work, didn't I?"

She didn't *get it*, Tyne realized suddenly. Her mother truly didn't comprehend that some of the things she said, some of the names and phrases she chose to use in certain contexts, could come off sounding offensive to others. Had that been caused by her upbringing? Tyne's grandparents had died when she was a young child, so she had no way of knowing what kind of parental influence her mother had had. It could have been that her mother's parents were bigots too, and that her mother was so comfortable in the standards set for her that she wasn't able to see that those standards could be raised. But if racism were a learned trait, why hadn't Tyne picked it up?

Was it plain ignorance on her parents' part? Ignorance had nothing to do with lack of brains or education. It was possible for people to be bright and ignorant at the same time. Was her mother's an entire generation that society had to make allowances for? Tyne dismissed that idea immediately. This type of shallowness had nothing to do with age. She'd met plenty of older folks who were open-minded and accepting of others, people who had adopted a "live and let live" attitude, not just when it came to race but also religion, politics, sexual orientation, whatever. However, she'd also encountered people, of all ages really, who seemed bent on building walls rather than bridges.

Her mother had invited Zach and his friends swimming. And if she'd made a habit of throwing a party for the landscaping crew, then maybe she *had* become a little more enlightened over the years.

Her mother sighed. "Tyne, I really wanted tonight to be special. I had hoped we could get through the evening without—"

"I agree, Mom." She stepped forward, offering a warm smile and holding out her arms in invitation. Her mother eagerly stepped into her embrace. "Tonight should be special," Tyne said. "Tonight *is* special."

CHAPTER EIGHTEEN

Lucas stood near the deep end of the pool watching Zach bounce on the diving board. Tyne's father had noticed Zach eyeing the pool, and he suggested Zach use one of the suits in the pool house and take a swim before dinner. The teen jumped at the chance. Zach launched himself into the air and made an awkward arch with his body, his hands pressed together above his head. The elaborate splash made Lucas grin surreptitiously; the kid obviously needed some practice.

"Looks like he's enjoying himself." Richard Whitlock joined Lucas, a bottle of beer in each hand.

Lucas accepted the beer with a nod. "He is. Thanks for inviting him to swim."

Richard regarded his grandson for several long seconds. "I hope he comes to visit often."

The man was probing, wanting to know if Lucas would be a help or a hindrance when it came to him developing a relationship with Zach. A mulish streak kept Lucas silent. He tipped up the bottle and drank. He didn't feel obligated to alleviate the fears of the person who had forced him and Tyne apart sixteen years ago, who had so drastically changed their lives.

Because of Richard Whitlock, you have a law degree.

He scowled, strangling the life out of the voice in his head. Benevolence wasn't high on his list when it came to Tyne's father.

"Lucas," Richard said, "I want you to know I feel bad about how things happened when you and Tyne were kids. I also want you to understand that I only did what I thought was best for my family, what was best for my daughter."

Both men watched Zach climb out of the pool and traipse back toward the diving board, water dripping from the hem of his borrowed suit, the tips of his fingers, the locks of his dark hair, and even his nose.

"I'm going to try a jackknife," the teen announced.

"We're watching!" Richard reassured his grandson.

Lucas smiled, but he was sure it looked as forced as it felt.

He remained silent while Zach jogged the three steps to the end of the board. The instant his son hit the water, he turned to Richard. "It would have been nice to know she decided to keep Zach. That she was planning to raise our child on her own. I might have been able to help her. From what she tells me, they had a hell of a rough time of it."

Richard's gaze slid to the ground, his chin dipping a little closer to his chest. His sigh was heavy. "I was angry. I wasn't thinking straight. And it only got worse when Tyne continued to be so damn stubborn. I was sure she would come around. Finally see that we were right. That our plans were for the best. But she never did."

Lucas shook his head, whispering, "Thank heavens for that."

Patricia Whitlock called out her husband's name. "The grill's hot. Time to put the steaks on."

The man glanced at Zach, who was once again hauling himself onto the ladder, and then looked Lucas directly in the eyes. "You probably won't believe me when I say this, but I agree with you. Wholeheartedly."

Watching him walk away, Lucas felt his gut knot. He didn't trust the man, didn't know if he could ever or would ever trust him. Tyne's father had proved himself to be selfish and egocentric; the kind of person who looked down on others, who only watched out for his own interests.

The magnanimous voice he'd choked off attempted to revive itself, and Lucas blanched as the voice reminded him of his own selfish behavior years ago. Did he dislike Richard Whitlock because of the man's character and the things he'd done? Or was it because some of the man's traits reminded him too much of his own?

"Hey, ah, hey. You okay?"

His son's voice knocked him out of his stupor. He fixed a pleasant expression on his face. "I'm good. That was a great dive."

Zach laughed. "You weren't lookin' 'cause if you had been, you would have said I sucked." He pointed to his cherry-red belly.

"Ouch." Lucas chuckled. Zach must have hit the water hard to make his skin turn that shade of pink. "You're right, I missed it. I was talking to your grandfather."

"That's okay."

"Zach," Lucas said softly, "I've noticed that you use a lot of 'heys' and 'you's' when you talk to me."

His son went still.

"I don't want you to feel self-conscious when we're together." Lucas could smell the sharp scent of chlorine. "I understand that you've grown up without a father around, Zach. I realize that calling me 'Dad' might be awkward for you. It's okay for you to call me Lucas, if that's what you want. If that's what will make you feel comfortable."

"Zach!" Tyne shouted. "You'd better dry off and get yourself dressed. Dinner will be ready soon."

His son's jaw muscle tensed and Zach blinked, completely ignoring his mother. "Is that what you want?" he asked.

The question startled Lucas. "What I want?" he repeated, buying himself some time. "Well, actually, no. I'd love for you to call me 'Dad.' But only if it's something you want to do. I don't want you to feel pressured into doing it, though."

"Zach!" Tyne yelled again.

The teen lifted a hand to let her know he'd heard, and when he looked back at Lucas, he was smiling. "I'll work on it," he said; then he snatched his towel from a nearby Adirondack chair and jogged off toward the pool house.

∽

Tyne sat in the passenger seat of Lucas's car, certain she could have floated back to Wikweko without these four wheels and this gas-powered engine, the feeling fueled by the sheer joy of seeing her parents again. No doubt about it, the beginning of the evening had been rocky, and there had been a bump or two along the way as well, but for the most part she was really happy about how the reunion with her parents had gone.

After dinner, they had enjoyed thick slabs of Black Forest cake, which her father had raved about, with freshly brewed coffee. While her mom had engaged Zach in lighting the citronella torches surrounding the patio, her father had had a second piece of cake. He'd suggested Tyne think about buying an empty storefront on Oak Mills' Main Street and opening a bakery. Tyne had laughed, but she'd also glowed from his compliment.

They had spent another couple of hours simply catching up. Wanting to keep the focus on the positive, everyone avoided the messiest parts of the past. That, Tyne decided, was what had made the evening such a great success. It was as if they'd all made a silent pact to keep the conversation centered in the here and now.

"So, ah," Zach piped up from the back seat, "how come no one warned me that my grandparents are freakin' racist?"

Tyne's gaze shot to Lucas. The humor lacing her son's question had Lucas shaking his head and grinning.

"Your mother tried to tell you, Zach." Lucas glanced at her. "She did try. But it's difficult to point out the bad traits of the people you love."

She smiled at him, sliding her hand over top of his where it rested on his thigh.

"When Grandmom talked about that one commissioner as 'that colored fella,' I almost choked on my cake." Zach tugged on his shoulder harness, making a light whizzing sound with the belt. "I thought she was joking. But nobody laughed."

Tyne sighed.

"Funny thing is," Zach continued, "she didn't say anything bad about the man. In fact, she said he was her favorite of all the commissioners. Weird."

"That sums it up, son." Tyne looked over her shoulder into the back. "Weird. I can't figure it out, either. My mother swears she doesn't mean anything by it, but—"

"That doesn't make it any less wrong," Lucas pointed out.

"Exactly." She nodded, hoping Zach could see her in the dim light of the dashboard. "Hon, I've been embarrassed by the way my parents act for as long as I can remember." She let go of Lucas's hand, twisting in her seat so she could more easily look at Zach. "But at the same time, they were deeply concerned about my well-being, they were kind and loving, and they tried to give me everything a girl could possibly want."

There would have been a time—a time as early as yesterday—that her heart and mind would not have been open to such an admission.

She grinned. "Your father once called me a spoiled brat."

Lucas looked into the rearview mirror. "And that was true." He leaned toward the driver's side door as Tyne *tsked* and swiped at his arm.

"What I'm trying to tell you, Zach," she said, "is that people have good traits and bad traits. Good habits and bad ones. You embrace the good, and do your level best to recognize the bad so it doesn't affect you."

Zach was quiet for a moment before saying, "It's like Uncle Jasper said about life. You gotta take the bitter with the sweet."

"You got that right." Lucas flipped on his turn signal and made a left.

"Come on now." Tyne nudged his shoulder. "They're not that bad." Her facial muscles pinched as she asked, "Are they?" The look in his dark eyes made her groan and laugh at the same time. "They can be awful, I know."

"They're not all bad," Zach said. "They obviously have wads of cash."

She just turned and looked at her son.

"That house, that patio, that outside kitchen and bar," he said, justifying his statement. "That bad-ass pool."

"Zachary!"

"All that land. The pool house is set up like an apartment, Mom. Did you see it? Someone could move right in there. There was a refrigerator and a TV, and, like, everything you'd need." Her son reached up and tapped Lucas on the shoulder. "And, Dad, I sneaked a look in the garage. They've got a Hummer. How cool is that? A *Hummer*!"

Tyne's lips parted and she sucked in a quick, silent breath. Not because her parents owned some exorbitant, gargantuan vehicle, but because her son had called Lucas "*Dad*." The word had rolled right off his tongue. Lucas, however, barely seemed to notice. It was as if her son had always addressed Lucas with the affectionate moniker.

"Zach," he said, glancing once again into the rearview mirror, "possessions don't say much about a man. What matters is who he is."

Something between a grin and a smirk twisted Zach's lips as he gave the window of the BMW three sharp raps. "I'd say you like possessions just as much as Granddad does."

Tyne saw the muscle in Lucas's jaw tense.

"Money can't buy happiness, Zach," she told her son.

"Your mother is right." Lucas's gaze remained on the roadway ahead. "I don't mind admitting that I lost my way. It's really hard to live in today's world with all its modern technology—wristwatches with GPS, cell phones that call you by name, electronic tablets almost as thin as a sheet of paper, you name it—where 'he who has the most toys wins.' Hell, it's almost impossible not to get caught up in all that grabbing, snatching, and wanting. I don't mind saying I got my priorities screwed up." He braked the car at a four-way stop, the headlights of the car facing them lighting up his face. "Got them screwed up *big time*." His gaze darted to the rearview mirror, obviously wanting to connect with Zach. "I'm sure my uncle is ashamed of what I've become. I'm one of *them*. Someone looking for acceptance, someone hell-bent on acquiring the respect and esteem of others by buying condos and cars and building an impressive bank account."

When the road was clear, Lucas drove slowly through the intersection.

"Don't be mad at me." Zach's head drooped forward. "I was only pointing out that your BMW was pretty sweet."

"I'm not angry with you." Lucas accelerated along the country road toward home. His sigh was loud and long. "And your point is well taken. I'm the last person who should be lecturing you about not letting possessions possess you."

"Guys," Tyne said cheerfully, striving to lift the sudden drop in the mood, "we had such a great evening. Let's not ruin it."

However, the last few miles to Wikweko were made in total silence.

CHAPTER NINETEEN

The coral light of pre-dawn steadily swept away the darkness as it ushered in Friday morning. Lucas had slept fitfully, awakened at least half a dozen times by crazy dreams. In the last one, a woman dressed in Amish garb hoisted herself up into a gleaming, tank-sized SUV, and stomped on the gas pedal, rutting his front lawn with perfect donuts.

He kicked the twisted sheet aside and sat on the edge of the bed. He reached his hands high and stretched his torso, thoughts of his mother wavering through his foggy mind.

What would his life have been like had she been the one who had raised him?

First and foremost, he would have had a mother. He would know what kind of person she was rather than spending all these years wondering.

She'd have cooked his meals, hugged away his hurts, read him bedtime stories, tucked him in at night. It's impossible to say just how a mother's love might have changed whom he'd turned out to be.

The carpet muffled his steps as he padded to the window.

The Yoder house had had no electric lines attached to it that Lucas remembered. That would have meant no

TV, no refrigerator, no radio, no lamps, no electronic toys. But primitive living never killed anyone, and he wouldn't have missed what he'd never known. He would have spent a lot of time outdoors, and he surely would have learned to work with his hands. Probably farming or carpentry or some other trade.

He'd have had a simple, wholesome life. Not too unlike his adolescence here at Wikweko.

Of course, there would have been no high school. Everyone in the area knew the Amish educated their kids only to the eighth grade. No high school would have been fine with him in some respects; teens could be cruel and tended to close ranks against anyone who looked the least bit different. But that would have also meant there would have been no football games. And without football, he'd have never made that great play—the one that had compelled Tyne to approach him with the compliment that had initiated their relationship.

He smiled, hardly noticing the glorious pink clouds streaking across the blue-gray sky.

His life had been changed by the sweet and innocent girl she'd been. Because of her, he'd discovered parts of himself he had never known existed. She'd taught him to love, to care about someone more than he did himself.

Then there was Zach. His smile broadened. The kid was great. Yes, he had some issues, but who went through their teen years unscathed by some kind of trouble? He sure hadn't. Problems aside, Zach had a good heart. And he was damn smart. Clever enough to quickly figure out that Lucas and Richard Whitlock weren't all that different, and assertive enough to voice the opinion. Lucas shook his head, remembering how his son had called him out on the drive home last night. Zach had the kind of common sense and intuition that would take him far in this world—as far as he wanted to go.

His son had called him "Dad" twice last night. Once in the car, and once before he'd trekked off to bed. Even now it was difficult to describe how hearing Zach speak that word made him feel. He'd never experienced that kind of joy. Even stepping into a courtroom for the very first time hadn't thrilled him as much. Hearing Zach call Richard "Grandad" had caused Lucas to grind his back teeth together. The fact that Lucas didn't much like—or trust—Tyne's father mattered very little. In fact, Lucas was forced to realize just how hungry Zach was for a family. A whole family. So as long as Richard treated Zach with kindness and respect, Lucas would do what he could to forgive and forget.

A vivid image of his mother swam through his head.

As idyllic as a childhood spent growing up on a peaceful Amish farm might sound, Lucas decided his current life had afforded him too many blessings to give up.

He reached for a clean pair of jeans and pulled a T-shirt from the dresser drawer. If he could change anything, he'd fix the mistakes he'd made in this life. He'd have set his anger aside. He'd have gotten in touch with Tyne, some way, somehow. He'd have been there for the woman he loved, for his son, through all those difficult years.

Walking through the living room, he heard water running in the kitchen.

"Hey," he greeted. "You're up early."

Tyne's long blond hair was tousled and sexy as hell. Her blue eyes were still heavy with sleep; her skin, pale as heavy cream. The silky T-shirt thing she wore did little to hide the outline of her rounded breasts, brown smudges of her nipples showing through the material.

"I didn't know you were up," she said. "I'm making coffee. It'll just be a minute."

He'd have been there for the woman he loved...

For the woman he loved...

The thought sang through his head, coming to him, not in the past tense, but in the present. The here. The now. *The woman he loved.*

She tipped the filled carafe over the water chamber of the coffee maker, set the empty pot on the burner, and flipped the switch. "Listen, Lucas. Thank you for last night. I know you didn't want to go. I really appreciate it."

He approached her, close enough to smell the warm, lemony scent of her skin, and kissed her cheek. She blinked at him, her blue eyes widening further with each lowering and raising of her eyelids. Damn, but she was gorgeous.

"I didn't mind," he told her truthfully. "I'm going to run into town. Have coffee with Jasper. Is that okay with you?"

"Sure," she said.

Staying right here and stripping that little top off her body sounded like much more fun. But he had some things to tell his uncle, things that had needed to be said for far too long.

∽

Light blazed from the window of Jasper's back door and Lucas saw his uncle sitting in the first-floor studio. He rapped twice, and Jasper let him inside.

"You're working?" he asked.

Jasper nodded. "Been up since three. The hawk in my head woke me."

"Hawk?"

The older man grinned, ushering his nephew into the brightly lit studio. "Accepted a job yesterday. Man drove in from Doylestown and brought this." He placed the flat of his hands on either side of a great log that sat square in the center of the studio floor. "Took four of us to get it in here. It's from an oak tree that's been growing beside the guy's tavern for as long as he can remember. The tree blew over in a storm, and he saved a chunk. He read my interview in *Pennsylvania Magazine* a couple years ago. Wants me to make him a woodcarving. His tavern's called The Hawk's Nest."

Jasper stared at the hunk of wood, his gaze roving up and down as if he could actually see a bird of prey hidden beneath the rough bark.

"Congratulations on the job. I can come back another time," Lucas offered. "I don't want to interrupt you."

"No, no." His uncle turned to face him. "That hawk will be flying around in my imagination for days before I pick up a chisel and mallet. I have a pot of coffee brewed." Without another word, Jasper headed to the far side of the studio, where an automatic coffee maker sat on a countertop, its glowing red light indicating that the burner was still hot.

Lucas accepted the mug his uncle poured for him. "I came to tell you that you were right."

Jasper's expression remained staid, and that didn't surprise Lucas. His uncle had never been susceptible to knee-jerk reactions.

As a child, he'd hidden things from his father: a less than stellar report card, a detention notice, a broken toy—anything that might garner his dad's disapproval. Lucas had felt loved and cared for, but his father had been a little on the hot-tempered side. After his dad had been killed in the accident on the interstate and Jasper had become his guardian, it hadn't taken long at all for Lucas to realize that the two men, although they'd been brothers, were as different as night and day.

Just a few months after losing his dad, he rode home from school, a teacher's note scalding his thigh through his trouser pocket. Lucas devised several fantastic stories to explain why he wasn't responsible for the fight he'd gotten into with Barry Sullivan. However, rather than the expected raised voice and swat on the back, Lucas experienced a very different scenario. Jasper had read the note and listened to Lucas's side of the story, and then his uncle had asked a slew of calm, thought-provoking questions. Being forced to think about his behavior, to admit his responsibility in the situation—even if only to himself—had been more agonizing and more effective than any punishment his father had ever doled out in the past.

After that, Lucas hadn't feared coming to his uncle in times of trouble, or when he needed to talk out some issue or other... or, like now, when he wanted to make a confession. Years of witnessing Jasper's unruffled manner assured Lucas that there would be no judgment. There would be no scorn. No violent reactions. Not even a single "I told you so."

The biggest hurdle he had to conquer was his own prideful unwillingness to admit he was wrong.

As expected, Jasper perched himself on a nearby stool and took a sip of coffee as he waited.

"It took coming back to Wikweko to see it," Lucas began. "It took meeting my son. Getting to know him. It took spending an evening with Richard Whitlock—"

Even that name from the past didn't elicit a response from Jasper. The man was good. As nonreactive as that solid mass of red oak.

"—to realize—" He clamped his lips shut, gazed down into his coffee mug, then forced himself to look at Jasper. "To realize what I've been doing."

He set the coffee on the counter. "It started in college. I cut my hair, and I listened to how my college friends talked, mimicked them, and changed the cadence of my voice. I worked hard to use proper grammar when I was speaking and in anything I wrote. I wanted to be accepted. I wanted to fit in." Reaching up, he scrubbed at the back of his neck. "When it came time to write my first résumé, I didn't use my full name. Lucas Hawk is what I chose. I wasn't trying to hide the fact that I'm Lenape. I mean, look at me. I'm Indian. No one could miss that. It was, well...I thought I'd have a better chance at success if I treated who and what I was with a little...subtlety."

Ceramic grated against Formica when he scooped up his mug. He swallowed a mouthful of coffee. "I'm not going to say that I was never discriminated against. That wouldn't be the truth. But I never let that stop me. If anything, it made me study more, work harder. I never lost sight of my purpose. After landing my job, the firm printed business cards for me: 'Lucas Hawk, Attorney.' My success was printed right there on those cards. And when I was promoted two years later, the firm had a name plaque made for my office door: 'Lucas Hawk.'" He sighed. "I didn't protest. In fact, I never said a word. I didn't see any harm in it. I was moving forward, reaching my goals, making the big bucks. What did it matter that people weren't using my full name?"

His mouth felt dry. "Then I met Zach." Lucas shook his head. "That kid is amazing. He looks exactly like me, Jasper. He's Indian. Lenape." Again, he paused, this time to rake his teeth against his bottom lip. "When I brought him home and you started spending time with him... he talked about what he'd learned from you. And I began remembering all that I learned from you while I was growing up too. You gave me a history. A family. Something real and tangible to hold on to. You gave me dignity. Self-respect. I was proud to be Indian." His gaze trailed to the log in the middle of the room. "Somewhere, somehow... I lost sight of it. All of it."

Quiet blanketed the studio, the *tick, tick* of the old clock on the wall, keeping a steady rhythm.

"I think it must have been very difficult for you, Lucas," Jasper said at last, "to have been so young and to have had a white man look you in the eye and tell you that you were not good enough or worthy enough to have what your heart desired."

Neither man spoke for several seconds. Jasper sat, drinking his coffee, and Lucas thought over all that he'd told his uncle. He couldn't, in good conscience, blame Tyne's father for the things he'd done, for the attitude he'd adopted regarding his own identity. In the end, he was responsible for his actions. No one else.

Jasper had taught him that, and Jasper was a great teacher.

"I'll fix it," he promised his uncle. "I'll fix it for me. And for Zach. I want him to know, to see, that I'm proud of who I am. I want him to be proud of me." He caught Jasper's eye. "Like I'm proud of you."

The old man went still, his throat convulsing in a swallow, his obsidian eyes growing moist. Lucas smiled when he saw his uncle grappling with his emotions.

"I appreciate all you've done for me," he continued. "You became my father when my father was no longer here for me. You didn't have to do that, you didn't have to take on that responsibility, but you did. Without question. And I thank you."

A poignant smile crinkled Jasper's wizened face. "You've already thanked me many times."

Lucas stood there, staring, a frown on his brow.

His uncle got up off the stool and set down his mug. The wooden box he pulled from the cabinet had been glossy all over at one time, but years of handling had worn away the shine from the front, centermost area of the lid. Jasper opened the box and dumped its contents across the workspace.

Cards. Of every size and description. Birthday cards. Father's Day cards. Get Well cards. Some were handmade of folded construction paper colored with crayons or markers, their messages written in boxy letters by an unskilled hand. Most had been store-bought. But every single one had been signed by Lucas.

He grinned, picking up one card, then another. "You saved all these?"

Jasper gently touched one, its spine dried and cracked. "More valuable than a treasure chest full of gold."

Sliding closer to his uncle, Lucas draped his arm around the older man's shoulders. "You've been just like a father to me." His uncle's head dipped, and Lucas asked, "What? What is it?"

Jasper shook his head. "It's nothing."

Putting a bit of space between them, Lucas remarked, "Doesn't look like nothing to me. Something's bothering you."

His head hung low, Jasper nodded almost imperceptibly. "It's about your father. And Ruth Yoder. I had hoped not to have to say anything, but you've been in touch with her."

Lucas lifted a shoulder. "It's hard to say where that whole situation might go. I may never see her again."

His uncle began gathering the cards with care. "But you might. So you should know the truth."

Taking another backward step, Lucas leaned his hip against the cabinet.

"When Ruth Yoder came to Wikweko with her father, she was as innocent as she could be." Jasper placed the cards in the wooden box. "My brother had a wild streak, and he got the idea to seduce her. There weren't many times that your father and I had words, but we argued about that. Bitterly." The wood made a tapping sound when the lid was closed and latched. "He skulked around like a thief for several months, and then he came home scared witless, saying that Ruth told him she was going to have a baby. We didn't see her or Reverend Yoder again until they rode into Wikweko with you."

Jasper slid the box into the cabinet and closed the door. "You might see her, Lucas," he said. "You might even have the chance to get to know her some day. I don't want you blaming her when it was all your father's doing. He cared nothing for her. Only wanted to steal her innocence, which he did. I never wanted you to know about his disgraceful behavior."

Lucas reached up and lightly scratched his temple. "Like I said, it's hard to predict what will happen. If I'll see her again or not. I hope I do, but...who knows?" After a moment, he added, "As for my father. I don't know what to say." He shook his head. "But if I've learned anything these past three weeks, Uncle Jasper, it's that I have no right to judge anyone about the choices they've made in the past."

CHAPTER TWENTY

Tall trees, lush with green summer foliage, shaded the trail and cooled the air. Loose gravel littered the hard-packed dirt path and made walking a little treacherous. A stone became lodged between the sole of her sandal and the bottom of her foot. She skipped a step and then wobbled on one foot while she worked it loose.

"I'm sorry." Lucas offered some balance with a firm hand on her elbow. "I should have suggested you wear sturdier shoes."

"It's fine," she assured him breathlessly, directing her gaze at the ground where the reddish earth of the trail collided with thick, mossy underbrush. She'd had an inkling where they were headed, and excitement skittered along her nerves like static electricity as she wondered if *he* remembered the significance of these woods, this place. She suspected he did because he'd been acting peculiar since returning from Jasper's earlier this morning.

Conversation had been animated over the breakfast she'd made of Creole omelets and warm apple-citrus compote. He'd thanked her, over and over, complimented her cooking several times too, and engaged Zach almost nonstop throughout the meal. She'd sensed that Lucas's spirited mood was covering some sort of anxiety, and that had left her quite curious.

Her interest had only increased when he'd waited until Zach had left to visit friends to invite her to go for a drive. Clearly, he wanted to be alone with her.

He'd driven through Oak Mills and then he'd turned south along the river. Easy conversation filled the twenty-minute trip. They'd talked about Zach and the radical change he'd made during his stay at Wikweko. They'd discussed what to expect when Zach faced the judge in just ten short days. He'd told her about his visit with Jasper, and about his uncle's exciting new commission. He'd also explained his realization of how his overwhelming need to succeed in his career had compelled him to downplay his ethnicity and that he now knew that, in doing so, he had betrayed his Lenape heritage. When he'd told her he'd decided to change that, his spine had been straight, his shoulders square.

When he'd steered the car onto the grounds of the state park, a shiver raced across Tyne's skin. She hadn't been here for... oh, Lord, so many years it was scary.

"Do you remember this place?" he asked her just as they broke through the trees.

She smiled, hugging herself. "Are you kidding me?" The high bluff offered a magnificent view of the Susquehanna. Good thing she wasn't afraid of heights. "I could never forget."

With a gentle hand at the small of her back, he guided her toward a nearby boulder, the same large chunk of granite they had perched on when he'd asked her to go steady with him back in high school. Although she had tried everything—painting the ring with clear nail polish, gluing felt to its inside surface—she hadn't been able to wear the plain metal band he'd given her that day. She'd been crushed, but she'd blithely shrugged it off in an effort to alleviate his embarrassment.

"I still have it." She looked up at him standing there. "The ring you gave me, I mean. It's in my jewelry box."

"Don't know why," he groused. "Damn thing turned your finger three shades of green. Made you look like your skin was rotten."

But she could tell he was pleased that she had kept the token of their affection.

He settled himself next to her. "I brought you here so we could be alone. I want to talk to you. About some... things. Several things, really. And first, I, um, I'd like to talk about Zach."

"We talked about Zach in the car."

He nodded and looked away. "Yeah. Yeah, we did."

"Lucas, you're making me nervous. What's this all about?"

A tiny frown drew his brows together, darkened his gaze. "I don't know how you're going to feel about this. But, well, I might as well go ahead and say it." He inhaled deeply. "I'd like for Zach to use my name. He's my son, which makes him a Silver Hawk. I'd like him to be able to call himself that."

Tyne's eyebrows arched, Lucas's request utterly blindsiding her.

"Zach's found a connection in Wikweko," Lucas hurried to say. "I think having a name to go along with that connection is important. He's Indian. He's Lenape. He should have a Lenape name. He should have *my* name."

A stab of annoyance shot through her. "Zach is my son too, Lucas. He's half white, remember."

He immediately looked contrite. "I know, Tyne. I'm sorry. I didn't mean to...I'm really sorry."

Pressing the heels of her hands on either side of her, she scooted to make some space between them.

"Tyne, don't do that. Don't move away from me." He took her hand, flattened it between both of his. "Don't be angry. I was only thinking of Zach. He's made great strides. He seems to have found his place here. He's made a bond. He's made friends who understand him. Who appreciate how he feels and what he's experienced."

She couldn't deny that everything he said was true. Her son seemed happier, more content, more at ease, here than he ever had in Philadelphia. He and Jasper had developed a wonderful relationship. This place, these people, seemed to bring out the best in him.

"Of course," he told her, "I understand that we can't make definitive decisions when we've been here less than three weeks. But you've said yourself that Zach has truly changed."

The river below rolled by at a lazy pace. She sighed and then turned to look at Lucas. "Your son would be absolutely thrilled to use your name. You know it as well as I do." For some ungodly reason, tears blurred her vision. "That child—" She stopped suddenly, repressing a wave of solid emotion. "He's not a child. I know that. But I can't help thinking of him that way." She swiped at the tear that slid from the corner of her eye. "He's been looking for a father all his life. I was able give him a lot of things. But I couldn't give him what he wanted, what he *needed*, most."

Lucas squeezed her fingers. "Tyne, you have to stop this. You gave our son everything you had to give. There's no reason for you to feel guilty."

Another tear slipped down her cheek as past regrets tore at her heart. "I kept the two of you apart. I didn't tell you about him, Lucas. Our child is fifteen years old, and—"

"I knew, Tyne."

Surely she hadn't heard him correctly. But the categorical quality of his tone made it almost too clear. Her fingertips felt chilled when she pulled them from his grasp. "What do you mean, you knew?" She searched his face, not really expecting an answer to the unnecessary question. But when he didn't respond, she pressed, "You *knew* I had Zach?"

"I knew you were pregnant."

He reached for her, but she drew away.

"Tyne, I was told you were pregnant, but I was also told you were getting rid of the baby."

"Who told you that? No one else knew. No one who would dare tell, anyway. When were you told? Before I left Oak Mills?"

He scrubbed at his forehead, and then raked his fingers through his hair. "Let me explain." His exhalation was rough. "There's a hell of a lot to explain."

"I'm listening."

He looked out over the bluff. "I'm not sure where to begin." Then he turned to face her. "When you stopped talking to me, stopped taking my calls, I went nuts. We hadn't fought. You seemed a little distracted that last weekend we were together, but I thought everything was fine.

I got annoyed when I didn't hear from you and it seemed you were avoiding my calls. I imagined you out partying with your college friends, and I decided to leave it alone. Give you some time. But after a couple of weeks I couldn't stand it and called you again. Your roommate told me you'd moved out of the dorm. That she hadn't seen you. She didn't know if you'd moved off campus or what. I tried to ask her more questions, but she blew me off. I didn't know what had happened, but I knew something was wrong."

He was looking at her, but she had the distinct feeling he wasn't seeing her.

"I called your house and got nothing but the runaround from your mother. At first, she claimed you weren't home. On the third call, she admitted you were home, but that you couldn't talk. Then after half a dozen calls, she started saying you refused to talk to me." He lifted one hand, palm up. "Tyne, I didn't know what was going on. All I knew was that I had to see you. I went to your house and had words with your mother. She said you didn't want anything to do with me anymore. That I should go away. And stay away. That I should stop trying to see you. I got so angry. I brushed past her. Started searching the house. Calling your name. I was..." He shook his head, exhaled in frustration. "Desperate. And scared."

Of course, Tyne hadn't been aware that he'd called or that he'd come to the house. She'd suspected he would. Would have been stupid to think he wouldn't. They'd been serious for three years. But she figured that one firm lecture from her father would have Lucas running. She'd also been certain that once Lucas learned she'd dropped out of college, that she'd left town, he'd leave things alone."

"Your mother picked up the phone. Threatened to call the police." The hand resting on his thigh tensed into a fist. "Still, I refused to leave until I had a chance to talk to you. That's when she finally admitted that you'd left Oak Mills. She wouldn't tell me where you'd gone, but she did say that you wouldn't be back any time soon. Then she told me you'd made some decisions. That you'd come to your senses. That you wanted nothing more to do with an Indian. That I should forget about you and get on with my life. She said that's what you wanted me to do."

Tyne slid her palms over her upper arms and squeezed tight. She'd never imagined her mother would be out-and-out cruel. But that had probably been the only way to make Lucas resign himself to the fact that their relationship was over. Tyne couldn't blame her mother entirely, not when she'd done exactly what Tyne had wanted. Oh, she hadn't meant to hurt Lucas. But she had thought it best for him to forget about her and to act as if they'd never been together.

"So I went away," Lucas said. "But it wasn't over. I went to see your father. At least half a dozen times, maybe more. He visited Jasper to see if he could get me to stop hounding him. Then your father called me to his office. I thought I was finally going to get some answers." He slid his hand down his thigh and cupped his knee.

"That's when he told me. That you were pregnant."

Tyne sucked in a sharp breath.

"I guess he knew I wouldn't stop, wouldn't let up," he said, "until I knew the truth. He said you'd decided to give the baby up for adoption. That you'd already met the parents. That this is what you decided to do, what you wanted to do, and if I caused any problems, I would only be hurting you."

Strain pulled at Lucas's face. Never would she have guessed that her father would tell Lucas about the baby, about the adoption. Her father had fought her so hard, had pushed her and prodded her to have an abortion. On the day she'd left the house, he'd been so furious that he hadn't spoken to her.

"That alone would have been enough," he told her, "to get me to stop asking questions. To leave you alone. If that's what you wanted, I wouldn't have gone against your wishes. I'd have walked out and never looked back. I think I would have, anyway. Who the hell knows what I would have done?" He tilted his head, scanned the expanse of the Susquehanna, and then looked back at her. "Then your father sweetened the pot. Told me if I stopped trying to contact you, if I left all of you alone, he'd see that my tuition was paid. Four years at Temple." Again, he gazed out toward the horizon. "A college degree sitting there on that desk in a fat, manila envelope."

Even though sunshine dappled through the leaves overhead, Tyne felt chilled to the bone as she listened to Lucas talk.

"So you gave up your son for the price of tuition."

She couldn't have punished him more had she slapped him hard across the face.

"But... Tyne... you have to understand... I was told..." His voice drifted, whatever words he'd wanted to say evidently lost in stormy agitation.

The sigh she heaved came up from the depths of her soul. "I'm sorry, Lucas. I had no right to say that. Everything you were told was the truth. I've already shared my nightmare with you. I nearly aborted our son. I nearly gave him away. I have no right to condemn the decisions you made back then. No right whatsoever."

Neither of them spoke for several minutes. Birds chirped in the treetops, and a chipmunk scrabbled across the path behind them.

"I was surprised," Lucas said, "when I realized you thought I didn't know. And then I had a devil of a time trying to tell you. What I did, the decision I made—picking up that money and walking out of that office—makes me look like such a... callous shit."

She uncrossed her arms, stretched out her hand, and touched him on the forearm. "Don't say that. You look no worse than I do for the awful things I considered."

"Yes, with 'considered' being the operative word. You ended up doing the right thing. And that's what matters most."

"What is this?" she asked, a grin quirking one corner of her mouth. "A competition?"

He only looked at her, not a hint of humor on his face. "Why didn't you tell me, Tyne?"

It had been the most difficult decision of her life. "The last time I saw you, you were so excited. You said you'd finally saved enough money for your first year of college. You'd have to live at home, you said; you'd have to commute, and you'd have to continue to work, but you were so happy. I didn't actually know I was pregnant then. My period was late and I was worried, but I didn't want to spoil our weekend. I loved you so much, Lucas." She shifted on the rock. "After I was sure...I was absolutely sick. I was going to ruin everything for you. I felt I would be a burden. Just at a time when you seemed to be getting yourself on track."

After a moment she groaned, swiping her hair back over her shoulder. "Lucas, what did we do? Could we have twisted our lives into a more tangled knot?"

His silence drew her attention, and she swiveled her head to look at him.

"I think," he murmured, "the question should be, can we untangle it?"

Her smile was soft and sincere. "We're working on it."

"Yeah." He nodded, capturing her hand in both of his and sliding his fingers up her bare arm. "We are working on it, aren't we?"

There was a measuring in his eyes that made her heart flutter.

"Tyne, I know you wanted to wait. You wanted us to get to know one another again. But I don't need more time." His dark eyes intensified with awe as he shook his head. "When I'm with you, I feel as if no time has passed at all. I know you, Tyne. I love you."

Her breath caught, held.

"I know what's in my heart," he said. "Just as surely as I know my own name."

With all he'd come to realize over these past days of their living together in his small ranch house, she understood the depth of meaning in his statement. She trusted him, believed that he meant what he said, and wanted nothing more than to reveal her feelings for him as well. But a strong maternal instinct held her back.

She glanced away. "Lucas, I'm worried. This is moving too fast. We have Zach to think of. If we try and fail…" The rest of her thought faded when she saw the firm set of Lucas's jaw.

"We're not going to fail. Not again. It just won't happen."

"What about my parents?" she asked. "From the looks of it, they haven't changed much. But, Lucas, I can't shut them out of my life anymore. As imperfect as they may be, they're still my parents. I love them."

"I know you do. I can live with that. I can't sit here and tell you that I'll ever feel about them the way you do, or that I'll be rushing over there every Sunday for a family meal. But I can tell you I'll do my best to respect your love for them. And I'll always appreciate them purely for who they are. Shutting them out of our lives would be a mistake."

She didn't miss his choice of pronouns.

"We've already made all the mistakes, all the bad decisions, we're going to make." His thumb smoothed hot, tiny circles on the back of her hand. "In fact, I say we make a pact right now. We promise not to make *any* decisions without talking things out, you and I. What do you say?"

Tyne studied his gorgeous face, his warm, intense eyes, her heart filling with so much happiness, she felt it might split in two. She pressed her palm to the side of his neck, slid it up to his jaw. Then she leaned in and kissed him softly before whispering against his mouth, "I promise."

"Ah," he said, "you've done it again, Amëwë. Got me right in the heart."

Her eyes went round. "You remember?"

He slid his arms around her and pulled him up tight against him. "Like I could ever forget."

∼

"All rise," the bailiff announced.

Everyone, Tyne, Zach, Lucas, and the assistant state's attorney, stood as Judge Taylor entered the small courtroom and seated himself. The uniformed officer called the room to order, declared that court was now in session, and ordered all of them to sit.

"Folks, because we're running behind today," Judge Taylor said, studying the file in front of him, "I'd like to get right down to business. So, Mr. Zachary Whitlock, tell me what's been happening."

Zach slid out his chair and stood. Tyne gave him an encouraging smile.

"Well, Your Honor, ah, Judge, ah, Sir," Zach stammered. He stopped talking, turning bright red in the face.

The judge leaned forward. "It's okay. Any of those will work." Without cracking a smile, he added, "But we don't need all three at once, understood?"

"Yes, sir, Your Honor." Her son's eyes widened, and he clamped his mouth shut, his cheeks and neck flaming to crimson.

"Relax, son," Judge Taylor told him. "Now, tell me what's been going on in your life for the past month. I see from your file that you succeeded in keeping your nose clean, so that's good."

"My dad took me to his hometown—Wikweko."

"Ah, yes." He peered over top of his reading glasses. "I remember now. And your mother? Did she go along?"

"She did, sir. And I met my family. My dad's uncle. He's Lenape. And my mom's parents. My granddad is the mayor of Oak Mills."

"Meeting family is good. What'd you spend your time doing?"

"My dad taught me to shoot a bow. And I went camping. My uncle taught me to build a shelter and start a fire to cook the fish we caught. I learned about edible plants. I played the water drum during a powwow. I heard all about my Lenape history. I whittled a bird out of pine wood."

Zach continued his litany of activities until Tyne could see the judge was fighting the desire to glance at his wristwatch.

Finally, her son said, "I learned a lot of things, sir. But the best thing I learned, I think, is that I'm responsible for me."

Judge Taylor perked up.

"I told you before," Zach continued, "that I didn't know those guys I was with the night I got into trouble. And I wasn't lyin' to you, sir. I *didn't* know them. But when I said it, I have to admit that I was trying to, like, blame them. 'Cause I was scared, and all I wanted was to get out of trouble. But I learned that what happened to me was my fault."

Her son had the judge's full attention now, and anxiety squeezed Tyne's stomach until she felt nauseated.

"I learned from my Uncle Jasper that I should never jeopardize my integrity. That my choices matter." Zach glanced at Tyne and then at Lucas. "I learned the same thing from my parents. I figured out that they made some bad choices when they were young."

Lucas turned questioning eyes on Tyne, and she arched her brows and lifted her shoulders the tiniest fraction.

"They made choices that they regret. And it helped me realize that my uncle was right." Zach rested his fingertips on the tabletop. "I've decided that I don't want to get old like them and regret the choices I made while I was a kid."

Lucas looked pained, his dark eyes glittering, his lips twitching, as he looked over at Tyne and mouthed, "*Old?*" Her cheeks puffed and she clamped her hand over her mouth. The last thing she wanted to do was laugh. Not at a moment like this. When Zach was trying his damnedest to do a good job of explaining himself to the judge. She faced forward and studied the overly stiff collar on the bailiff's olive uniform shirt.

"So I'm going to be careful," Zach said, "about what I say and do, and who I hang with. 'Cause like my Uncle Jasper says, when it comes right down to it, all a man has is his reputation. If he ruins that, he's got nothing."

Judge Taylor gazed at Zach for a few drawn-out seconds, nodding. "Excellent."

Something in the man's voice made Tyne look his way. An awkward smile cracked a fissure across his marble-like features.

Then the judge murmured, "Wonder if this Uncle Jasper of yours would mind if I sent a few dozen young people his way." He picked up the forms and typed pages that made up

Zach's file and tapped them smartly on his desk. "I'm satisfied by what I've heard." He directed his attention to the prosecutor. "Is the State satisfied?"

"Yes, Your Honor," the woman said.

Judge Taylor nodded. "I'm going to file your case on the stet docket. What that means, Zachary, is that if you keep out of trouble for a full year, then these charges will be automatically dropped and expunged from your record. If you get yourself arrested, however, you'll face whatever charges you're up against plus these charges. Is that clear?"

"Yes. Sir." Zach let his hands fall to his sides. "I understand."

The black-robed man closed the manila file and handed it to the clerk. "I'm feeling good about this one. I don't think I'll be seeing you again, Zachary, so you have a good life. That's all." He rapped the gavel.

On their way out of the courthouse, Lucas slid his hand in Tyne's. They paused just outside the door and watched their son descend the concrete steps.

"Damn," Lucas whispered. "Would you look at him? His head is high, his shoulders are square." He looked at Tyne. "This feels good."

She smiled. "It does, doesn't it? He did a good job in there." Nothing in the world could beat being proud of her son. Well, almost nothing. Being able to share that proud-parent feeling with Lucas was pretty damn great too.

EPILOGUE

"Perfect day for a wedding," his uncle said, adjusting his navy tie. "You nervous?"

"Not a bit." Lucas smoothed his hands down the lapels of his jacket. "If anything, I feel like this has been too long in coming."

A fresh crispness snapped in the cool spring air. Crocuses and yellow daffodils bobbed their colorful heads in the large planters placed strategically along the street. The two rounded the corner, and Lucas's step slowed when he saw the plain black buggy sitting outside the Oak Mills Courthouse. Jasper lifted his hand in greeting to the woman sitting inside.

"I'm going in to find Zach and Tyne," his uncle said. "You have plenty of time."

"Thanks," Lucas murmured, then veered toward the street.

The horse nickered and bobbed its head when he approached.

"Ruth?" He was too surprised to smile. "Thank you so much for coming. I sent the invitation to let you know what was happening. I have to say, I never expected you to attend."

"I thought of contacting you. I've written you half a dozen letters." Ruth Yoder captured a wayward strand of hair and tucked it neatly under the white band of her pleated cap. "But then I decided a surprise would be better."

She reached her hand out to him and he took it. The full skirt of her black, cotton dress billowed slightly, and he glimpsed her sturdy, polished shoes as he helped her down onto the sidewalk.

"Your father?" Lucas asked.

Her mouth went flat. "He went to be with his Maker. Six weeks back."

"I'm so sorry." Then an age-old Lenape sentiment came to mind, and he murmured, "May your heart find peace."

Her hazel eyes filled with sad resignation. "He was very ill there at the end." She took a deep breath and gazed up at the courthouse, swallowing back her grief.

"I brought you something," she said, turning so Lucas could look into the back of the buggy. A beautiful quilt sat folded on the back seat. "It's a wedding ring pattern."

Lucas's throat constricted. "Thank you so much. Did you make it?"

She lifted calloused hands. "Amazing what these rough old things can do, isn't it?"

He stepped forward and leaned in, gingerly touching the colorful fabric. "It's amazing. Tyne will love it."

"Now," Ruth began. She tugged at the waistband of her dress. "You said I have a grandson. Will I meet him today?"

"Oh, yes. I'm sure he's inside. With his mother. And his grandparents. And my uncle."

"That was your father's brother?" she asked.

Lucas nodded.

"I hope I get to talk to him today."

"I'm sure you will. Tyne's parents have planned a small reception at their house later this afternoon. You're welcome to come."

"I'd love to." She reached inside the buggy and slid something from the floorboard. "I brought this for your son."

The small, leather-bound album looked worn. Lucas opened it and sucked in his breath when he saw the yellowed newspaper clippings. Unexpected tears sprang to his eyes.

The first was an article that depicted him as a boy of eight. He was holding a certificate and wearing the medallion he'd been awarded in an elementary school science competition. Lucas still remembered the weather display that had won first place in the event.

Another was a group shot that had been taken when he and a group of his friends had raised money to help pay the hospital bill of a local boy who had been injured in a fall. Chase had lingered for weeks, but in the end he hadn't survived. The sound of Mrs. Halloway's heart-wrenching sobs at the funeral were forever emblazoned in Lucas's mind.

There were several pages of clippings from high school sporting events: football and track. His high school graduation picture made him smirk. His hair had been longer than Tyne's back then.

"How in the world did you get all of these?" he finally asked his mother.

There was a lovely secretiveness in the twinkle of her blue-green eyes. "Father forbade newspapers from the outside to be in the house." She shrugged. "But a mother has to keep up with her child, doesn't she?"

She slid her hand up his forearm. "I may not have had the privilege of raising you, Lucas, but I love you. I've always loved you."

With trembling hands, he closed the album and set it on the floorboard of the buggy. Then he turned and wrapped his arms around his mother. She hugged him as if her very life depended on it, as if this were the last human touch she would ever receive.

When they parted, her gaze was so watery, tears trailed down her cheeks. "I never thought that would happen."

Lucas pulled a handkerchief from his pocket and offered it to her. "I'm glad you were wrong."

She laughed through her tears. "So am I."

"Listen," he told her. "I want you to know it's okay. I understand what happened. I realize your religion made it impossible for you to keep me with you. I don't hold that against—"

"My religion?" she asked, tilting her head a fraction. "Lucas, I didn't give you to your father because of my religion."

Refraining from reacting to this unexpected revelation was nearly impossible.

"I became pregnant with you during my rumspringa." She paused, moistened her pale, bare lips. "During our seventeenth year, we're given the freedom to experience the world. It's a time when we're released from the church. It's our belief that only informed adults can truly accept Christ and the church and the Amish way. We can't reject something we've never experienced. So, for a time, we're not bound to the Ordnung. The rules." Again, that secretive smile passed her lips. "Much to my father's complete displeasure, I took full advantage of my months of freedom.

"It was not the first time a young girl found herself carrying a child out of wedlock. Usually, such an occurrence would have resulted in a hasty marriage. But I could not marry your father. That was never a possibility. He was...not one of us. I would have been shunned." She folded his handkerchief into a perfect square. "Besides, even if it *had* been an option, I fear your father would not have married me. I loved him, Lucas, but I do not believe Ry Silver Hawk felt the same about me."

Remembering what his uncle had told him, Lucas found his gaze drifting from his mother's.

"My father was a hard man. His Ordnung was the death of my mother. The doctor said she died of pneumonia. But I believe she was worn out. She gave up. I was duty bound to stay with him, Lucas. I was his daughter, and I was called to honor him and take care of him. He had no one but me."

Her tone was even, matter-of-fact.

"But I could not allow you to be subjected to that," she told him. "It almost killed me to hand you over. But I had been to Wikweko. I had witnessed how your community clings together. They take care of one another." She used the folded handkerchief to wipe an errant tear from the corner of her eye. "I knew you would be happy. And very much loved."

Lucas stared at Ruth Yoder, her eyes, cheeks, lips devoid of makeup, and thought she was absolutely beautiful.

He cleared the thick emotion from his throat. "I was," he assured her. "And I thank you for giving me that."

She smiled and hugged him once again. "I am sure you must have a thousand questions about me. Because I know I have a thousand about you. But we really shouldn't keep your bride waiting any longer."

"Yes, it would be a shame if she decided to turn tail and run now." He laughed. "We moved back to Wikweko, you know. I just opened an office there."

"That's wonderful." Ruth checked that the horse's reins were secured to the meter post.

"Tyne is thinking of opening a bakery. But she hasn't decided yet."

"I am a fairly good baker myself," his mother told him. "I may offer her my services. I have lots of free time on my hands these days."

Arm in arm, they ascended the courthouse steps.

"Mom." Zach tapped his mother's shoulder, excitement elevating his whisper. "Mom! Here he comes. Who's that with him?"

She shushed him and promised to answer all his questions later. But for now, she feasted her eyes on Lucas as he held open the glass door for his mother.

Tyne smiled at Lucas. "I thought you'd changed your mind."

"Are you kidding me?" he said. "Let's get this show on the road."

Looking at Ruth, Tyne's smile widened. She leaned forward and kissed the woman's cheek. "I'm so happy you're here," she murmured. "I know Lucas is too."

Her gaze skipped from Jasper to her dad, her mom, her son, and finally to Lucas's mother. Love saturated every nuance of her being when she looked into Lucas's eyes. "It seems the family is finally all together."

His soft kiss was swift and sweet. "Seems so." He kissed her again. "Can we please get in there and make this official? I've been waiting long enough."

Holding tight to Lucas with one hand, her son with the other, Tyne was ready to say *I do*. She was ready to be a family. A whole family. At last.

— END —

A NOTE FROM THE AUTHOR

Dear reader,

I hope you enjoyed my story. *Reclaim My Heart* is very special to me. I was afraid the book might never see the light of day. You see, my father was diagnosed with cancer while I was writing the story, and I became his primary caretaker. It's difficult to write about love and happily-ever-after when you're watching someone you love succumbing to that terrible disease, and there's not a darn thing you can do about it. So I set the book aside.

After giving myself time to grieve, I decided to work on Lucas and Tyne's story, and I'm so glad I did. I fell in love with these characters, especially Uncle Jasper. I hope you liked them too.

If you found the book entertaining, please consider leaving a review. Good reviews help other readers find books to enjoy. And I'm not going to lie, good reviews help me too.

Find me online! I love to hear from readers.

I have a website: www.DonnaFasano.com. Subscribe to my blog posts and you'll receive news, fun and inspirational quotes, recipes, chances to win great books and prizes only offered to my fans, and much more.

Facebook: http://www.Facebook.com/DonnaFasanoAuthor
Twitter: http://www.Twitter.com/DonnaFaz
Pinterest: http://www.Pinterest.com/DonnaFaz

All my best,
Donna

ABOUT THE AUTHOR

Born in Elkton, Maryland, Donna Fasano met her knight in shining armor—a logical scientist type—when she was still a teen. They married, raised two children, and currently live in Northern Delaware with their wild-dingo-of-a-dog, Roo. Donna loves to read and has an eclectic taste when it comes to fiction. She collects cookbooks and loves to use them. She hikes, bikes, and kayaks (physical activity is necessary due to her love affair with food). Donna has been writing romance novels and women's fiction since 1989. Her books have sold nearly 4 million copies worldwide, and she is pleased to be able to say she's a *USA Today* Bestselling Author.

Printed in Great Britain
by Amazon